SUNSHIP

ISBN (Paperback): 978-1-7399995-4-4
ISBN (eBook): 978-1-7399995-5-1

Published by Leporello Books

SUNSHIP

MAGGIE MORRIS WYLLIE

To Royo, again, for all his help.

'Omnia vincit amor: et nos cedamus amori.'
'Love conquers all: we too must yield to love.'

Virgil

CITY OF THE MARBLE GODS
A.D. 46

PROLOGUE

It was sometime during the sixth month of the consulship of Asiaticus and Silanus that I was brought back to the house on the Quirinal, my mind so completely gone that even to this day I remember nothing of my journey or of the men who bore me all the way from Britain. Though now I understand them to have been a unit of veteran auxilia, awarded honourable discharge and thus headed for the City in order to claim their long-sought dues.

Rome was more stifling than ever that summer; the heat had forced the household to the coast a full month earlier than usual, which meant, thank all the gods, that I was delivered into the hands of the elderly houseboys who'd been left behind to manage whatever there is to be managed in a home devoid of orders. But now all chores were set aside. I might have been brought home to die but the old boys had other ideas, and set about their task with gusto, smearing my wounds with pounded elm bark and forcing infusions of borage down my throat, taking it in turn to sit by my open door to watch for any sign that might signal a worsening of my condition.

And, little by little, some vestige of my sanity returned.

As August drew to a close and the cramped space of my sleeping cubicle became more foul-smelling, a couch was carried out into the garden – with me upon it, I might add – and placed in the shade of the little fountain with its marble satyrs. And, lying in that night-time place, a multitude of stars suspended in the vastness of the firmament above, how reasonable it had seemed to watch whilst a cluster of the flickering lights detached themselves from the galaxy to start a silent drifting towards me, as I knew they would. Other lights, on some other night, in some other place, but not stars of the sky. Might they be a pattern of torches held aloft by warriors on the far side of a darkened valley?

A glimpsed reflection of a memory lost, weird chimeras darting in and out of my mind; slain horses lying on a riverbed, men with antlers sprouting from their heads. I found myself submitting to … and here I seek specific words … anguish … despair. But then again, such boundless melancholy is experienced by so few that means to describe it lies beyond the scope of language.

Then came voices, murmuring down through my torment.

'Are you awake, Siva?'

'Can you hear us?'

I asked if I was dreaming still.

'No,' they told me. 'You're home now, safe.'

But though I was back in the old, familiar house no longer did it feel like home.

Sirius nights, suffocating in the perfume of lilies and sounds of the City. The clatter of wheels and the lowing of bullocks, the noise of the crowd, like the droning of some great hive of wasps, tambourine players hollering songs of the moment, or so I took them to be. 'Oh sister. Oh sister' was one such ditty, repeated over and over until I swore that if I were forced to listen to it just one more time I'd take a knife and slit my throat.

Sometime later, I asked where I'd been.

'Britain, Siva. Don't you know?'

I recalled my life until a certain point which seemed to me like yesterday. But nothing after that.

'It's two years, now, since you set out,' was what I seemed to hear them say, though I knew they must be mistaken.

But they insisted they were right.

A timescale vast as that behind me, yet I remembered nothing of it. I was lost, the gods had abandoned me.

'Just give it time,' the old slaves said.

But time was a luxury I didn't possess, though I can't say I knew why that was. The sands of the clock were running out fast and once the last grain had fallen it would be too late.

Too late for what, though?

But as things turned out, far from deserting me as I'd supposed, the gods had taken pity on my plight, had resolved to return the lost part of my life to me, for only they could have contrived to place Petronius on a certain point on the Vicus Sandilarius, at a certain moment of a certain hour of a certain day …

* * *

About a month after, I'd started to recover. About a month after I was able to settle into at least a couple of hours of sleep during the unrelenting interval strung out between dusk and dawn. In fact, about a month after I began to act a little less like a man gone out of his head, Asselina sent a note.

'I heard you're back a month ago yesterday. If you don't come to see me I'll never speak to you again.'

By her first words, which I had to read three times to make any sense of their meaning, I assumed she was letting me know that she'd only just heard I'd been back in Rome for a month now, though in fact she was wrong; I'd been back far longer. As for the last part of her message, I rather imagined it was meant as a threat.

I remembered her, just as I remembered everything before the stretch of time blanked from my mind. I could remember her room in that dilapidated building, its walls covered with gaudy pastoral scenes, trees hanging with fruit, birds perched upon branches, flowers and yet more flowers. Less money spent, a little more thought, and the effect could have been quite charming, but Asselina and concepts such as moderation would always be at odds. I had liked her though, she was fun. In any case, since my life had become too much of a humourless thing, I felt I might be able to turn my back on my worries and bury myself, quite literally, in the here and now, which is why I went to her in the cool of that early dawn.

And how, I've often wondered, would the next part of my life have unfolded had I not raised myself out of my lethargy, not stayed precisely the hours and moments I did and, if after leaving her, had not been accosted by a voice from the past.

It was late morning by now and having picked my way down from the Subura, I was on the point of risking what was left of my life by stepping out amidst the thronging crowds on the Sandilarius crossing when I heard a horrible voice shrieking my name across the teeming thoroughfare. Its shrill screeching cadence could have belonged to none other than that outrageous old rascal, Fabius Licinius Rufus.

A litter and the slaves balancing its weight had come lumbering and wobbling in my direction and a hand had reached out from between its hangings to strike me with a spongy object.

'If you,' and the hand struck out at me again, 'haven't been trying your best to avoid me, my mother's a whore. Now get in, and quick.'

It was mighty obvious that getting aboard was my only option, since until I did the entire crossing would be forced to suffer, for he had a voice did Fabius. What's more, the crowd had started to laugh at the sight of the outlandish foreigner, freedman's cap poking up in the air, being swiped across his face by a slipper.

Once inside its safe confines, I held my hands up, woefully aware of what was in store for me.

'Don't start,' I warned.

'Whatever can you mean?'

'Just don't, that's all.'

'Dear, dear, a little testy this morning, aren't we? Such ages since I've seen you like this, Siva my treasure. One year, eleven months and three days to be precise ... but, then again, who's keeping track?' And he handed me the offending slipper, indicating that I should fit it back upon his foot.

How shiny black his toenails were painted. What wouldn't the Asselinas of this world have given to command such outright vulgarity? No wishy-washy bad taste for him; Fabius was Rome at her best.

And his next words, 'No more than a personal observation, my sweet, but don't you look ... a ...' and here he sniffed the air as though some unpleasant odour was assailing his nostrils '... tad dishevelled? Did someone tie you in a bag and throw you into the Tiber? Is that where you've been all this time? If not,' and here he settled his copious backside into a more comfortable position, 'why then they should have for that's the perfect place for you.'

He did have a point though; he was calling to mind, I supposed, the Siva of old, he of the impeccable demeanour, of the long plaited hair and eyes lined with kohl, the very same Siva whom for such ages he'd been trying to get into his bed despite the fact that time and again I'd told him that, strange though he might find the concept, I happened to be a lover of women.

But this had been a mere detail, fit only for ignoring. When he'd come back for the umpteenth time and for the umpteenth time he'd been rejected, he'd only mouthed the same, unbowed response, something along the lines of, 'Oh what a wicked waste,' or 'One mustn't cease to live in hope'.

Fabius had been good for me though, his scandalous behaviour had served as an antidote to my stolid and decorous life and so I'd continued being his friend, despite the fact that if Marcus had found out he never could have approved. Worse still, had even so much as a whisper about whom his son's freedman chose to spend his time with fluttered about the ears of his father, well, that's something I'd rather not think about.

'Home for weeks now and not a word from you. Not one reply to my countless invitations, delivered by the hand of Zeno himself, to come and watch my new performance. Every night I peered out from the stage in eager expectation, only to have my heart wrenched so cruelly from my body, for you weren't there. No Siva Ostorius, I shan't forgive you, no matter how you urge.'

For the sake of all that was holy, couldn't he see I was ill? In all the time that I'd been back, I hadn't so much as ventured out.

'Oh, poor darling, not been out. Been in though, not ill enough for that.'

A moment in his company and already he'd managed to rile me.

'Sacred gods,' I marvelled, 'can't you even go down to the Subura without the whole place gossiping about it?'

'Gossip? Who, me? Surely by this time you know that I never indulge in gossip and hearsay,' and he'd laughed down his nose in that irritating way of his. 'In any case, don't flatter yourself, your antics in a whore house are hardly interesting enough to be considered gossip. You want gossip? I'll give you gossip. Hundreds of tales are dashing about the City, all about Britain, some less true than others I'll be bound. And here you suddenly appear, the very one to testify as to which are and which aren't.'

'Are and aren't what?' By now he had completely lost me.

'False. True. Oh, forget it. What should you care anyway since they'd all pale into insignificance were they to stand beside those of one who's actually been there.'

Now he was sulking.

I kept my mouth shut.

My silence shocked him, I suppose. As we rocked along inside the claustrophobic confines of the litter, I felt it impossible to blurt out the truth, that the one year, so many months and so many days he spoke about in such accusatory tones had completely disappeared from my mind. He knew me too well though and, sensing something must be wrong, he shed his huffed and petulant tone and tried to cajole me into merriment in that old way of his.

'I've heard accounts of Britain, oh yes indeed, stories to make one's blood run cold. But – and here I promise you it's true – I said to every last one of those scurrilous tale-mongers, *I shan't believe a word you say until Siva Ostorius comes back and I can hear it from the horse's mouth*. Or in your case, donkey's.'

'Donkey's what?'

'Mouth, darling, mouth. Unless, since your trip to that island of Hades you've taken to speaking from any other orifice.'

From his expression I could tell that only now did he seem to be grasping the fact that he was confronting an altogether different being from the one he used to call his friend.

'My dear,' he went on. 'Look at me. You're altered. You're not Siva anymore. What can have happened to promote such a change? You left elegant, refined, and come back looking like some low-living,' and here he paused mid-sentence in order to seek out the perfect word, at long last settling upon 'degenerate', which, coming from him was rich indeed.

'Does this mean you don't love me anymore?' I wondered out loud. 'Am I to have some peace at last?'

'Love you now, a nasty, scruffy, unshaven ...' and again he cast about for just the right word, 'ruffian' being the one he came up with. 'Sorry, my lamb, but now I must look for another. And to think, there I've been, keeping myself for you all this while.'

Despite my confused state of mind, I found myself smiling; it's impossible not to when you're with Fabius.

'You smile. Oh, but perhaps I'm being cruel? What about the inner Siva though?' And leaning forward he caught my cheek between his finger and thumb and called out, 'Yoo-ho, Siva, are you in there?'

I slapped his hand away. But on he continued, undaunted.

'The Siva I remember, quick-witted Siva, diviner of future events. *What will you be up to in one year eleven months and three days?* I might have asked you back then. *Oh, let me see, that's the time I've set aside for a little boating trip out on Venus' mirror ...*'

What foolishness lurked within the depths of Fabius' skull.

'... or some such thing you'd have replied. Ha, I applaud the fact that for once you'd be wrong. *What will you be doing in one year eleven months and three days?* No, Siva my treasure, not passing time with trifles such as boating or any other gentle pastime, but staggering across the Sandilarius looking like, like, a ...' and here he paused to ransack his cache of extravagant vocabulary for another adjective fitting enough to describe my new persona, '... hardened criminal.'

And that was the moment, the perfect moment, the moment he struck out his foot and kicked me so hard as to jolt me through the litter's gauzy curtain onto a thoroughly irritated looking chap pushing oil vats along in his handcart. I was suspended now, half in, half out of the swaying contraption.

'Oh, come sir, join us do, down here in the land of the ordinary mortal,' the oil vendor barked whilst struggling to keep his load balanced.

And with this I heard Fabius' braying laugh; he so enjoyed the banter of the street-wags.

I look back to that moment and wonder. Did the gods prompt him to kick just when he did? Are we placed upon a predetermined path in life, along which we're set to struggle till the end, a path from which we cannot deviate? And should we stumble off that path, will there always be a hand poised ready to place us back upon it? Chance, fortune, providence, the gods are they all rolled into one? When I dipped out of the curtain of Fabius' litter that morning, after the kick had been so deftly discharged, I saw the face I knew would save me. Not the flushed and angry one belonging to the oil vendor but another face, an ordinary face, not a face from the part of my life I could remember but one I knew better than even my own. And the wide, astonished eyes of the face had returned my gaze and the small man to whom it belonged started to push his way towards me through the throng, mouth open, shouting in a peculiar language which I seemed to understand.

'Siva … Stranger. Look it's me … Siva, look, it's me.'

We were together on the brow of a hill, looking out over an undulating swathe of land towards a far horizon. The small man, the one I'd just seen thrusting his way towards me, shouting my name, was leaning against a great pile of wood. I knew it was a beacon, ready for lighting. And then the image left me and I found I couldn't breathe.

Fabius, peering out from the curtain, advanced and receded in front of my eyes. I tried to tell the bearers to stop but my voice wouldn't work.

'Stop!' squealed Fabius.

I clambered down and started to push back through the crowds; he was here in the Vicus, the little man who held the keys to the lost years. I heard myself shout, 'Petronius.' But who was Petronius, and how could I be so convinced that if I found him my torment would come to an end.

But he was nowhere to be seen.

*

You've become a madman, the creature staring out from the mirror seemed to be saying.

I held its gaze and wondered. Was this really me? Did some vestige of my old self remain within me still, no matter how I'd changed from the Siva of before, the Siva who'd lived in this house, a member of the Scapula family for half my life?

Loath though I was to admit it, Fabius had been right in his summing up of my new appearance. I fingered the stubble on my face. Were these my eyes? Was this my nose, that my mouth? I wanted to cry out but managed to control myself for the consequence of such behaviour would be proof, if proof were indeed required, that contrary to my almost normal demeanour of that morning, no longer was I fit to be part of a noble family's household. And though the old boys would try to prevent it, I'd be taken away and confined somewhere far from Rome, a comfortable place where I'd be well treated, but away from the City nonetheless and any hope I might have of finding the little man who'd run after me shouting, 'Siva ... Stranger. Look it's me,' in that odd but familiar language.

My name was Siva, though the face staring out at me hardly seemed to be his at all; that had been a tranquil face, devoid of emotion. And Siva Ostorius had worn his hair long, had plucked his eyebrows where the hairs ran along the bridge of his nose. His features had been fine, his shoulders slanting. Such a pity he'd been a lover of women for only think what fortunes were to be made in the beds of the Fabiuses of this world. This new face, filled out and rough, cut all over with scars, set on its thickset neck upon powerful shoulders, wasn't mine, might it belong to the one called Stranger? Yet Asselina and Fabius had known me; Asselina with joyful amazement, Fabius with lashings of bogus dismay.

And the slaves had known me too.

'At least you're alive,' they'd tried to comfort. 'The very one who claimed he'd never survive army life.'

But I knew it wasn't the army that had done this to me. And who was the little man out on the Sandilarius crossing, who I seemed to know?

That night in the garden, it felt as if the very stars were pressing down upon me from the heavens above, such were the tortures of my mind. Who was I? Who could I be now? And in what felt destined to be another failed attempt, so often had I tried to enter back into myself during those past interminable weeks, I held my arms close to my side and sucked my breath deep into my chest, inhaling to the count of seven. Numbness engulfed my mind, and as the oppressive weight of the glimmering lights above seemed to lift, I found myself experiencing that most comforting of sensations, akin to drunkenness, that I had known so well.

I was tumbling backwards, back, and back. I was free again, skimming out across a void, darkness beneath and darkness above, faster and faster. I was a bird with outstretched wings, hovering above a silver landscape. And, looking down, I wasn't in the least surprised to see the figure below, crouching in a leather tent, and know it was me. I was back again, I'd returned to that forest's edge, the dawn that marked my second birth.

The anguish was gone, my mind was clear. The lost years raced into my mind. Again, I faced Cal. Again, I rode with him to the place they call Nemeton, again I hung my sunship on the golden branch, and again and again, until the waking touched me as they'd say in the still unconquered lands, and I knew that I wanted nothing else but to stay there and dream it all forever.

ISLAND OF THE PAINTED PEOPLE
Two Years Earlier, A.D. 44

CHAPTER ONE
THE MISSION

I was crouching in my leather tent at the edge of a forest with nothing for company save the incessant pattering of rain which covered our camp in a blanket of misery.

Though the guttering lamp gave out little to no heat, I'd been huddled over it since darkness had fallen, every manner of ghastly thought creeping into my mind, my only comfort stemming from the fact that thus far I'd avoided having my hair shorn. For though Gratius had taken such glee to inform me that a head full of lice was not what I wanted, at least I had increased my chances against the perishing cold, having wrapped its front section around my neck and tucked the rest under my army-issue waterproof cloak thus providing an extra layer against the frigid chill. Under these two layers I wore five others, two of oiled felt, two of wool and under them one of silk, none of which, I may add, did much to help me for still I was frozen to the marrow of my bones.

But what, in the name of all the gods, was I doing there in the first place?

It was Marcus' fault; he was the one who'd summoned me to that place of miserable torment. I counted it as an act of wanton treachery, and didn't think I could ever forgive him.

My name at that time was Siva Ostorius. My last name belonged to my master but Siva was my own, which will tell you that I wasn't Roman.

All had been normal in my calm and organised life until that early morning when he had sent for me. I was set to accompany him to the senate and, being used to last-minute changes – mainly of time – I had my writing case ready and was dressed in my linen kilt and silk-fringed tunic. My hair was plaited as usual, I had lined my eyes with kohl and my sunship hung from its chain round my neck.

In the land of my birth I had looked just like everyone else; those inhabitants of my memory wear vivid colours – turquoise and pink are the ones I see when I close my eyes, colours of jewellery or the tasselled belts of the white-clothed priests of the temple. But in all the years I had lived in my new one, I'd never known how it felt to look like a Roman, my master having decided to keep me exactly the way I was when first he set eyes upon me. I don't know if this was an idea he'd had from the start or if it was one that came to him later. But earlier or later, I'd been happy enough to adopt the somewhat mystical guise he dreamt up for me to use as a weapon against his adversaries. As I stood beside him, tablet and stylus in hand, my strange appearance would divert their attention from what he was actually saying; his words seldom being as straightforward as they might have seemed.

In that seething, jostling City known as the centre of the world, only those who lived on the periphery of life accepted me as a person in my own right. Others regarded me as an exotic being, or perhaps an inconsequential oddity, yet I was content to look out from behind my painted face. My life was easy and predictable; I had no choices to make, neither did I want any.

When I arrived in his room, I found the great man pacing the floor. He turned when he heard me and looked at me somewhat apologetically. 'Plans have changed, my Siva,' he said. 'Gratius will come with me today, you have more urgent things to attend to.' He paused. 'A message has come from Marcus.' I might have said earlier that Marcus was his son, but perhaps I should add that in many ways he was more like a friend. 'He is well and the campaign is going to plan.'

I thanked the gods for this news, though things could have changed ... who knew what might have happened to him in the meantime; but I couldn't allow myself to think in this way.

'The important thing, however, he asks me send you to him.'

If I hadn't known better, I might have thought it was the festival day of Hilaria and this was one of his jokes. But it wasn't, and a great horror rose up inside me. I only just managed to find my voice. 'But ... why, sir?'

'It seems that you're the only one who can help him with some crazy plan. He's set it all out in a letter, but it would take too many words to explain what it is, and half a day for you to read them. I'm willing to go along with his wishes on condition that he returns you to me in April.'

This made no sense; how could I get there – and back – by then? But wait a minute, this was ridiculous. Surely, I'd wake up and find I'd been dreaming.

'Don't worry,' he said, 'you're going by boat. It's only just autumn, the seas are calm, with a fair wind it should take you two weeks at most. Come, I will show you.'

He led me to his table, upon which lay the same unrolled map that Marcus and I had studied together. Then it had been to plot his journey, along the Aurelia to the Alps and through them into Gaul. I might explain here that this had taken place the year before when he set out with Claudius' legions to take his part in the invasion of Britain.

But now my master placed his finger on a new starting point, tracing it close to the coast, round the bulge of Hispania and sweeping it over a stretch of water to the spot so recently marked as the camp of the XX Legion.

'It will be a different experience for you, and one I hope you'll enjoy.'

Hope was one thing, reality another. I forced a smile upon my face.

'It's an honour,' I managed. 'And it will be good to see Marcus again.'

'You'll be a rational presence in his life for the next stretch of time,' he replied, 'and I thank you for that. Gratius will set out the details; I have pressing business or I would do so myself. You have two days to prepare for the journey. May the gods go with you.'

All I could do was thank him.

I stumbled back to my room and slumped on my bed. 'By sacred Jove, Marcus, what have you done to me?'

The first days of September had been set to continue as they had until now, with duties marked out in my master's library, accompanying him to an ally's house – or more likely a rival's – writing up his notes. And then there were the joyful things, floating in Fabius' little bathhouse out on the Via Tusculanum, sitting on the roof at night, charting the heavens.

But now here I was and in little more than a day I'd be turning my back on it all; my fate from now on was too dreadful to imagine.

What did I know about Britain? An island filled with sorcery and horror, they called it, set at the edge of the world, though amongst those who understood such things, we knew it was round and therefore didn't have edges. But even though they were wrong on this count, words like fearsome, mysterious, barbaric crowded into my mind. And then there were tales of talking trees and stones that walked ... and men who pulled the moon from the sky with hooks made of silver.

I did my best to console myself; Marcus was there and I would be with him again. But somehow this didn't seem to help.

Gratius came to my room later that day. My bed was piled with towers of neatly folded undergarments, tunics of silk and fine-spun wool, laced Persian boots, my star-map, shaving knife, toothpicks, medical recipes and potions; little bags of things like myrtle and hericium, dried venom of various types, the smaller of my crucibles, a pestle and mortar ...

Then there was the food; dates, dried apricots, a pot of pickles, fig jam, two cheeses.

'What's all this?' he wanted to know, making no secret of the fact that he thought me beneath his contempt, he being the model of all that was Roman.

'My stuff,' I stated the obvious, then worried that I might have sounded offhand; it was never wise to ruffle Gratius' feathers.

'You've to take what you're wearing,' he replied with an air of elegant indifference, 'and that ... black stuff ... for your eyes, your army kit, which you'll be given. That's all. Don't cut your hair, keep it as it is.' He turned his lips down as if in sympathy. 'But you do know that it won't be long before it's full of lice.'

He flicked his finger at my sunship. 'You're to take that too, and if you want my advice, I'd keep it out of sight or it'll be gone before you know it.'

I didn't really want his advice, but I supposed it might be a good idea to take it. 'I'll find someone to bring you your marching pack.'

Pack wasn't such a terrible word; marching was the one that got me.

When he left, I sat down on my bed amidst my piles of packing. All would have to be abandoned. But apart from its fearsome reputation, the other thing I knew about Britain was its wet and freezing climate, and if I'd learned anything during the twenty-two years of my life it was that desperate events require desperate action. The particular action just needs thinking about, so as far as the clothes were concerned, the thing to be done was to wear as many as I could. Everything else had to go. I was particularly sorry about the food but consoled myself with the fact that the pleasure of eating was low on Marcus' list of priorities. And as for the rest, he was bound to have loads of it; three carts filled with his personal effects had followed his legion on its journey to that hideous place only a few months before.

It was the new slave-boy Ares who appeared at my door a little while later; he seemed rather nervous. 'Please, Siva,' he said. 'I've been sent to help you and tell you what's on this list.'

He looked at my stacked-up piles in dismay.

'Were you thinking of taking all that?'

'I was, but I'm not anymore.'

'I only asked because you'd never get it all in.' He placed what looked like a large leather satchel upon the heap of forbidden belongings and said, as if it were the worst thing in the world, 'There are only a few things you're allowed.'

'I know, I wish they'd told me.'

He looked at me with great sympathy.

'I still have to bring your army clothes.' He checked his list and repeated what Gratius had just taken such glee to inform me. 'But you've to take what you normally wear as well and the paint you put around your eyes.'

'I can't believe this is happening.'

He did his best to console me. 'We've heard that it's only till April and that you're going by boat. And whilst you're away, we'll pray for you and offer cakes to Salus.' But even though he didn't succeed, I smiled and thanked him all the same.

'Shall I stay with you for a little?'

I told him not to worry, I was fine. I just had to look upon it as an adventure and I would tell him all about it when I got back.

If I was sure then; he turned to leave, but then he stopped. 'I forgot to say but,' he pointed at my neck and repeated what Gratius had just said 'you've to take that as well.'

I told him I would.

'I hope you don't mind if I ask what it is. I've been here for a while now and have seen you wear it.'

'An amulet,' I held it out. 'It's called a sunship.'

He stepped towards me to look at it closely. 'It's beautiful,' he said. 'I've never seen anything like it before.'

I took it off and held it up.

The little ship, carved from a slice of carnelian hung from its copper disk. 'Look,' I placed my finger on the disk, 'that's the sun,' I moved it to the little crescent-shaped stone suspended beneath it, 'and that's the ship of a god called Ra.'

A moment's silence then he asked, 'What's he doing?'

'Bringing light into the sky. He sails across it every day.'

'It isn't Roman?'

'No,' I said, 'it's from Egypt. It's all that's left of my old life.' And thinking that he might feel sad for a life he'd once had himself, 'But look,' I said to cheer him. I opened the disk. 'It used to hold perfumed wax.'

Even after all that time a shadow of the scent of blue lotus floated towards us. For half a moment I could see the delta, its banks planted out in green ribbons, the butter yellow of the sands, a canopy of stars stretched above me.

'You're lucky to have such a wonderful thing.'

'But I've got something else you might like.' I took my Persian boots from the pile and handed them to him; he was tall so I thought they might fit. 'They're yours if you'd like them.'

'They said you were kind and now I know it.'

Just then a voice shouted, 'Ares!' He was wanted back in the garden where he'd been helping to water the fruit trees.

'Good luck there,' he said, 'but you've got your sunship and it will protect you.' He turned as he left. 'Maybe you should keep it hidden. I've heard its rough out there. Someone might want to steal it.'

When he'd gone, I rolled up my linen kilt and tunic and wondered when I'd wear them again.

CHAPTER TWO
TO THE EDGE OF THE WORLD

The next day found me at the port. Having been given my army gear, one pair of hobnails were on my feet, the other was tied inside a heavy and dank-smelling waterproof cloak. I wore leather breeches, which chafed my legs, and a red over-tunic of military design. I had longed to dress like an ordinary Roman, but this wasn't what I'd had in mind.

The sun had only just risen but I was sweltering, having opted to wear all five of my tunics under my clothes for fear they'd be confiscated. And so, filled with trepidation as to what lay in store, I reconciled myself to the unimaginable and stepped onto the gangplank.

The boat was a large one filled with supplies, of which I was part. My freedman's cap did its duty and I was treated with respect and the usual suspicion, given my own space, and fed fairly regularly. I used these first days to listen to conversations between the sailors for I realised that despite the weekly sessions spent with my master in the Senate House, and thinking it quite unimportant, I had absorbed not so much as a single fact about the invasion.

The voyage turned out to be a test of utmost endurance; I'd

only ever crossed a vast expanse of water once before, on my way to my new life in Rome. Then the pointed prow of the skiff had sliced through green, sun-dappled waves and the wind had been from the south. This time was different though. After two days, the wind turned against us and up and down and up we reared on mountainous waves, and for the following days dread reigned supreme.

But worse was to come. As great bleached ghost cliffs came into view, rising like palaces out of the waters, mere dread was swapped for utter panic and my body was wracked with a shivering and shaking as the boat lurched mightily this way and that. Storm clouds, the colour of cuttlefish ink, tumbled down upon the ocean, and before the wind turned into a tempest, the sails were furled and the boat used the oars. A drum started beating loudly and steadily and my heart went out to the mariners ordered into action below me.

The searing blasts grew stronger. At first, I tried to cling onto the rails with the thought of vomiting over them, but one of the sailors saved my life. From then on, grasping a wooden bowl to my chest, I curled up in my corner. I didn't even have strength to pray.

By the time we made land, at a dockside as unlike Ostia as was remotely imaginable, I had been rendered a babbling idiot. I'd imagined that nowhere could have been worse than my small corner of boat, but I had been inordinately mistaken. Mud, sand and who knew what else was mired into a soupy mess, upon which hundreds of feet squelched daily. Then there was the shouting, braying of pack mules, banging of pulleys, trundling of machinery and smells from pigs alive and slaughtered. Add to this the stink of human excrement, for think how many latrines had been dug, the only thing preventing the great many stinks from becoming overpowering stenches was the wind blasting in from the sea.

Gratius' words hit me hard now, and I made sure that my sunship was tucked well down between the folds of my five tunics.

I had been told that when we berthed, I was to travel on one of the pack-carts waiting on the wharf side. Fifty or more snaked beside the boat waiting for instructions to load.

I could but thank the gods that I was assigned to the fifth in the queue, in charge of an elderly soldier. Reluctant to have me anywhere near him, I sat on the bare planks behind his load of crates. As we bumped along the half-finished road, they slid this way and that, forcing me to move my position every few minutes. Flat countryside stretched all around, and a grey sky hung above us. By the time we reached our destination the only thing keeping me alive was thoughts of food, bed and safety. Marcus came a good way after.

It's true, the anticipated perception of a forthcoming event is almost always contrary to the way it turns out. And so it was then. This was the first time I'd come face to face with an army camp and found it difficult to remember what I'd imagined it would be like; certainly nothing as nightmarish as this.

In my feeble state I was unable to take in much about what seemed to me more like the prison blockhouse down by the Tiber, my first scant impression being of crossed towers protruding at either end of massive gates. A standard inscribed with a leaping boar and the words Leg XX whipped in the wind above them. The carts were guided onwards. When mine reached the checkpoint, it was explained that I had been sent to join one Marcus Ostorius, and we were waved through. Back in the City, my position would have assured me help to clamber down. But not here. Due to my time spent on rolling waves, followed by trundling along in the cart, by the time my feet reached the ground I could barely stand upon them.

I was told that Marcus' quarters were in one of a small row of what looked like barrack buildings they said were the headquarters. 'Look, that one with the eagle banner hanging outside it.'

I pushed the leather door-flap open, and there he was, bent over a table. A basket of dispatches were spilled on the floor, tablets stacked in untidy piles to left and right. How he detested work that had nothing to do with battle, training, weapons, or the like.

'… Marcus.'

Despite the fact that by now my throat felt as if it had been scoured by a salt stone scrub, with my voice reduced to little more than a whisper, he heard me. But when he turned, it wasn't Marcus but Quintus Paulinus, one of his fellow officers whom I happened to like enormously, a consequence of the fact that he so obviously hated military things, almost as much as I did. His father had carried some minor honours from various campaigns, and like all sons of army men, poor Quintus had been sent out to foreign fields with orders to follow in that good man's footsteps. And here he was now, in what was no more than a draughty hut, in some far-off land, set against an enemy he couldn't care less about defeating. But if Marcus wasn't around then he was the very one to restore my faltering spirits.

He looked ecstatic to see me. 'Praise be Siva, here you are … and in one piece, thank all the gods.'

He took my pack and guided me to his camp bed. I

stretched out upon it and closed my eyes. By now my head thumped as loudly as the drum that had beaten the oar stroke. I managed to ask where Marcus was, before falling into the arms of Hypnos, and therefore didn't hear his answer.

I had slept for six hours, Quintus took great pleasure to tell me. I felt as if my bones had been smashed with a mallet and unable to muster the strength, he helped me sit, and when I could speak I asked him again about Marcus.

'Don't worry.' He did his best to smile, but a flicker of something inside me suggested that worry was something I shouldn't entirely cast aside. 'I'll explain it all, but first you must get yourself to the bathhouse. By Jupiter, you look strange dressed like that,' he added. Did he mean even stranger than I had before?

I could only agree.

Leading me out along a corded pathway, he waved at the building work in full swing around us. 'As you can see, we're still under construction; it'll take a few more months until we're up and running.'

Even though this was the baths used by the upper echelons, we entered what seemed more like a stone-built outhouse than anything else. In one corner stood a stove, one of those contraptions you fire up with bellows, which, as he told me the hypocaust system had not yet been completed, served to heat the water for the hot pool and the room itself. Undecorated and purely functional, it was nothing like any back home.

I thank the gods that this was the time for the evening meal, and we were alone. As my sole purpose was to get myself clean, after I'd cast off my clothes, I handed him my sunship and stood while the bath servant mopped me down. He saw the slave brand on my arm, and I can't imagine what he thought. I longed to lounge for a while in the steam room but, desperate to find out about Marcus, I spent only a moment or so in the cold pool before I put my filthy clothes back on and we made our way back to the hut, where I promptly took them off again.

Wrapped in a blanket, my legs comfortably bare, my army issue hobnails no longer on my feet, I was ready to eat with a still joyful Quintus.

Bowls of seaming lentils sat on the table before us. I grabbed one, and without waiting to skim the fat from its surface, rammed its contents into my mouth.

Quintus took a spoonful from his own before pushing it towards me. I accepted his offer and set about its contents with gusto. He waited until I had scraped the last lentil onto my spoon before giving the news. 'I'm sorry, old chap, he's not here. You'll have to make a bit of a journey to reach him.'

Those endless days rearing up and down upon waves, squelching through mud at the landing place, the cart ride of Charon, only to find he was somewhere else, was a heart-crushing moment I can tell you.

'He's up on the frontier.' And as if to cheer me with wonderful news, 'You're to join him.'

Whatever torture I'd suffered till now paled to insignificance.

'Don't worry.' These words again. 'There's a double detachment of auxilia going up country for outpost garrison duties.' I tried to batten down my shock. 'But not for a couple of days,' he added as if to console me.

Double detachment and outpost garrison duties were words from a foreign language to me. I could only assume they were taking me with them. I can't imagine what my expression must have been like.

'Sorry, old chap, but you'll be alright.'

I couldn't entirely agree with him. But now came the crunch. 'Why did he send for me? Do you know?'

'It's to do with a tribe called the Brigante. They're tremendously powerful. It's thought that their leader, a woman called Cartimandua, could be persuaded to join Rome. The thing that stands in our way are her priests. They're believed to have mystical powers, divining the future amongst other things, and are really the ones who're in charge. Anyway, all they've witnessed of Rome so far is the military side of things, and from what Marcus said, he wants to show them a different one.'

But what on earth did he think I could do?

'Be proof that Rome isn't entirely composed of columns of marching men, that religious people are here as well, that they'll have the chance to spread their own beliefs throughout the Empire. Tempt them into submission, in other words.' He chuckled. 'He wants to make them think that you have powers greater than theirs that you could use to destroy them.'

Unable to miss my expression, he tried to mitigate any damage he'd made. Perhaps there was some logic to Marcus' plan. 'Your knowledge of the stars could be used as evidence – or false evidence – for his claim.'

Ye gods, this was crazy. 'It sounds ridiculous to me.'

'For Rome,' he said, 'but not here.'

The sooner I got to Marcus the better; he was surely going out of his mind. Or had already. I thought of the little bag of hericium, back there in my room, just when I needed it here.

Quintus was shaking me awake. I failed to hear the first part of what he was saying, which seemed to involve the word hurry '... the weather's changing for the worse.'

Why was he talking about weather?

'They're leaving now.'

I blinked up at him.

'The auxilia, they're leaving … you have to hurry.'

But hadn't he said I'd have a couple of days before I set off?

'I'm sorry.' It was clear that he was. 'But things have changed.'

There was hardly time to pull on my breeches. He helped me with my hobnails, my waterproof cloak, after which he took my pack from his table.

'I'll see you when you get back,' he said, as he thrust it into my arms.

When did he think that would be?

But 'soon' was all he said before abandoning me to the guard who'd appeared to accompany me down through the gates to a patch of ground where my travelling companions waited.

'They're Macedonian,' he confided in a low voice as he handed me over. I couldn't work out if he thought this a good thing or not.

I knew little about the men who stood by their horses save for the fact that Marcus had always liked auxilia, perhaps because their ranks were composed of foreigners, like me.

CHAPTER THREE
THE WAX MAP

My trip to the frontier started not too badly at all helped by the fact that the young captain in charge seemed more than somewhat astonished when I informed him, in Greek, that I was the chap who'd been assigned to his protection.

Having digested this information, he looked me up and down. Didn't a fellow who could speak his precious language every bit as well as he, deserve the best of treatment? A good mount had already been found for me, but now, having proven myself, I was invited to take up a position beside him behind the unit's out-riders, two gentlemen of ferocious appearance who, in addition to their standard uniforms, wore wrist-shields and had short-bows slung across their saddles.

The captain had been told my name, but now he asked to make sure. 'Just Siva then, are you?'

He was used to convoluted Roman names, or so I assumed, and I thought I should explain. 'Well yes, to my friends, but my full one is Siva Ostorius Scapula.'

I promptly wished I hadn't bothered trundling out that long and convoluted title. I might have been wearing army clothes but now he knew I was a slave. Alongside this young captain, not much older than me, who'd doubtless fought battles on many frontiers, I felt diminished. Thank all the gods that my cap, filthy by now, with its point all bashed, was back in the hut with Quintus and not still on my head. A badge of dishonour, or so I felt then.

Whether for want of finding something to say on the subject of being a slave or because he knew Marcus, he whistled through his teeth. He followed this by introducing himself. 'And I'm Leonatus.'

There was no road out of camp, not even a path, which meant we were forced to heel our horses on through miry, waterlogged grassland. And as if this weren't enough, on reaching a somewhat higher plateau, and looking back across the distance we'd covered, we could see storm clouds rolling in from the sea.

It was upon us in moments, and in moments we were drenched. My army issue waterproof cloak might not have been the most elegant of garments, but I was thankful for it now.

'Pull it out to cover your horse's flanks,' said Leonatus. 'Look. Like this.' He helped me arrange mine just so, with spectacular results; the waterproof fabric slanted, tent-like, from my shoulders and the rain just glided off.

That early evening, we made camp. I reckoned we must have covered close to twenty miles, quite a feat taking the terrain into count, which had been a virtual quagmire all the way from the camp gates. The Macedonians, however, were frustrated in the extreme, having hoped to make twice the distance at the very least.

On the boat across the ocean, listening to those conversations about army life I had made a monumental discovery ... the power that drives the mighty forces of the

Empire is rivalry, pure and simple. Rivalry between centuries of any particular cohort, between cohorts of any particular legion, between cohorts of separate legions, and on, and on; the greatest rivalry of all being that stoked up between the legionaries and auxilia, such wrangling being the very lifeblood coursing through their veins.

A unit from the II might have built a ditch in record time. Records are made to be broken, however, and when the inevitable happened and the previous feat was bettered, if by a fellow unit it would be accepted, but only just. If by a unit from another century it would be too, but far less so. If by a unit attached to a rival legion, barely tolerable, but if, dear gods, by a unit of auxilia, why then a pall of thorough resentment would settle on the shoulders of the trounced, and the poor old Thracians, Iberians or whomsoever would be made to pay dear. They beat us, we beat them, ditches dug faster, miles marched further. The men in charge were not so foolish.

Leonatus was thinking fast. It had taken a unit from the IX three days to make it to the frontier. This being the case, he'd set his lot the task of doing it in two, but now it threatened to be closer to four.

'It's this shithouse of a marsh,' he said. 'We'll have to get onto drier ground.' Which wasn't such a bad idea, if only someone could tell him how.

During the last part of that day's trek, as we forced our horses onward, the rain driving against our backs, we'd been able to make out a faint suggestion of hills blurred on the horizon. This being the case, it was decided that the main body of our unit should stop off here by a forest's edge and make camp; the trees would give at least some protection.

A patrol of scouts would head out towards higher land, see if they could find a dry track for tomorrow or, failing that, one less sodden.

Leonatus went too, and though by now evening was settling in and soon it would be too dark to use their bows, the archers went with them, which bore out Marcus' analysis of the men of the auxilia as opposed to those of the cohorts. A centurion would never have conceived of flaunting rules with such bravado; if a scouting job was called for then only scouts would do it. I could only presume that the Macedonians knew things that I, in my naivety, couldn't even have guessed.

I stood back watching as camp was dug by those left behind, feeling more useless with each passing moment. We'd stopped whilst a glimmer of light still hung in the sky and now, I realised why. Only by witnessing for myself the digging of an encampment ditch round a paced-out square, the earth from the ditch forming a rampart behind it, did I grasp the meticulous precision required, which would have been all but impossible when the last trace of light had gone from the sky. Despite this, however, the entire operation took no time, the men all working together. Up went the tents next, each to be shared by an eight-man crew. Leonatus had more space, there being only five in his; me his archers and the company trumpeter … a chap you wouldn't want to argue with.

In the haste of that morning, I'd brought no food, but my camp mates didn't seem to mind sharing what was, up till then, the least appetising meal I'd ever faced – bread and oil and a handful of boiled beans. I fell into conversation with the trumpeter, getting to grips with how it should be eaten, watching as he set about the task, covering the bread with his twelve beans or so, finishing off with a drizzle of oil.

Dusk had melted into night when we heard the patrol riding back, horses snorting, the quiet voices of men thanking the gods to still be in one piece. Leonatus appeared through the tent flap and greeted me politely. Had I been him I would have stretched out, dead to the world, but his staying power was remarkable. Now came his archers; they sat together by a small shaded and guttering lamp, heads close together, poring over a sizeable, double wax tablet. Until then I knew nothing of plotting charts, was familiar only with those of the lands of the Empire, complicated diagrams requiring much deliberation.

This map was different though. It was, to my unpractised eye, simply a triangle scored into the square of wax in its frame, inside which were groups of symbols which Leonatus was attacking with a stylus grasped between his broad soldier's finger and thumb.

There came a point when I could bear it no longer.

'Excuse me … but perhaps I could help.'

He and his archers turned round in unison, and patient looks were upon their faces.

'It's only that, well, you see, I'm rather good at this sort of thing. Marking down details, I mean.'

Now they turned to one another, eyebrows raised.

Leonatus made a space beside him, close to the lamp. The moon was full and shone through the gaps in the tent, adding to the light.

'Just tell me what you want marked, and where.'

'Another line of marsh, just here,' said he.

'Marsh?' I questioned.

'Crosses,' he said, pressing his fingertip to an empty patch of the triangle. 'Down here.'

'Six more?' I asked. 'Same as the line above?'

He nodded and I crossed away, but had to stop after three had been marked, his stylus was so old and useless I'd have thrown it away several hundred tablets before.

'Do you have a knife?' I asked, somewhat ridiculously, and he handed over the one on his belt. I whittled the blunt tip until it had been brought back to some kind of life. Then I started again, my second three crosses being of such elegant proportions I could see they were glad that I'd offered my services.

'One small hill – a square I mean, here and two there,' continued a much-impressed Leonatus.

And so deftly were my three squares marked that I felt I'd earned enough points to allow me to ask what, in fact, we were doing. This, I presumed, was some kind of chart.

'It is, and we're marking down our own observations,' he said, 'since we're going to cut up country tomorrow. It's a plotting table, you see. These marks,' he meant the squares and so on, 'represent hills, rivers, marshland, high ground. When we get to the garrison a fresh one will be drawn up, showing our new route, and that will be given to the unit we're replacing. They'll take it with them on their next excursion, add their own notes, and so on and so forth. It's how maps are made in the army. With first light we're leaving the route laid out for us … mark it here.' He curved the air with his finger. And now it was one of the archers' fingers stabbing the wax above a series of circles. 'North of the forest.'

I market it down.

'So, this is what Britain looks like,' I said, thinking how little the toppled triangle resembled the uneven edges of Britain on the map in my master's office.

'Not all Britain, we don't have any idea what that's like,' he answered, 'it's just a bit of the southern part.'

'Oh, I see,' I said, but I didn't really.

'Look,' said he, pointing to a large square to the left of a line marking what I took to be the coast. 'There's Dunum.'

'Dunum?'

'Camulodunum where we came from and,' he moved his finger a smidgen, 'here's where we are now, roughly, of course. And this,' he pointed a good way further up, 'is the frontier. Or it is at the moment.' The line beside it ran down in an arc, surrounded, completely, by crosses. He placed his finger on one of them. 'And here's the outpost garrison station, where we're heading.'

'What's beyond it?' I pointed above the topmost edge of the tablet.

'We call it the land of horror.'

A moment passed. I might have asked him what he meant but thought it better not to. Instead, I moved my finger a little southwards. 'And below it?'

'Brigantia. Enemy territory.' Now he was stabbing a point further down. 'And that,' he said, 'is the camp of the II.'

From what I'd picked up on the boat, this was Vespasian's legion. 'It's in Calleva, friendly country. But they won't be there much longer. They're off west as soon as they've worked out their plans and got rid of the enemy tribes closer to them. It'll probably be when winter is over.'

West was beyond the left of the tablet. 'It's their job to clear the place out. It makes me feel almost sorry for them.' He didn't sound sorry at all. 'The northern frontier's one thing. I don't fancy their chances out there.'

He'd completely lost me by now.

His finger moved back down all the way to Camulodunum, over a few crosses further south, past a thick, squiggly line. 'Major River ... Tamesis,' he informed, our ships are sailing on it already.'

CHAPTER FOUR
THE CAMP AT DAWN

It was barely light before a glimmer of warmth began to seep into my body. I had started to doze off, to dream. I was in the house on the Quirinal. It was the feast of Saturnalia and breakfast tables were piled high with food: caviar, walnut bread, pickled artichokes, salted ham. But just as I stretched my hand out towards them, they changed to plates of squares and crosses.

I came to slowly, the idea that any time now the camp would be stirring made me all the keener to stay where I was.

So, no surprise then that lying there, my mind focused on the faint flush of comfort creeping upwards from my feet, I heard nothing of them, but Leonatus did. I was jolted into life by three sets of feet kicking into my side as he and my camp mates stamped over me and hurtled out into the dawn. The trumpeter sounded alert and a great thundering noise, akin to that of stampeding cattle, came blasting towards us.

Looking back, I'm astonished at my calmness of mind; perhaps it all took place too quickly to be aware of anything much. As I got to my knees, I tried to gather my thoughts; startled, disorientated but not frightened, not at that point. I grabbed the knife I'd used to sharpen Leonatus' stylus ...

though what I thought I'd do with it, Mars only knew. And when I did stumble out into that arena of terror, what I saw before me would haunt my sleep for weeks to come, until I'd become so accustomed to blood and gore and pain and death that I was able to cast off the memory of the whole episode as if it were an old pair of shoes. Tied to their stakes within the ditches, the horses' shrieking added to the clamour and yells of the men; Leonatus roaring out orders. The trumpet blasting, over and over.

Those of our men not yet hacked to pieces stood together, a roof of shields over their heads, stabbing out as they'd been trained. It was mighty obvious, however, that tactics like these would do no good, as all around, slicing into them were the biggest men I'd ever seen. I was tall by Roman standards, yet they dwarfed even me.

If I can remember my first fleeting impression of a British war-party it's a glance of a memory of whiteness of skin and wildness of hair, the hair being what struck me first; the colour of plaster dust sweeping up from their heads like gamecocks' crests, and gold round arm, neck and waist.

And as delayed terror struck me full on, I found myself rooted to the spot. Beside me, a sword sliced through the trumpeter's neck; a slurping sound and his head whirled into the air. A spray of blood spurted over me and the only thing certain was that I'd be next for the same kind of treatment.

So, what are your thoughts when approaching your death? I was too dazed to think of anything much, the notion of trying to defend myself, even had I known the first thing about combat, futile indeed.

I stood, arms by my sides, tiny knife useless in my grasp as the one the gods had ordained would be my executioner stopped splitting open the last of my comrades still on their feet and walked towards me, shifting the hilt of his sword in his hands. It was like some drawn-out theatre piece unfolding bit by bit when the whole thing must have been over in no more than a glance. Strange how a terror-filled moment can be suffused with such clarity of thought. Big as the rest, with muscles sculpted onto a lean, spare body, and from his scalp stood white sharp-ended spikes of hair. Then there was his skin, paler than I thought skin could be, and across it was laced an intricate mesh of blue patterns. The hair, the patterns on his skin, his blue painted lips, and gold; thick armlets of the stuff, and a rope of it fastened around his neck. He wore nothing else.

During that long moment I was aware of a measured questioning in his expression. And I was right, for along with his obvious distaste at coming face to face with a creature so feeble as to be making not the slightest play at defending himself, he seemed every bit as intrigued by my appearance as I was by his.

He stopped in front of me and I saw his face; a serpent coiled its blue painted way across it.

Our eyes met, and as if he'd been stopped in his track by some invisible force, there he stood and for so very long that I found myself wondering if by some lucky chance the gods had struck him senseless.

But the gods weren't with me; the mighty sword was raised in the air and with barely time to gather my breath I looked into his eyes ... green they were, the colour of glass ... before the force of metal whacked into the base of my neck. A curtain drew over my eyes and did I fall or did the ground spin round to unbalance me? When one is dead, do minutes merge into hours and then into days? In what seemed an eternity but must have been no time at all, I expected to find myself being ferried over the Styx but instead there was smoke and a smell of gore, like the stench of the butchers' stalls in the meat market.

Then the pain struck.

Lying there in the mud, my agony wrapped around me, held me still and silent. With each beat of my heart came an explosion and I only wondered how long it took for a man's life to trickle away with his blood, and mine was all around me, seeping into the ground.

To die out there, on the edge of a barbarian forest, no pain now only a spinning inside my head and a blanked silence. But slowly, from somewhere within this mute world, I was dragged back into consciousness. Sound trickled out of the silence; screaming and clamour wrapped around me again. I opened my eyes and my anguish returned in all its splendour. I was aware of something above me. A foot pressed down hard on my chest. I gagged and the presence moved away. Next the force of freezing water struck my face and shoulders and words were spoken at me, words devoid of meaning, but before I was able to gather my scrambled thoughts, arms were round my shoulders pulling me to my feet. Dead weight that I was, I tumbled back onto the ground. The arms gripped round me again and I was hoisted upwards.

The glare of pain forced my mind to return to that place of numb refuge. I sensed a kind of jolting movement and a dull, repetitive sound like hooves striking soft ground seemed very close to my ear.

Time passed. The jolting ceased and I was dragged back onto the ground. The hoofbeats faded into the distance. I opened my eyes and was just about able to make out branches stretching above me. I was deep in the forest; the mud I supposed I'd been lying upon wasn't mud at all but a mixture of leaves and pine needles. And just as it had as I'd lain on Quintus' camp bed, a drum beat at top volume inside my head.

No terror or panic; these were my last moments of life. I was perched on the threshold ... what would death be like? Would my soul be given permission to walk through the iron roof of heaven?

I sensed a shape looming above me. A face came into focus and a hand was close to my neck, a strangling hand or so I thought, but all it did was rub my cheek as if to wipe off its colour.

My chin was grasped, and green eyes stared into mine. The owner of the face was talking at me, enunciating clearly, and I wondered if he was attempting some type of Latin. Perhaps, but if so, it was a strange type and he spoke with such an odd accent that even I, with my multitude of languages, had no hope of following it.

Frustrated by my lack of response, he took me by the neck of my cloak, pulling my face close to his, saying just four words this time. It was Latin now, I was sure. Had I been able to rouse myself sufficiently to conjure up a reply, the gods know I would have. I was desperate to speak to this man, but my voice had disappeared completely.

He repeated his phrase, and I caught some glimmer of sense in it now. 'Man. Are. You. What?'

And all I could do was reply with my silence; the last thing I needed at that most important of all the moments in my life. He gave up at this point, let go of his grip, crashing my head to the ground. And now I knew I'd have to smarten up if I were to stay alive. I'd have to listen and listen hard, try to work out what he was saying for only then might he and I be able to enter into some kind of understanding.

What was he doing now? I managed to prop my head up and watched for a while, thinking hard, as he picked sticks and branches from the ground, piling them together. When the pile was sufficiently high, he bent over it and striking a flint, produced a flame which he blew upon, coaxing it into life. And now from my worm's-eye view I saw him moving, stretching out on the ground almost out of sight. By pulling myself up a little more, my line of vision altered, and I was able, but only just, to see him lying motionless on his stomach.

A kind of madness washed over me then, and I fancied I could hear a voice, distinctly like Marcus'. 'Go now. Run,' it seemed to be saying. Madness indeed, as in the first place, I could barely stand, and in the second, just where would I be running to? Logical thought having flown from my mind, I attempted an escape of sorts, lurching noisily from the clearing towards the darkness of the forest.

He was upon me in an instant, his feet making scrunching noises on the carpet of leaves. My legs worked furiously, rather as legs do in dreams where you can't make distance no matter how you try. I felt heat from his body and the blow of his elbow against my neck. He pulled me round, and in the split second before he crashed his forehead into mine, I saw that his blue painted serpent had horns much like that of a satyr.

CHAPTER FIVE
A PLACE CALLED NEMETON

I came to through a pattern of lights flashing up from somewhere deep in my head, and I knew that I was good for nothing, I could move neither body nor limb and my skull was pierced with shards of agony.

I forced my eyes open and there he was, back in his old position, prostrate beside what now I could see was a riverbank. There was a glint of silver in his hand; he'd picked a fish out of the water. I'd never seen anything like it before, it was a big one too, as long as the distance between his fingertip and elbow, lashing about in his grip as he walked up from the water's edge. I knew just how that poor fish felt, at the mercy of our mutual captor. Mercy, he had none though for the rock came down on its head, and its motionless body was placed beside the flames. And no more than a moment before it had been alive and swimming in the river.

There's nothing worse than the smell of cooking for making an ill man sick to his stomach. And what's more, I could tell he was about to share his meal with me; to stay alive one must eat and, quite plainly, he wanted me alive. Simple as that. Though for how long I didn't know.

The painted man crouched by the fire. The charred shape

of the fish was pushed about in the embers then lifted out by its tail. I watched as he pulled flesh away from bone, took a chunk in his hands and rammed it into his mouth. It seemed that violence was good for the appetite. After a second chunk had been prised from the now white pungent mess of bones and skin, down he strode to the riverbank, indicating the remainder was for me.

The thought of moving, never mind putting a morsel of that fish in my mouth made my stomach heave. I had to get clear of the sickening smells, so even though every part of my body was racked with pain I was able to find strength to get up on my feet. And then another strange thing took place; back my captor came and pulled my arm round his neck. I felt the dry warmth of his skin and the power of his grip as he guided me to the river. But, by the time we'd made the twenty or so steps the ground was spinning again. I lost my balance, and to steady myself grasped out at the nearest solid object, the neck of the sturdy little war-horse with whose rump I had lately become so familiar.

The sparking settled, and feeling the ground firm once again I opened my eyes, but then I wanted to shut them again. Was what I saw in front of me real or some nightmarish illusion conjured up from somewhere within my battered mind? I forced myself to look at the thing tied to the horse's harness … the head of the company trumpeter or, should I say, what had once been his head but was now a mangled mass of bruises. One of his eyes was out, leaving a concave hollow above his cheekbone. Whilst sharing his bread and oil and handful of beans, he'd told me he was from Pydna, how he longed for home, for the warmth of the south, to feel the aches dissolve from his bones as he sat in a tavern by a dusty crossroad, to wait until the cool of the evening touched the town and the first lamps were lit, before venturing back to bed where he'd lie with the doors thrown open onto the night.

Now his night had come and I hoped he'd be carried back to the south in the arms of Up-Aut, would never feel cold or far from home again.

I was learning. Having lived in Rome for twelve years now, and for part of this time during the reign of Gaius Caligula, I should, I suppose, have been well versed in brutality, but I wasn't. Apart from a couple of instances in my life, witnessing the savagery of the slave market, and once, somewhere along the Appia, coming upon a crucifixion marking some old-time patriarch's funeral, I was a relative innocent. The bleeding apparition was enough to upset me properly, and for a very long time. I looked upon that severed head and was struck with absolute sorrow.

In fairness, however, I did manage to summon to mind the hymn of Ra and up-turning my hand to where I thought the sun might be if sun indeed there was, I attempted a silent mouthing of his death-rhyme.

> Praise be to thee, Oh Ra, Oh Timu.
> Thou hast risen and put on strength,
> and thou settest in glorious splendour into the underworld.
> Thou sailest in thy boat across the heavens
> And thou established the earth

From here on, the horse carried the three of us onwards, his master, his master's prisoner and what once had been a good soldier but was now my captor's trophy. As we journeyed through the forest, I scrutinised the painted man at close range.

Though big by Roman standards, his body was spare with none of that exaggerated brawn sported by the prize fighter; I imagined he looked like a hero of Marathon, perhaps, or an acrobatic tumbler. Now a nose's length away from the back of his head I studied his peculiar stiff and spikey hair, his neck ring, thick as a woman's wrist, fashioned from a deep, lustrous gold, the likes of which a potentate would sell his mother for. The sword strapped across his back was caked with dry blood and his skin spattered with it, but through its glaze I could make out indefinable whirling whorls spiralling round him like ribbons.

It was clear to me now these highly stylised designs were lost on a Roman's eye. 'Got these weird markings all over them,' I'd heard back on the boat. But I was Egyptian and their beauty wasn't lost on me.

And what of my surroundings? Rays of light slanted down through the trees whose leaves were not simply green as I'd always supposed leaves to be, but tinted orange, red and gold and spread like a multicoloured mosaic across the forest floor. Birdsong filled the space around us.

By this tree and round that one, down into a hollow and up to the summit of a rise; how he had the remotest idea where he was heading was a mystery to me. Only that slightly flinching muscle of his left arm let me know that he was guiding his horse along a well-journeyed path.

On we went until the sun, glimpsing through the branches above, entered its central position in the heavens. The horse was forced from its amble to a halt and my captor signalled that I should dismount. I did so, stiffly, for every bone in my body had seized, but as I groaned, I caught the look on his face; a scowl, a drawing together of his eyebrows, a stare from those pale eyes. *Just think yourself lucky*, was his wordless warning.

What was he up to now, undoing the leather thong attaching the trumpeter's head to his bridle? He held it, dangling, and strode off into the forest shadows. He'd made no signal that I should go with him, but neither had he indicated that I shouldn't, and so I followed on, hesitating for only the merest of moments. But that was enough to lose sight of him.

The trees were tightly encircled by bushes and woven round with streamers of ivy. The birdsong had lessened, the light was almost entirely blocked out. I stumbled ahead, as straight as I could, trying my best not to trip over roots jutting up from the ground. A moment later and I started to wonder if the darkness was lifting or if my eyes were getting used to the gloom, but no, there ahead daylight flooded down through a gap in the heavy branches onto a clearing where my captor stood motionless, pressing his elbows to his waist, holding his forearms, palms towards the sky. In place of the birdsong, a deadly silence weighed down upon me.

I stopped in my tracks. This was wrong; I should have stayed where he left me. A critical thought came into my mind, 'Ye gods, Siva, get away fast as you can.'

Fascination fixed me to the spot, however. Only after what seemed like an eternity did he take a step forward and place his hand upon what I made out, only now, was the trumpeter's head, placed in a fork of the branch in front of him. It gaped out like an image from some ghoulish nightmare but the Briton's touch had been almost reverential, as though extended to some respected deity instead of a severed body part of one of the detestable who'd invaded his land. And as I watched, I saw something quite incredible; he held a cup to the trumpeter's lips as though offering a libation to the man he'd just slaughtered.

Only one thing was certain. I would have to seize the

moment, retrace my steps back to the riverbank, praying not to get lost in the darkness, for getting lost in a place like this would to be lost forever.

The moment came, but as I took a first step my shoulder brushed against a twig which caught a shredded patch of my cloak. I stretched to free myself but stopped in my tracks. There, on the tree just next to me, I caught a glimmer of a shiny object glinting in the dappled light.

And who could blame me for doing what anyone else would have done, for reaching up and plucking the mysterious fruit?

It was a circlet of gold, which seemed too large to fit even a Briton's arm, yet too small to be fixed round a neck, crafted in imitation of a twisted stem sprouting from a flower bud.

Lost in wonder, I traced a finger across it. What was it? And how had it come to be stuck in the tree?

Then I felt my eyes, which by dint of all that peering had become better focused, grow so wide as to almost pop out of my head. Hanging all around from twenty, thirty, forty branches was gold and silver, yet more circlets, drinking cups, music horns, knives on chains. And skulls, skulls hanging everywhere, some with shining coin-shaped slices of gold fixed into the empty sockets of what once had been eyes.

The newly familiar scrunching of feet upon leaves pulled me back to reality. As he approached the spot where I stood, I could only hold my ground and wait in trepidation. Now, for some reason, he seemed more human, his shoulders slumped forward as he walked towards me and moved his palm across a wound on his chest. When he saw me, however, he straightened, and catching sight of the golden bud clasped in my hand it was as if he lost all reason.

Still balanced on the tightrope stretched between my old life and my new, still so much a part of disciplined, stoical Rome, I thought it impossible that a man could roar so loudly, not even one of the drill sergeants out on Mars Field. And with his roar came the memory of that early dawn, still only a matter of hours before though it might have been a lifetime away. Fury, wrath, anguish, he howled words that required no translation. Body racked and shaking, he threw back his head and stared towards the treetops.

The roar, then silence. I held my breath. Moments passed and during this brief interval I set my mind to work more quickly than ever it had worked before. He lowered his head, opened his eyes and putting my plan into action, I took a step forward and holding my hand out, palm upward, with the bud balanced on it, I approached him rather as one might a guard dog, offering a sweetmeat, hoping the beast won't bite off your fingers.

Yet more moments passed, he stopped shaking and mumbled something, accompanied by a gesture directed at one of the trees behind me. He was telling me to put the circlet back in its place, or so it seemed, even though the tree he pointed to was not the one I had taken it from. And so, I followed his instruction, balancing the object on my outstretched hand I took a step backwards. Backwards I paced, a slow and silent movement perfected during my years of servitude, a movement I could have performed in my sleep such countless times had I withdrawn just so from the presence of a certain breed of nobleman, or woman for that matter.

Then I wondered, for it seemed I had two choices. Should I place the circlet on the tree to which he had pointed, anywhere at all and get it over with, or should I put it back where it belonged?

The temple-trained part of me settled for the latter and I made a rash decision; this, after all, must be a holy place and I suspected that any gesture I made now was bound to be scrutinised by his gods. We're steeped in religion, we Egyptians, and so can be trusted to sniff out sacred things from miles away. I could hardly believe that I'd lost my sense of intuition just when I needed it most. My gods had flown in the face of other gods; gods of the desert and gods of the forest meeting in this silent place. But to be fair, this was the land of the forest gods, and here they ruled supreme.

Now it was my turn to point at my captor's choice of branch. Shaking my head, I moved my finger a little way to the right and waited for his permission. A flicker of his eyelids and I put the treasure back in its resting place. And with this action, intuition returned. I should offer up something of my own. All I had was my sunship, the last thing in my life that I wanted to lose and, though was a simple object when compared to the beauty around me, I knew that a sacrifice of some significance was required of me now.

No time for hesitation, I tugged it over my head, wasting precious moments untangling it from my hair, clasped my captor's wrist and dropped it into his palm, an offering from my god of the sun to his of the forest.

He took a long time looking at it, before stepping forward to hang it on the branch beside the bud. And I was glad that Ra was with me; his copper sun disk glistened beside the gold all around it, and his little ship hanging beneath it shone as deep an orange as the evening sky flickering through the branches above us.

Was the worst behind me or was it still to come?

CHAPTER SIX
BEYOND THE GATES OF BEL

The forest was behind us now, and the sun, a swollen bronze orb, was sinking beneath the horizon in front of us, and there in a clearing on the shoulder of a hill was a settlement of sorts with smoke from ten or so fires wisping into the dusk. We stopped at this point. I was ordered down and my wrists were bound with the same leather thong the trumpeter's head had dangled from, all those nightmare hours before. For him, at least, the terror was passed and now I wished I had died with him too, for I was sure that the foreign hill, a little way across the valley, would be my place of execution.

The Briton signalled that I should walk behind him now; a tricky task with wrists tied together. He took his seat, adjusted his sword on his back and kneed the horse forward. To begin with, the going was manageable, the horse ambled onward with a slow, steady gait whilst I hobbled after it, as best I could. Just short of the settlement though my captor let out a screeching whoop and set it to a trot, forcing me into a galumphing run, striding behind him with inelegant, huge loping steps.

As we entered the place, I was vaguely aware of figures ranged from left to right gazing silently on. I say 'vaguely aware' since, by now hardly able to open the swollen slits of my eyes, I could make out only fuzzy outlines on either side of me. We came to a halt; my binding was untied and I slumped against the horse's rump.

Whatever else happened, I was beyond caring.

I was put into a wicker cage. It was small and I sat squashed inside it, arms grasped round my knees, unable to move. As one of the blood-curdling stories I'd heard on the boat came to mind, I knew that death was not the thing I feared but the torture that was bound to come first.

All I could do was plead with the gods. What heinous pact wouldn't I have entered into with them just then if only they'd agreed to whisk me back to Fabius' little bathhouse. Eyes shut, I tried to evoke the steamy comfort of the pool, of how it felt to lie back in the water, wisps of vapour rising upwards to escape through the circles carved into its ceiling.

But dreams were dreams and I'd have to put up with reality.

Half dead, anyway, bruised, battered, sick and weary I was past caring that I had reached the end of my life, when a child came bustling authoritatively towards me, elbowing his way through the gaping crowd gathered around me. At least, at first glance I thought he was some poor, deformed child but when he stopped in front of my cage, and I peered at him through my bloated eyelids, I saw I'd been wrong. He was a hunched and tiny man who looked as though he were the oldest person in the world. I could hardly think what was most strange about him, his height – or lack of it should I say – or his wizened, shrivelled face. Like a bird, a tiny bent bird with features hidden behind a mesh of wrinkles, he squinted at me from behind his hood, his minuscule frame quivering and shaking as if wracked with palsy. Now he bent forward and, through the bars of the cage, he prodded me with his staff, much the way animal-handlers prod tigers or leopards. I'd always thought it peculiar that no matter how tough the handler appeared, the prod was sure to be followed by a little backwards jump, lest goaded by his action the beast broke out into the open to grasp his tormentor by the throat.

The prod came first, followed by a slight readjustment of position a little further off, then a gaze towards me to judge the reaction of the peculiar creature trapped inside.

The ancient birdman took up his staff again, pointing it into the air. With his signal, my cage was hoisted up the side of the hut to which it was attached, and I found myself suspended well above head height of the crowd. Despite my swollen eyes, I was able to discern that, quite unlike the jesting, taunting faces of a Roman mob, those gazing up at me wore ominous expressions of foreboding.

That tent, pitched behind the camp ditch not so many hours before seemed nothing less than a haven of bliss.

An icy darkness swept in. I longed to lie down but the confines of my cage limited me to a squat, as I've said, knees drawn tight to my chest. I tried to will myself into oblivion, inhaling to the count of seven and pushing my breath out, slowly, slowly.

But now, colder than the wind whistling round my cage, I felt what remained of my spirit plummet. 'This is it,' I said to myself, death seeming now like a blessed relief. I looked up through the roof of my cage and saw, set against the night sky, a somewhat altered zodiac, stars glinting from an eerie firmament patched with cloud, and a moon darting out of sight behind the scudding, silver shadows to reappear and disappear again. Life and death. Life and death.

It was as if I'd become one with the wind, was being swept up in its arms.

*

It took a while to work out that the bright, circular object shining above me wasn't the moon but a lantern suspended from rafters, and that I was lying beneath it on a pile of straw.

And now a face appeared above me, blocking out the light. It was a familiar type of face, the type of face to be seen in the City a thousand times every day. It had bushy eyebrows, a largish nose, small mouth and shortened forehead, above which dark grey hair stuck up in all directions; hair which, quite simply, had never recovered from repeated shearing by an army barber and, as such, was considered a badge of honour, a mark of the legions.

The face's owner had a thick neck, thick arms and narrow, slanting shoulders. I knew that if I stood beside him, he'd barely reach my chin.

A finger scratched the forehead of the face. 'Wot have we here then?' he said in Latin. 'A young gentleman of the Hebrew persuasion, if I ain't mistaken.'

He spoke a dialect from just west of the Viminal, a spot where one never likes to find oneself alone after dark.

The scratching finger was taken from his forehead and placed against the face's cheek. 'No let me try again, Syrnian, that's what you is,' and the owner of the face began to chuckle, his chuckles turning into wheezes and his wheezes into deep, hacking coughs.

The lantern-light, the coughing, the hammering inside my skull, added to which a fire was raging in my throat, my tongue stuck to the roof of my mouth.

'I'd be incredibly grateful,' I managed to whisper, 'if you'd let me have a little water.'

When yet more moments passed, the owner of the face gestured widely and turned as if to make a proclamation, the very way an orator might when, standing on the rostrum, he readies himself to address an audience of dubious intellect.

''E speaks. 'E speaks. And a right la-di-da one he is too. Excuse me a moment won't you, till I translate a bit for my lordship here.'

Only then did I see the little birdman standing behind him, all swathed in his colourful cloaks. The birdman's voice was high-pitched, his words like none I'd heard before.

'You're to stay with me, guv,' said the owner of the face after long moments of listening had passed, 'that's wot he says. Until tomorrow that is, and then you're off to meet the war council. And a deal of talking you'll have to do then, and no mistake.'

The ancient birdman turned and disappeared into the dark beyond the lamplight, but the little Roman settled down beside me. The rim of a cup was pressed to my mouth. Rivulets of water ran down my throat; I felt a little less like dying.

I shut my eyes to block out the lantern bobbing in the draught above him. I must have slept for when I opened them again, he was gone and the hammering inside my skull had too. I glanced round and could see that my prison was a small building with a circular wall woven from what looked like reeds. The same wind that had whistled round my cage whirled the straw from my bed and wafted dust all around. There was nothing much else, apart from a sweet smell, like rancid honey and the overwhelming dread welling up inside me.

I fell back into a kind of terrified half-sleep and dreamt of the trumpeter's battered head dangling from the roof above me. But just as it opened its mouth to tell me something of infinite importance, a shuffling noise pulled me back to reality.

The little man's face peered down at me again.

''Spect you're hungry?' he stated the obvious, and pulling a curtain strung across a gap where perhaps a door should have been, shouted into the dark. There was no response. He shouted again, louder this time, and after some moments a young boy thrust through it, jug in one hand, dish in the other. After placing them on the ground beside me, he seemed keen to hang about gawking, but the little Roman chased him off and watched as, mustering sufficient energy to pull myself into a sitting position, I propped my back against the woven screen behind me. If it hadn't been there, I'd have had to lie down again for my strength was gone completely. I thanked him profusely and set about the food with gusto.

It was meat of some sort, on a bone, which I tore off and thrust into my mouth. In defence of my poor table manners, all I can say is my last meal had been the bland but identifiable hunk of bread and the beans. The bone I was gnawing at now might have been a dog's rib for all I could tell, but I crunched it up all the same. The contents of the jug, however, turned out to be un-watered wine, of a really fine quality to boot, arm-and-leg kind of stuff. And, as I slurped and swallowed, I took a clearer look at my gaoler.

Small but of a normal enough height as far as the City was concerned, his clothes were as unlike those of a Roman as could possibly be imagined. He wore a version of the auxilia's breeches, and I suppose of mine too, but where ours had been leather his were of wildly checked wool. His shoes covered not only his feet but the lower portion of his legs, and around his shoulders was a kind of shawl, the ends of which were tied on his chest in a neat double bow. A funny blue hood hung down from the back of his neck.

With the gnawing hunger gone from my belly, and my head returned to some semblance of normality, I forced my brain into action; to have even the slightest chance of surviving what was ahead of me, I'd have to establish some basic facts. I knew nothing about Britain, save for wicker cages, painted men, forests hung with skulls ... and the little Roman, who was he?

'I hope you don't mind,' I whispered, 'but I wonder if I might ask who you are.'

'Name's Petronius,' he said, 'of the legions of the late ... nutcase ... Gaius Caesar Augustus Germanicus.'

Caligulas legions? Their farcical attempt to conquer Britain was still a subject of great amusement. I screwed up my eyes to see him better.

He misinterpreted my expression.

'Shocked you, has I sir? What an idea that is, escaping from your precious army.' He fixed me with a beady eye. 'Lay a wager, so I would. Bet you're glad you're not back there with your chums.' And with that he disappeared.

This was the moment I set my partially recovered mind to thinking. 'Your precious army. Your chums.' This hit a note; they thought I'd been part of Leonatus unit. I had to separate myself from the legions. Make them believe that I was as much a hostage of Rome as I was to them. But how?

The answer appeared in the form of one of my master's stratagems, which floated up from somewhere deep in my brain. *Offer up something to your opponent to put them off their stride. Make it appear as a sign of weakness, that they are the ones with the strength.* How often had I watched him as he turned a bitter situation to his advantage.

Here was my chance; perhaps my only one. I'd have to start thinking … even I was surprised with what I came up with

'I'm sorry,' I said, when he stepped back though the curtain, 'but there's something you should know.'

'On you goes then.'

'You think I was with the auxilia unit. Well, I was … what I mean is …' I made a show of stumbling on. 'I was with them but I had no choice. They were transporting me to the frontier. I'm a slave, you see. I hate Rome as much as you do.'

Which had the very effect I had wanted. 'Wait here,' he said, as if I had any choice in the matter.

When he returned, the birdman was with him.

'Told his lordship wot you just said. Now you has to tell him.'

'I don't belong to the legions,' I said. '… I didn't choose to be with them.'

The birdman spoke in his language.

My gaoler translated, 'Wot you called, any road, 'e wants to know.'

'My name is Siva Amun Ra.' Better to give my old one than anything vaguely Roman, far less Ostorius Scapula.

'And if you're not Hebrew, and neither is you Syrnian, where is you from?' was my gaoler's next question. 'Looks like some poxing foreigner so you does.'

Which only made me wonder from whose point of view I looked foreign. If from the Britons', then he'd be a foreigner too.

'Egypt,' which, with luck he could just about manage.

There was quite a long silence.

'Gypt, Syrnia, same thing to me.'

'Why did they make you a slave?' he asked next, translating the birdman's question.

And as if they were coming to my rescue, Quintus' words sprang into my mind ... *their priests are believed to have mystical powers, divining the future amongst other things.*

'I was a priest,' which was partially true, and for good effect I added, 'of the temple of the Upper Kingdom.' This was a figment of my imagination as such a place didn't exist. I ploughed on. 'You may not believe me but I have the gift of reading the stars and to tell what is about to happen.' Pure fantasy, of course. 'They were taking me to the frontier to divine the path they should set upon next.'

No need to convince the little Roman; he'd be familiar with the Augurs. Reading the entrails of chickens, ox livers and flights of birds across the sky.

I waited for this to be translated from Latin, but there was no need. The birdman's eyes widened. He might choose to speak in his language, but it was clear that he knew mine as well.

Next time the little Petronius person stepped through the curtain, carrying a bowl, milk sploshing over its rim, I had my questions ready.

'What will happen to me now? Am I to be hung back up in that cage?'

'Oh no,' said he, 'they'll make you a god of sorts, talk about that already there is. Either that or they'll give you the chop.' He hesitated. 'But you ain't no Roman, you're from Gypt.' He rubbed his chin. 'Well there you has it. The holy guys will hold a council with their pontifex and all you has to do is speak up for yourself. Tell them you weren't with them there auxilia boys. Not really. At sunrise, that's when they'll stand you up in front of them and ask you stuff. Just keep your wits about you, that's all.'

How would they know what I was saying? These holy men, did they speak Latin by any chance? I hadn't missed the birdman's expression as he listened to my tale of Egypt.

'Wouldn't be surprised if they do, my old son, wouldn't be surprised if they do. But they're not about to admit that to no one. The princes speak though, some speak good, the others, well ... But that's what I'll be there for. No don't go worrying on that count, I'll guide you through.' He gave me a truculent look. 'But later, like, if I find out you was part of that lot after all, I'll slit your throat for you, so let that be a warning, god or no ruddy god, I'll have you so I will.'

I felt sure he'd be true to his word.

'And the chap who captured me, where does he fit in?'

He laughed a wheezing laugh. 'Can't be described as no chap.'

'Know him then, do you?'

'Who doesn't. Name's Calgac, means swordfighter and fighter he is, but we call him Cal.'

'Not terribly nice then, I take it?'

'Nice? What's nice got to do with anything? Nearest as can ever be got to Tog, he is, and I only thank the great god Bel that he weren't taken too, back down there by The Waters. Just about manage without Tog, we can, but if Cal were gone, there wouldn't be much left in life, so there wouldn't.'

He was silent for moment.

'Trust him, of all folks,' he said next.

What did he mean?

'Bringing you back. Only he could have thought that one up.'

Now was my chance. 'Why did he? They killed all the others, you know.'

'Dunno. Maybe for the weird way you look ... or that.'

And, putting my hand on my chest to where he was pointing, my fingers traced the shape of something that shouldn't have been there. My blood ran cold in my veins. 'But ...'

'But what?' He peered at me, uncomprehending.

'I left it in the forest.'

'Well it ain't there now ... What is it, anyroad?'

I tried to batten down my shock. 'A sunship.'

He pressed his finger on the disk.

'That's the sun,' I forced myself to keep talking. 'And that's the Bark of Ra.'

'Bark avra. What's it doing there?'

'Sailing across it.'

'A story, is it?'

'No ... the priests of my country say it's true.'

'Is he stronger than Jove?'

I couldn't tell him, one way or the other.

'Might help me anyways tomorrow.'

And with that he disappeared back through the curtain into the dawn.

I had witnessed many types of magic in my life, in Egypt and the temple in Rome, but those had been theatre pieces ... this was real. I took the sunship from my neck and looked at it closely. Nothing about it had changed. I opened its copper disc, all smudged by Petronius' fingers, and caught the faded smell of blue lotus.

The gods had been with me all the way through my life. Surely, they wouldn't abandon me now.

When he'd gone, I tried to fight sleep but felt myself falling into dark space, reaching out, trying to catch something. Stars twinkled below me in the void of the heavens perhaps. And now I was tumbling, down and down, onto the horns of Taurus.

CHAPTER SEVEN
SIVA DARK STRANGER

A pallid light seeped through the basketweave roof. It took a moment to swim up towards it. And when Somnus released me, I tried to unravel my dream. What did the dark space mean? Or the horns? But there was no time to ponder upon this; the curtain was parted and I was tilted to my feet by a couple of giants, Petronius in their wake. My weakened state made me as shaky upon them as the little birdman himself. I managed to mumble my well-rehearsed plea to Petronius. 'I wonder if you'd be kind enough to make sure they know that I'm not with the legions, that I was brought here as a slave, that I'm as much a victim of Rome as they are,' as out I was guided, into the dawn.

'I will my old mate, don't you worry.' His fearful smile didn't fill me with confidence. 'But first you're going to the war council and maybe they'll let you tell them yourself.'

I was led to a circular building. Torches lit the smoky space inside. So numbed with terror was I that I could barely place one foot in front of the other. A group of men, all large, fearsome and wild in appearance, stood from their benches as we entered, not in respect, but to better see their peculiar captive. Strange what visions flash into your mind at such moments, a senate war assembly, tribunes in their bordered togas, maroon shoes laced upon their feet.

The least ostentatiously turned out of the men stepped forward. He had a craggy, handsome face. I guessed he was about thirty or so. Though plainly dressed, something about him told me he was their leader; perhaps it was because he looked like a thinker.

'You say you're a slave?' He spoke in fairly understandable Latin.

I paused for too long.

'Speak,' he said next and I heard my master's words. *These weak and snivelling miscreants dragged before me, with their tremulous please for mercy* and I knew I could not falter.

'Yes.'

'That you are not Roman. That you do not belong to their legions?'

'I am not … And I do not,' I answered loudly.

'You may not be part of them but you may support them.'

'I do not.' It seemed that he might be persuaded.

He waved the company away, and when they were gone, he pointed at my sunship.

'And this is the object you offered to Bel?'

With no idea who Bel might be I asked if perhaps he would explain its reappearance. But no.

'I am told you have powers to read the future?'

'I come from the land of Egypt, where many possess that knowledge.' I hoped he wouldn't know the truth.

'My name is Caradoc,' next he said. 'I lead the fight against the invaders.'

Here was my chance. With no thought as to where this might lead me, preposterous words came out of my mouth. 'Would you permit me to join you?'

With no hesitation, he countered, 'How well do you know Rome and its leaders?'

'As much as any slave … perhaps more.'

'Then give me a reason to believe you. Perhaps information about their strategy and if you answer wisely, I may consider your request.'

Did it matter what I said? How would he know it was true? But I decided against this path and thinking upon my master's insights, *an immediate answer devoid of consideration lets me know they are saying the first thing that comes into their heads.*

I asked if he would give me a moment to think, but I wanted to anyway.

Five heartbeats passed before I replied. 'If the Great Caesar had one overriding strategy, it was to divide and conquer.' And remembering what Leonatus had referred to as 'friendly country', meaning the tribes who had turned to Rome. 'You cannot have separate factions; you must stand together as one and you may have a chance.'

He didn't reply, and for such a long time I felt myself consumed with dread … I had answered badly I was going to be hung back up in my cage.

And when he eventually said, 'I may take you up on your offer' a flood of relief cascaded through me.

He held my gaze. 'But first I will test you. We will speak later.'

By now the light had turned to silver which seemed to be breathing through the misty, tree-lined horizon. The giants who had led me here came forward and, heart beating so loudly in my ears I felt they could hear it, I was led, stumbling forward. I could make out a circle of fires in the centre of a grassy expanse, around which were ranged a hundred or so men, so huge, so terrifying to behold, each one adorned with gold, some with helmets, some without, some with coloured cloaks wrapped around them, most, as far as I could see, with moustaches that hung to their chests.

And what did I look like to them? I was filthier than might be imagined a filthy man could be, my hair matted with blood and vomit. I stank, my clothes were in tatters, my face puffed with bruises and my mouth felt twice its former size. In keeping with my altered demeanour, my prayers were now somewhat tempered. Whereas in my cage I had pledged all I owned to the gods if they'd only transported me to Fabius' bathhouse, at that precise moment I'd have been simply euphoric to be back to my normal, everyday self, wearing my kilt and silk-fringed tunic, scrubbed and clean, my hair washed and newly plaited.

In my ghastly, putrid state it dawned on me that the only one amongst them who had an inkling of what I looked like before he'd reduced me to this sorry state would be my painted captor. But for him to see me I'd have to see him and that was the last thing I wanted to do, either then or anytime in the future.

My gods were still with me, however, for he wasn't there.

As I made my unsteady way forward, all around was silence save for the crackling of flames and Petronius' voice at my shoulder. 'Easy does it, old son, easy does it.'

When we stopped, I found myself before a group set somewhere off from the others.

Standing to one side was the tiny birdman, on the other, three strange thin men with heads shaven back as far as their ears and cold expressions in their eyes, which seemed neither to look nor to see.

Petronius spoke; his voice was loud, the language he used peculiar to my ear.

The little birdman approached and holding the point of his staff to my chest, lifted my sunship. Petronius moved towards him and pointed at the pale white globe, which by now had risen over the hilltop, and spoke in his language. He could only be telling the story of Ra, setting to with a great many words, of which of course I had no understanding, and when several minutes had passed, the little birdman turned his back on the sun, now hovering higher in the heavens and pointed his staff. With his signal, one of the men whom I presumed to be priests came towards me. Something golden flashed in his hand. A few more paces and I could see the knife plainly. Behind me now, he grasped my head and pulled it back. I had seen many goats have their necks cut this way.

'Accept my soul,' I prayed to Amun.

But my neck was spared ... he cut off my hair, and I was filled with great exultation for death wasn't ready for me yet.

When the sun was higher in the sky I was led to a river by the priests, Petronius to the fore, carrying a box of beaten gold, inside which the filthy and tangled sacrifice had been placed.

On reaching its bank, the little birdman had taken it from me, then kneeling had lowered it into the water. I could hardly bear to watch as an object of such value sank beneath the current.

Petronius, misreading my reaction, chirped up, 'Don't go worrying my old mate, hair grows back, so it does.'

A prayer had been offered to some god or other and I was handed a basket of acorns.

'Idea is,' explained he, 'that you should spread them in the forest. But only when no one's there to see, mind.'

I gazed at him, puzzled and he qualified his instruction. 'So one'll spring roots, become great oak. Gift to the forest, like.'

'Should I do that now?'

And a look of incredulity that one could be so dense. 'No, no. After dark, that's when, after dark.'

With my appearance, my name was changed too. Petronius told me, from now on I'd be known as something impossible to pronounce, which he told me meant Dark Stranger, member of two tribes, no less, the men of gods called Bel and Camul.

And that's how I got my name.

CHAPTER EIGHT
A NEW FACE

A startling reflection stared out from the polished bronze mirror; a new face covered in swellings, welts, wounds and gashes. My hair was gone and in its place stubble. I ran my hand over my new bristly head, rather liking the sensation.

'By Pollux,' Petronius looked up at me with fresh eyes. 'Done good, so you has. No posh boy now, so you aint.'

Here I was now, clean for the first time in what seemed an eternity. And, thanks to the little man, who'd set about it with pumice stone and sharpened knife, I sported, alongside my new, naked head, a face shaved as professionally as any on the Clivus Victoriae. I wore a woollen tunic and a pair of long breeches, one leg a pattern of multicoloured checks, the other squares of black and green. The only Roman things left were my hobnails, which looked ridiculous sticking out below the breeches.

I smiled secretly into myself.

'Next thing, you has to learn up their lingo, and learn it up pretty soon, or you're never going to be one of them. Not never. Just listen to me and copy along.'

I could only wonder about that.

A swarm of questions buzzed in my head. I wanted to know about his legion, why he'd deserted, and about the Britons, about the place all hung with skulls, the little birdman, the reappearance of my sunship. What I wanted to know most of all though was what was in store for me next. The chap I'd spoken with the night before, he of the thinker's face – who'd told me his name was Caradoc – had said we would speak again. There were so many things I wanted to know, but I hadn't been alone for long enough with my little friend and there had been no chance to ask him.

'Is there somewhere we can talk?'

He thought for a moment. 'The lookout's a good place. We can take our turn at watching over it.'

And when I asked what we would be watching over, he drew his eyebrows together as if to say, *Do I need to explain every last thing to you?* 'The beacon. In case it needs lighting.'

I followed him out across a space, filled with flocks of hens that clucked around our heels, at the edge of which rose a small hummock. This was the first time I'd walked freely since my ungainly arrival and I found it hard to keep up with him.

We climbed to its summit and settled down beside each other, leaning our backs on a great pile of timber, cut to various sizes, which I presumed was his beacon ready to light.

I summoned that part of me I regarded as Roman to make wise use of this chance opportunity. I had no idea what lay beyond my prison, but now, high on our vantage point, looking out over a vast panorama, I could see the lay of the land. Once I had worked out my escape route, I'd compare it with Leonatus' chart.

Having a fair idea of the sun's position on my way here, I knew we were west of the place where I'd been captured. But were we north too? If the sky was clear enough that night, it would tell me. I cupped my eyes with my hand; the sun was straight ahead. Turning to my left, I looked out towards the southeast. If I made a run for it, which I planned to do just as soon as I could, that's the way I'd have to go. Ahead of us, the forest stretched southwards. I turned again to look behind me and saw that it did the same in all directions. Getting away from here in one piece would be the hardest task of my life. I had detested the camp of the XX, but now it seemed like a realm of joy. I'd get back there if it killed me, which it probably would.

This was the first time I thought about Marcus. Would he know about the attack? If so, he'd be sure I was dead. I couldn't bear to think of his torment. Or how he'd find courage to tell his father.

But this was no time to revel in self-pity, or pity for Marcus either. I should be gathering as much information as I could.

I started with 'Where are we?'

But he misunderstood my question. 'A farm,' said he.

Never having been in one in my life I can't say it was what I imagined a farm would be like ... Fabius' villa in the countryside near Patavium, yes, his olive groves, yes, the small holdings, rather more like gardens, crammed full of rabbit hutches, beehives, rows of bean plants on my master's estate in Cumae, yes. Here, however, not too far below us a dozen or so fat sows rooted untethered, in the mud.

There wasn't much sign of anything growing in the long strips of fields. But in place of crops were people, hundreds of them, and ponies and dogs and tents and fires.

Looking down I retraced the path along which I'd been dragged on the evening of my inglorious arrival. Nine buildings were set out beside it, three larger, six smaller, all circular with roofs of evenly cut thatch bound across with leather strips, those of the larger houses being arranged in decorative layers, with paler shades of what I took to be straw at the top and darker shades at the bottom. Beyond the fields of people, the forest spread like a gilded pavement, stretching out towards the horizon as far as the eye could see.

'Were Ruadon's. Belonged to 'im,' he expanded, 'and no doubt will be again. Given over to Caradoc's men now.'

This was no help to me, but I forged on. 'Forgive me, but are they a tribe?'

'Don't you know nothing?'

'No. Well, yes … What I mean is I do know absolutely nothing.'

'Calls themselves the Catvelan … Catuvellauni to you lot..' I noticed he didn't include himself in the company. 'Means the War Chiefs.' And he left it at that.

Now came my next question; what was in store for me now, did he know? That morning, the chap I'd spoken with, he of the thinker's face … 'The man called Caradoc,' but I didn't get further.

'High Caradoc to you and me. Supposing you'd call him Dux back there in the City. He's the new leader seeing as Tog's dead.' I must be a simpleton not to know that. 'Killed back in the Midway Waters. By your lot,' he added. 'A great one he was. Greatest of all.'

'Sorry,' I said.

'Suppose it weren't your fault,' he conceded. 'But now he's gone, see, and Caradoc, well he's taken over.'

'What kind of man is he?' I felt the need to ask.

At this he gave me the same kind of look he had when

explaining how British rules stated quite clearly that acorns had to be buried at night. 'A legend he is,' was all my little friend said.

I asked if I might help him in his fight against Rome.

'And?' Petronius looked at me doubtfully.

'He said he would set me a test.'

'Oh ...' he replied.

I didn't want to know what this meant.

But what about the little man, the more I knew about him, the better I'd be able to discover what he could unknowingly help me with my escape plan. *Fall into easy conversation. Listen to their story*, or so my master had said.

'So tell me about Caligula's legion.' By which I meant tell me why you ran away and how you managed to survive. It was still held up as the greatest of failures, but I knew very little about it.

'Didn't care nothing for it. No didn't care for it at all. Escaped, didn't I?'

Which, I supposed, was one way of putting it. Harsher souls would have called it desertion.

They got as far as the shores of Gaul. 'Two of our ships set off from there. I were on one. Then that crazy man changed his frigging mind. We was half a mile out when the signal flares was fired'

The other ship, he explained, had been able to turn around. But theirs was carried off course by massive churning waves. After my own nightmare passage, he'd no need to go into detail. Their oars were smashed to tinder wood and they were washed ashore. The enemy shore, that was. They'd been stricken with terror by tales of what lay ahead of them, bleeding forests and a race of blue-skinned ogres.

Having seen the ogres and bleeding forests for myself, I knew what he meant when he added that, as things turned out, the tales had more than a little truth in them.

As far as the shipwreck was concerned, the Britons had scoured the cliffs looking for survivors. And once found, they'd been cared for. Not simply the officers, as might be supposed, but the common soldiers too. They'd been fed, clothed and supplied with a means to get back to the other side of the sea. The men of the island even went so far as to send messengers out along the trade routes, securing their safe return.

'Didn't want no excuse, did they. Didn't want none of that madman's rescue parties next on their patch.'

And return they had, well most of them, there being some amongst them who'd chosen to stay, 'just because they liked it here', had joined the army in the first place only as a means of escaping drudgery and hopelessness; even I knew that a soldier's life was some several steps away from dole and circuses.

The Britons were fine people, he said. Peculiar, yes, impetuous, yes, boastful, strutting, conceited, yes, but they were also people of honour and they'd no silly senate houses, no idle, protected sons. All had the same requirements made of them. Every man, or woman for that matter, was given their place, and they'd face up to anyone, even the noblest amongst them to hold onto it. Of course, I put this into my words.

'Been here all this time so I have. Never would want to go back to the City.'

Pulling his hood over his eyes to shade them from the watery sun, he sat for a moment in deep contemplation. 'But they're a weird lot, them Britons. Some things I won't never understand about them, won't never until the day I die.'

I couldn't let him fall asleep; there was still so much he could tell me.

'So how had I got out of the cage?'

'Oh, that had been lowered,' he said, 'on the orders of the very same men who'd put me there in the first place. Them boys, they're called wisdom carriers,' he informed, 'seeing as they carry the wisdom of oaks.'

'Oak trees?'

'What other oaks is there?'

'And the minuscule fellow, who looked like a bird?'

'Goes by the name of High Atha.'

'Who would you say is his counterpart in Rome?'

'Come again?'

'Who is he most like back in the City?'

He thought long and hard and came up with a rather astounding analogy.

'Mother Vestal,' was his reply.

I took a few moments to digest this bizarre piece of information before I continued. 'I wonder if I might ask a few more questions?'

'On you goes then.'

I took my sunship from my neck, and hoping to make better headway than before, 'I don't understand it. I left it in the forest. And now it's back here. How did that happen, do you know?'

'Cal brought it.'

What did he mean?

'When you was taken out of the cage, they thought you was near dying. The way to stop you, they said, was to get that there thing back to where it came from in the first place.' He pointed at my neck. 'Don't know nothing about that 'cepting they said your god lived inside it. They sent him back there to get it.'

It took a few moments for this to sink in, and when it did he saw my shock.

'What was that terrible place, anyway? The trees were all hung with skulls and gold.'

'He never took you there,' Petronius stared at me, appalled. 'That place, well it's not for the likes of you or me. Type of altar, by their way of thinking. Called Nemeton, it is. There's no one let in there. Least no one who's ordinary.'

'He didn't invite me, I followed him.'

To which he looked even more horrified. 'It's a wonder he didn't slice off your head right then.' He paused for a moment. 'But, thinking it over he wouldn't be able to, ain't allowed to take no sword into that there 'oly place. Specially not that one ... called the Whisperer it is. Whispers through the air when it strikes.'

And though I longed to find out more about that nightmare place, time was passing and not knowing how long we would have together, I pressed on.

'And the golden box, what about that?'

'Were given.'

'By whom?'

'You joking or something?'

'No.'

'Who do you think it were?'

If I knew, I wouldn't be asking, I wanted to say. Instead I remained respectfully polite and told him that I didn't know.

'Must have been that there bash on your head.'

'What must have been?'

'Fact you never saw him making his pronouncement.'

'Who are you talking about?'

'He were there, unless it were an illusion. Stood up and spoke. Night you was first taken out.'

We could have gone on like this ad infinitum, so I changed tack.

'Are you talking about the little birdman?' I couldn't remember his name.

'You scares me sometimes,' he informed me. 'Cal it were, that's who.'

At this I felt my brain might burst.

Before it did I moved onto my very last question.

'What's Samhain?

He thought for a moment. 'Like nothing back there.'

I assumed he meant Rome.

'When will it take place?'

'Tonight,' he said.

'And when is it over?'

'When it finishes.'

CHAPTER NINE
CARADOC

I looked up and saw that the evening star had appeared in the sky. We call it Hesperus and I wondered if these strange people had a name for it too. I was sitting by one of the mighty fires set in a circle in the field; it was somewhat unsettling not having hair, my neck felt decidedly chilly.

Back bent, head slumped upon his chest, Petronius dozed beside me.

What was in store for me next? That morning the chap I now knew was their leader, he of the thinker's face, had said we'd speak again. If his previous line of questioning was anything to go by, when 'again' came he'd want to know about military things, tactics, plans and the rest. What should I tell was the question, 'should' being the operative word. At that time, in my mind, I was still part of Rome, still attached to a City, albeit to one I liked very little, to a people I grated against, apart from my master and Marcus, and of course my friends, friends whom I loved but who, like me, preferred to live outside the bounds of what was regarded as 'normal'.

And so, after much weighing up of this and of that, I thought it best to steer a middle course, to tell as little as I could get away with, what my master would describe as evasive strategy, crossing bridges as I came to them; less a case of misplaced loyalties than of simply staying alive.

And what of the test he would set me?

I was putting together my half-cocked scheme when riders came in from the forest. A clatter of hooves and Petronius woke. He looked round as if to say, 'I wasn't sleeping, you know.' And as if my thoughts of Rome were fusing with my little friend's dream, he snuffled and turned his face towards me, 'Never thought nothing about it,' and he was right, neither of us had mentioned the City up until then, 'but what's going on in the old place them days?'

'Miss it, do you?'

'Do and I don't, I suppose.'

'What do you miss most, would you say?'

'Easy one that,' and he screwed his face into an expression of longing. 'Them little patty cakes, that's what, and sausages, a pot of leeks all brown at the edges ... salt bread, pickled artichokes, garum ...' But whilst this was more than a torture to him, on he went nonetheless. 'Figs, purple-black, wrapped in their leaves, all gooey like. Used to come here too, so they did, from over, once upon a fair time past, when trading was still going on ...'

'Over?'

'Over the ocean, leastwise that's how they put it.'

Several young boys appeared at that moment to lead the horses away, whilst others came forward with water in cup-like ladles. And, as the riders entered the circle of fires, I recognised the man called Caradoc. His companions looked bone weary, but not him.

Massive pots were carried out now, again by the young boys, and placed at various points near the fires. Caradoc was served, but the others were left to take their own share, piercing long forks into the pots, and digging out pieces of meat. I went last, with Petronius.

As far as the meat was concerned, you simply held it in your hands and tore off pieces, which you then proceeded to ram into your mouth, washing it down with the type of beer close to one sold in taverns before the games. I can't remember the contents of the cauldrons being even vaguely tasty, but it was food and I was hungry.

'Weren't always like this, you know.' Petronius was harking back to days apparently not long past. 'I remember a time, so I do, when the gatherings was a real treat. In they'd come, from far and near. Singing there'd be, and music, and a bit of fisticuffs when tempers got 'igh.'

But just as I began to relax, to lull myself into thinking that I'd been forgotten, one of the young boys appeared in front of us and spoke with Petronius.

'Caradoc, 'e wants a word, but no need to worry on that count, seems it's all good.'

By the time the boy and I reached him, he was on his feet. He came towards me, and grasping my elbow steered me through the maze of fires, leading me up the hillside track until the blaze of voices was far below us and sat himself down on a rocky knoll. I followed suit, horribly nervous.

'So you're going to help, now you've joined us,' he stated rather than asked.

'As much as I can,' I replied. Were all my fine plans flapping out of my mind like wings from the temple of Jupiter Ammon?

He began by telling me what he knew about the invasion forces, how they functioned and so forth. His intelligence was based on a mixture of accounts, those handed down from memory of the last campaign, what he'd witnessed with his own eyes and the information supplied by Petronius and others who'd deserted the legions. This he went through with me, step by step, holding my gaze to note my reaction.

I was finding Caradoc's Latin less easy to follow than I had that morning, which I put down to the fact that now he was speaking at length, rather than uttering the odd sentence, but soon I had the hang of his accent.

First came the division of the army into its sections; legions and auxilia. As far as tactics were concerned, such basics as the tortoise and wedge had been explained to him, though he said it had been hard to imagine such formations until he'd come across them at a place called the Midway Water. He knew, too, that eighty men formed a century, that each was overseen by a centurion, that six centuries formed a cohort, the first cohort being the most important, since it alone was able to act as an independent fighting unit, consisting, as it did, of five double centuries, composed of eight hundred hand-picked men.

Of the auxilia, again, he knew more than I. All textbook stuff, but he left me far behind.

This was the point reality kicked in, put paid to my first notion of skirting around facts. Since I wouldn't have recognised a tortoise, wedge, or whatever other mode of combat had it jumped up and hit me in the face, what was there for me to skirt around? But surely this stood me in good stead as it proved Petronius' claim that far from a fighter, I was simply a slave.

Now came the time of my testing, however. Since I'd gone through the motions of joining his people, I couldn't let him think that I was holding back information. But what information was there to give? I struggled with memories of what I'd picked up from my master and settled on some trifling facts, not because they were trifling, but because they were all I could muster. Was he aware, I wondered, that four legions were here; the XIV, the IX, the II and the XX ... which being Marcus' and the one I'd been in if only for a day, I knew at least something about. The commander was a chap named Aulus Plautius, who, I felt it would be somewhat graceless to add had just been elected Governor of Britain. Then there was the XX under Vespasian. I reached the XIV and the IX and here I began to get muddled; who their tribunes were I couldn't remember, even if I had known in the first place. Now was the time I wished I had listened to Marcus endlessly droning on about army matters.

I could have kicked myself but kept on talking, someway or other, and when two or three sentences later my mind caught up, this is what I heard myself say: 'If you're to beat them you'll have to act soon, for with every month passing they'll get more dug in, more secure in their fortresses, more knowledgeable about the terrain, about your people. Then they'll set out against you.'

As I babbled on, however, I sensed a certain reluctance in Caradoc's eyes. At a guess I'd have said that he was a man who had no great love of battle, someone who'd seen what had to be done and had set about doing it. And when I thought about all the men who'd marched out of Rome, the eager campaigners, veterans and novices alike, something inside me felt leaden; foreign armies with marvellous commanders had failed miserably when confronted by her legions. So, what hope had the Britons?

The thought did strike me just at that point; here I was, sitting on a British hillside, in deep conversation with an enemy king. Was this really happening, or was I sinking into madness? It was as if Fabius' voice answered in the affirmative, *The balance of your mind has tipped right over, my sweet, just as I always predicted.*

I must have been gazing off into space as I'm prone to when thinking and had to rouse myself to answer. Marcus' fixation on his precious army came to my aid. 'Well, it's late in the year and ...' but of course, when speaking to him, I couldn't describe them as 'our' now, but 'their', '... their commanders will do anything to avoid a winter's campaign so it's my guess they'll settle in for a while, until the cold weather's over.'

'It gets a deal colder than this. We're iced or snowed in for long stretches of time.'

So, though blissfully unaware of just how severe his winters would turn out to be, I told him, 'The longer it's cold, the better as far as I can see, for it will give you time to group your men, plot your strategy ... one of my master's fixations ... and they'll be doing the same, not simply resting but shipping in more troops, drawing up plans, sending out mapmakers ...' At this, Leonatus' chart came to mind; Leonatus and his scarred nail-blackened fingers so clumsily clutched around his stylus, his non-Roman attitude to things of importance. 'Strengthening the place they know as Dunum.'

'Dun Camul, fortress of the god of war. It used to be my father's place, but it's been handed over to his enemy, a traitor they call Cogidubnus. We'll fight, and we will get it back.'

I could think of nothing to say to this, no words to tell him that I, too, knew how it was to be forced from my land, that I recognised his sorrow. But he was lord of these people and it seemed improper to utter what might be regarded as prattling banalities.

'Yes,' I said, 'they'll wait until winter is over, then they'll march west.'

It was on the way back to my place beside the fire where my little friend sat, head bent and dozing, great waves of relief coursing through me, that one of the young boys ran up behind me. He pointed over his shoulder. I was wanted back on the hillside.

As I gasped my way back into his sight, Caradoc walked towards me. 'You say they'll march west?'

'As far as I know,' I replied.

'What do you mean, exactly, by west?'

I knelt and picked up three longish twigs, which I formed into Leonatus' triangle. He stood unmoving, but after a good many moments, he crouched down beside me.

'Here's Dun Camul,' I said, marking the easternmost edge of the 'chart' with a stone, being careful to use his name for what Rome called Dunum. 'And here is another place, out to the west.' And though it had been somewhere vaguely beyond the left of Leonatus' tablet, I took a guess and marked it with another stone. 'I can't be precise but this is where I think they'll be going. The II Augusta, Vespasian's legion, I mean,' I added for the sake of saying something. 'Meanwhile, the XX plan to go north.' I placed a third stone on the triangle's topmost point.

'When Samhain is past, I want you to go on a mission.' He placed his finger on the western stone. 'To the place you have shown me. It's in the lands of the Durotriges. A woman has gone there. Her name is Cartimand.' Quintus' voice thundered into my ears. *A woman called Cartimandua.* Such was my shock, I all but missed what he said next. 'I want you to tell her what you told me this morning about your great Caesar's tactic … about how we must remain united.'

Did it matter that the blustering question I used to cover my shock was so utterly foolish? 'How will I get there?'

'You must not be concerned,' he said, 'you will be in good hands.'

But I was concerned, I was very concerned. Those waves of relief coursing through me only a short while before were whipped up, now, into seething anguish.

'He's sending me to meet a woman … her name's Cartimand … do you know anything about her?'

I was talking so quickly Petronius could hardly keep up with me. 'Calm down.' He grasped my arm. 'Calm down. You're still alive, ain't you, and that's the way you got to stay. What was your question again?'

'He's sending me to meet some woman. Her name is Cartimand. What do you know about her?

He tried to cover his shock, and after a moment, replied, 'Chief of another tribe … a big 'un, who lives in the north, beyond what you lot calls the frontier.'

'Why is she so important?'

It seemed he didn't want to tell me. 'Look at the stars and find out for yourself.'

He had a point but my elaborate story had come back to bite me. I thought quickly and came up with a ridiculous answer. 'It doesn't work for me, only for others.' I didn't quite know what I meant by this, but he seemed to accept it.

'Feared, so she is, by all the others. '

The mission dreamt up for me by Marcus had changed into one from Caradoc. The gods of fate were testing me.

'I'm confused, if her lands are to the north why am I to go west?'

'She's come down there for a while, or so I hears. You only needs to go that far.'

'Where?'

'Duro country. Lord Caradoc, he wants them Duros to up sticks and bugger off out of the place.'

'What place?'

'Their place, the Land of May. In case the cohorts go marching out there, raid their fortress and all.'

'The Duros are people then?'

'Durotriges is their name. Means the Strong Ones. Keepers of the Great Hill. But Keepers of the Sacred Gates too.'

'Where are they gates to?' I asked, quite reasonably, or so I imagined.

But 'To nowhere,' he answered, 'least nowhere that's real. They're called the gates of Ciern.'

This had become a Gordian knot I didn't have strength to begin to unravel, and so I changed course. 'When am I going, do you know?'

He didn't.

'And who am I going with?'

He didn't know either.

What he did know, however, was that we – whoever 'we' turned out to be – would be sneaking our way through Bantey country. 'And them Bantey, well you better watch out.'

It would take two days, perhaps even three if the mysterious Bantey were about, to reach the gates leading nowhere. Details, like who or what the Bantey happened to be, men, gods or something else, I couldn't cope with knowing.

I did think to ask if the men of the great hill had a leader.

Which, quite clearly, was the stupidest question.

'What kind?' I ploughed on, nonetheless.

But 'a good one' was all my little friend said.

'By Jupiter, Petronius,' I heard myself pleading, 'can't you get me out of this?'

CHAPTER TEN
SAMHAIN

But now, with the soft pounding pattern of a drumbeat behind us, our conversation about Duros and the like came abruptly to an end. Faces turned towards the silver fuzzed circle.

But the eeriest thing was the silence, for as they stood, faces turned towards the place from where it came, the feasters fell silent and even though I felt I had to be breaking some ancient taboo, I couldn't help whispering, 'What's happening?'

'Samhain. It's came now.'

With still not a clue as to what Samhain was, I changed tack. 'But what are they doing?'

'Waiting for the fires,' and with his words a dull mumbling rose from the crowd, a mumbling I recognised as one of expectation, which in every land must sound the same.

'Is it some kind of prayer?' I whispered again.

'Yes, to friend Granno.'

And from the pitch black of the forest, the drummer appeared, towering antlers fixed to his head, with, close behind him, young boys carrying bowls of fire.

'How can they do that without being burned?'

'Supposing I knew the answer to that one, I'd be a holy man myself.'

I was more than somewhat disconcerted at his lack of astonishment and told him so.

'Ah you just wait till you've been around them Britons for as long as I has then nothing'll disconcern you no more.'

A priest stood at the edge of the wood piled pyramids and threw the bowls into the largest of the stacks. A bright and scorching tongue shot into the night, and glowing fragments of leaf and twig sailed and sparked above our heads and we were allowed to go forward towards the first fire. As we approached, I could see a life-sized figure, woven from corn stalks, pushed amongst the giant logs and wondered about the significance of it all. A tribute to this year's harvest perhaps, with 'friend Granno' burnt as a sacrifice to entice abundance in the coming year.

Feeling that I should bestow some blessing of my own, a benediction from my past life to my new, if short-term one, I spoke the words of Aten aloud. 'When you have dawned, they live. When you set, they die.'

And with the heat of the flames all but grilling our foreheads, Petronius turned a shiny face towards me. 'You what?'

Once the last of the fires had been lit, the feasting began. Hunks of meat were passed around and more beer, for on this Samhain, for the first time in memory, as Petronius explained, no new supplies of wine were to be had, the war having put paid to such everyday staples.

He started unwrapping a parcel of cloth. 'Sometimes I treats myself,' he said, by way of explanation, 'and you as well tonight. Fixed them special.'

And in the parcel, open now, I saw a pile of crayfish.

He picked up one from the top of the pile and waved it in my direction as if to say, *dig in.*

'Don't we have to share them round?' I asked somewhat ruefully. There were more than enough for two.

He relieved me of my concern. 'They aren't partial to this kind of food.'

I was immensely glad to hear it though I wasn't sure that I believed him.

As we ate, we sat silently watching as ashes were taken from the fires' edges and smeared across the nearest faces. During this smearing ceremony, which demanded silence and contemplation from all, I felt something strike the back of my neck. I glanced over my shoulder but could see only darkness. There it was again. This time the object landed in front of me and when I picked it up, what did I see but a walnut. Someone had thrown it at me. But why? When I asked Petronius if being hit by nuts was part of the feast of Samhain, he responded, 'Never heard of it. But that don't count for nothing. Real weirdos they are sometimes, them Britons.'

Perhaps it was the type of prank Marcus was forever getting up to back in the City. If so, I'd learned enough from him to know that I only need sit still for a moment, seem absorbed in whatever was taking place in front of me, then turn round quickly to catch my assailant red-handed.

I sat, feigning engrossed captivation, then turned. There behind me, arm raised, poised to strike again, stood a girl. I knew she was a girl, even though her face was covered by the hood of her cloak, her hair escaping from it in tendrils. Her height, her slim body told me she was utterly feminine. Far from stopping mid-act as she saw me turn, she aimed carefully and this time the missile hit its target, right in the centre of my forehead. I bent over to pick it up from the ground beside me, wondering if I should throw it back. As I raised my head to look at her again, all I could see was the blackness of the forest stretching out behind me.

From that moment on it was impossible to pay attention to the ceremony being acted out in front of me. I watched, feigning interest, secret smiles rising within me, as the men took up handfuls of ash from the fires and rubbed it into each other's faces. Wooden masks were fixed, not over faces as might have been expected, but onto the backs of heads. I say masks but they were simply circles, fashioned from wood with slits slashed across them, two at the top and one at the bottom, to signify eyes and mouths.

'So they'll confound the spirits and they won't recognise no one. Now that their true faces have been blanked out and them false ones put on the backs of their heads. Confound the spirits, that's what it's about if you gets my drift,' explained Petronius.

I was settling myself further away from the spluttering cinders, Petronius had gone off to relieve himself; he had, after all, drunk twice as much beer as I and he was half my size, though perhaps I exaggerate. And now, after he'd left me alone, small, warm hands were covering my eyes.

I could only sit in silence as something was tied round my forehead and the hands scrubbed at my face. I opened my eyes and turned peering into the darkness. But nothing was out there, only the sound of soft laughter beside the forest's edge.

When Petronius came back, he let out a guffaw. 'Gods preserve us, what's been happening to you then whilst I've been away? Can't leave you a moment, I can't. Someone should have told them though, you ain't in need of any of that black stuff on your face, it's black enough to start with. And what's that on the back of your head? A horrible face it is. Ain't no spirit's fixing to come near you now and that's a fact.'

CHAPTER ELEVEN
THE HORNS OF TAURUS

It was still dark when we made our way along the path, Petronius and I, past the goose pen, round by the blacksmith's hut and through the field to the river. Two young boys holding sizzling flares came up from the bank to light our way towards a figure, a little way off, mounted and ready to go. And though his patterned skin was hidden under a hooded cloak, like the one I was wearing, and gone were the garish white spikes of his hair, I knew it was him and was struck with a kind of paralysis.

As I stood staring, he kneed his horse forward, two giant dogs pacing behind him at speed, leaving Petronius to give me a foot-hoist into a peculiar contraption of a saddle, like the auxilia archers', with pommels at front and back.

'Ye Castor, Petronius, is it only him and me?'

'You'll be alright, my old son,' he said. 'He'll take care of you, so he will.'

Comforting words, but I didn't believe them. Once I was safely mounted, Petronius handed me a blanket and a leather pack, inside which he'd told me was a knife, some flints, bread and a slice or two of dried meat. He tied it onto the front of my saddle. 'Took by one of them boys from that there raiding party you was on' – along with a water flask, whacked my horse's rump and off I half trotted, half cantered into the emerging dawn. A huge beast of a sword was slung over my back. Apart from the fact that it was something I'd never had cause to handle, it was unbearably heavy, added to which my legs became more chafed and raw as they rubbed back and forth on my horse's belly. I could only thank Chiron for those saddle pommels; they were all that stood between me and the ground.

I couldn't have said whether I was more terrified or embarrassed, ridiculous I know. There I was, deep in a British forest, trying to catch up with some rabid maniac barbarian and two great beasts of dogs, heading for gates leading to nowhere, which weren't actually gates in the first place, and what was I feeling? Embarrassed.

Though I'd felt like an idiot on my trip to the frontier with Leonatus and his men – I hadn't so much as known how to arrange my cloak across my horse's flanks to keep off the rain, had dithered on the sidelines whilst they'd shovelled great mounds of soil to form the camp ditch – I'd been with friends at least.

But I wasn't with Leonatus, I was with him. Forget about cloaks and rain and shovels and camp-ditches, he'd seen me scared witless, spewing up my meal of bread and beans, prancing along after his horse.

I had fostered a hope that somewhere on the journey, if we got out of the forest, into more open country I might find a chance to escape. But that was before I knew who my travelling companion would turn out to be.

During that first part of the morning's trek I was dragged, my soft, gentle spirit recoiling in horror, into a world Marcus would have relished.

And just as I had when I'd been with the little man on the

hummock, I thought about him again and couldn't begin to imagine his anguish. He'd have heard about the massacre by now, that I'd died with Leonatus, and he'd be distraught. He was tough but I knew his soft side. We were entirely different beings, but he had treated me as a friend, and as time passed, more like a brother. How could he possibly imagine that I had survived. One thing was certain though, I'd get back to him. At least, that was my plan. My conviction that this was a certainty helped me push thoughts of him out of my head; worrying about things over which I had no power did nothing but demolish what little was left of my spirit. And somehow, I'd manage to do the same with my task to come.

The sun rose over the distant trees a few hours into our journey, and shards of a hoard of Thracian gold were spread out before us. By the time we entered that gilded landscape I was shaking and weak with hunger but the ghastly thought struck me; stopping wasn't part of the Sword Fighter's plan.

So on we went.

We kept to the forest track for most of the time though now and then we were forced out across open country, and here the marginally less gargantuan of the dogs was sent out in front. Off she'd shoot, a streak against the hay-coloured ground, and on we'd follow, galloping through herds of deer who'd stand transfixed until we were upon them then, panicked, they'd scatter.

Danger was out there quite clearly, but as far as Petronius' Bantey were concerned, I was barely able to lift my lumping great sword from my back, never mind put it to any good use. Whoever they happened to be, if they came at us … well, I tried my best not to think about that.

But luckily, the gods travelled with us.

It was strange being back in that forest with the trees crowding around me again, the tangled undergrowth, the ivy fluttering like ribbons from the branches above our heads, a smell of witch hazel; a great shushing like many thousand sighing voices. The faded leaves were plucked by the breeze and whirled around us. Down they fluttered onto our shoulders, the Sword Fighter's hair, our horse's manes. Their stirring and whispering making me think of the rattle of papyrus disturbed by ducks or oars on the banks of our great mother Nile

As evening fell, we reached the bank of a wide, slow-moving river marking the edge of the forest. The Sword Fighter reined in his horse and dismounted. At intervals during the day he'd made stops like this, but only to relieve himself, or drink from streams or pools, and I'd followed suit, but now he took his sword from his back and laid it on the ground beside his pack, indicating that I should do the same.

Next he turned his attention to his horse, scratching her ears and rubbing her nose, unfastening her bridle. Never having done such a thing in my life, I watched and copied along, clumsily removing my own horse's gear, reins, saddle and bag. We worked in silence, avoiding each other's eyes.

Behind us loomed the forest and waist-high ferny undergrowth. In front was the river, and beyond it a grey stretch of land. An owl hooted, the river gurgled, our horses whinnied and snorted, tossing their heads, the dogs wriggled about on their backs, mouths set in human-like grins.

Whilst all this was taking place beside him, the Sword Fighter picked up a stick and started to root about in the earth. I stood looking on, feeling a thousand times more awkward than I had when watching the auxilia digging our camp. He made a hollow, then set about filling it with yet more sticks, twigs and handfuls of leaves, and unrolling his own leather pouch took out a flint. He struck it, it sparked, the leaves caught, the fire glowed, brightly at first then less so as the sticks and branches shrank into the makeshift fireplace.

Now what? I'd reached a point where I hardly cared. I was dead on my feet, fit to drop, supperless, onto the ground. So I did.

I woke with first light, or should I say with first noise, a squeaking of leather and jingling of bits. I forced my bleary eyes open and saw the horses saddled and standing at the river's edge and, beyond them, a landscape of dreams. The gurgling river meandered, unhurriedly, its surface strewn with leaves of varying golds and ambers. Beyond the far bank was a stretch of rolling land, a sweep of meadow, before the forest sprang up again. Such overwhelming beauty filled me with great waves of yearning. For what, however, I couldn't have said.

It took all my courage to follow the Sword Fighter into that river. He led the horses out first; a hard job for they plunged and showed the whites of their eyes. Then he came back for me and the dogs. I had the feeling they'd been ordered to stand guard beside me. We swam, or should I say, half trod, half drifted across the river, using one arm to propel ourselves, whilst we held our cloaks and rolled packs with the other, which only made me think what I could force myself to do when I put my mind to it. Until then, swimming had been a thing of enjoyment; warm sun-kissed water, or the rose-scented pool of the bathhouse. By the time we reached the other bank, I was on the point of being very ill indeed.

Amazing that in all this time we'd said not a word to each other. Amazing but true. And even here, wringing out our clothes – at least now I had no hair to worry about – my painted captor avoided my gaze. It was as though I didn't exist.

Sopping wet, we mounted our horses and travelled at speed across the meadow and skirted the edge of the forest. In front of us stretched a vast, treeless plain, and here was my first encounter with mist. It drifted around us, like steam from a cauldron but was bitter cold rather than warm.

Those sailors' stories about Island Britain.

And as we stopped by that great wall of cloud, the Sword Fighter acknowledged my existence for the first time since we'd set out. Half turning in his saddle, he signalled that we'd have to travel stealthily now. I saw, again, the green of his eyes, his face traced over with its now faded serpent and thought, *is this really happening?* But it was, and now we started across the strangest place I'd ever encountered, stranger even than the ziggurat-strewn plains of Ur, which till then had been the strangest of all.

And in strange lands, strange things invariably happen.

Stealthily we went then, the less enormous of the dogs walking the path ahead of us, and after a while great smudged shapes floated out of the pearly glow. Here was my chance to make some little stab at conversation.

I furrowed my eyebrows and asked, 'What are these?' in my quietest, most courteous voice.

'Gods,' the Sword Fighter answered, in Latin, and though she hadn't been called, the lead dog appeared at his side, giving me the distinct feeling that she didn't want to be out there on her own anymore.

The shapes firmed up and we entered a ring of huge rocks growing out of the earth. I felt a great urge to get down from my horse, walk round its circle, be part of the magic. But as I slowed her to a trot, he turned and glared at me. Then he rode on.

During that journey, crossing stretches of what looked like roads, wide as the Appia, cut into the ground, I felt my horse shiver beneath me. The dogs made small, bleating noises, and looked plaintively up at their master, but he ignored them and they slunk along in silence, heads down, as though unwilling to take in any aspects of their ghostly surroundings.

By the time we left the stone-planted plain, the mist had started to lift. A patch of sky gaped blue above us and in it I saw a hovering speck.

'Amun opened the doors of the heavens,' I whispered the comforting words, 'and I flew through them on the wings of a hawk.'

We entered scrubby woodland now, my horse settled down and the dogs were allowed to run free. Off they darted into the rust-coloured undergrowth, bounding in and out of clumps of bracken, noses up, tails thrashing.

The Sword Fighter was taking it slowly; I kept a good bit behind him. The sun sailed higher above the horizon and what had been a patch of blue was like a wide thrown sail. The scrubby land stretched out ahead, our breaths rose white in the fridge air.

Then the roar crashed into us. My horse reared up; I'd have been hurled from my saddle if not for its pommels. The dogs stood rigid, noses pointing. The Sword Fighter slid from his horse and pulled his sword from his back. He waved for me to dismount, and fast, and pointing to a clump of briar kicked out at the bigger dog, propelling him in its direction. We followed orders and made a dash for the hiding place, where he stood in front of me, ears forward, eyes fixed towards his master.

The gods only know what came over me next; lunatic curiosity and a need to prove myself, perhaps.

It took some time to clumsily fumble the too-heavy sword from my back, and taking what courage I had in my hands I stepped from the cover of the briar bush. The dog followed, his nose prodding into the small of my back, until we were out in the open. Here he took the upper hand and stole past me, hackles raised, leaving me to tag along behind him.

We'd just crossed a sun-dappled track, were wading through the bracken, closer and closer towards the bellowing when the ground moved. It simply opened like some wide, gaping mouth and next thing I knew I was plunging down into it. I grasped out in panic and scrabbled against its walls with my feet. But this was a mistake, for the more I scrabbled, the more they crumbled. A rush of pebbles spilled onto my head as I slipped even further into the abyss.

The immediate thing was to stay as still as I could. I grabbed at an out-jutting stone and, sticking my toes into the earthy side of the chasm, pushed my body against it and clung on for dear life, face wet from tears, sweat and snot. Time passed. I prayed to all the gods I could think of that they wouldn't let me lose my grip and crash down into the scream-filled darkness beneath me.

It was some kind of maddened creature, stamping around at the foot of the hole. Its horns flashed white, like Bithynian blades ... or the horns of Taurus.

Lifetimes passed; the screaming echoed around me. But now came a new sound, a rustling and shuffling above me, and blue patterned arms were round my chest, pulling me upwards, scrambling and sliding, tearing at the undergrowth, grass, stems, roots, anything I could get my hands on. Firm ground was under my knees, but only for a moment. A mighty shuddering came next, a chunk of ground gave way and now it was the Sword Fighter crashing down into the gaping mouth, grabbing my arm as he went. Amazingly enough, I managed to hold onto it for long enough to let him catch onto the out-jutting stone, just as I had been doing only moments before.

I was above the ground now, and he was below it. Surely the gods had looked down upon me, here was my chance I could get back on my horse and head off, but to where? I glanced around, the stone-planted plain lay to my left, the looming forest stretched out before me ... *and them Bantey, well you better watch out.* Any lunatic thought of escaping was dashed now to dust. But something else stirred inside me. I cannot say what it was apart from a conflict at odds with my instinct to run. Or, even at that early time, was it something more?

I knelt, stretched my arm into the hole and could just about touch the top of his head.

'Cal.' I said his name for the very first time. My voice came out shaky, like that of a woman who's been crying too much.

A frantic moment setting my brain into action; if I were Marcus what would I do? *Come on Siva, think.*

I got to my feet, ran to the horses. But just as I was unfastening the first of the harnesses, my fingers awkward, unable to function, the screaming, which had died away the moment the Sword Fighter's arms grasped round me, started again. I was desperate to rush back but knowing that Marcus would have taken a moment more to finish the job, that's what I did. Harnesses undone now, I fumbled around in my pack and found my flints.

Back to the edge of the hole, down on my stomach and

with trembling fingers I tied the harnesses together, struck one of the flints – a piece of equipment I'd never had occasion to use in my life – against some dry leaves as I'd seen him do. A spark flew out. Thank Vulcan it lit, and I transferred the sputtering flame to one of the sticks strewn around, making a poor but useable torch. I cupped the feeble flame in my hand and squinted into the now partially lit darkness. The Sword Fighter was halfway down, clinging on for dear life, and lurching about beneath him was not a bull, as first I'd supposed, but a leviathan of a beast I'd never had chance to rest eyes on before.

I stuck the torch into the lip of the hole but the light only angered it more. He pawed the ground and crashed his horns into its earthy border. A great shaking erupted but there was no time to wait till it stopped. I lowered the looped reins and tried my best to position them under one of the Sword Fighter's feet.

'Foot,' I said in Latin and saw a tiny movement stir within his stiff, still body. And sure enough, a foot went out and balanced on the harness. The strain on my arms was enormous and I knew I wouldn't have strength, not simply to support him but to haul him up and out of danger. Before he made that final movement, however, and put his other foot in the harness, inspiration struck. I called the dogs to me. The big one stopped his growling, edged towards me, and crouched on the ground by the chasm. The smaller one followed, though rather more hesitantly, and after winding one set of reins round my upper arm, I did the same to the dogs' shoulders. We'd pull together.

I shouted above the screaming. We strained, all three of us, and the Sword Fighter's body spun out from the ledge, no arms or legs supporting him now, his life resting in the hands of one puny Egyptian and the backs of two dogs. With that first weighty step on the harness, he sank down a little, and by the light of the twig torch I could see that now his legs were within hacking range of the horns. Thank Apis there was no movement below for long enough to let me adjust myself to this new weight, but as we began our pulling again the charge came.

We pulled even faster. Up came the swordsman. His hand felt out for my arm. He held tight onto it and now his head was out of the hole, now his shoulders, and now he was grasping at the grass, stems and roots, just as I had grasped. I leaned over, felt for his belt, and gave a mighty heave. By now my nerves were utterly gone.

Next thing he was lying face-down on the ground, shaking and trembling. For a moment I thought he was breathing his last. Then it struck me; he was laughing. I looked down at him as he rolled about in his state of side-splitting mirth, desperate to join in, but racked, still, with my old deeply ingrained sense of hesitant self-consciousness. But the more I stood looking on, an expression of acute discomfort on my face, the more he sounded like some deranged hyena, until I was unable to hold myself in check a moment longer.

'Ye gods.' My voice was bright and high now. 'Ye gods,' and though I hadn't a clue as to what he was finding so funny, I started to laugh at it too, beginning with a polite, gentle chuckle, but as it grew and swelled inside my belly, all sense of decorum was set aside, as wave upon wave of unbridled emotion swept through me, finishing me off, convulsed, squeaking out, 'Stop', for if he didn't I felt I would burst.

But he didn't stop, not until he was beat, and even then, he ground his laughter to a halt in bursts and starts. And when he spoke, though I had no understanding of the Briton's language at that point, I could tell that the words coming out of his mouth were nothing less than curses; loud, uncouth and obscene as any to be heard on the stage of the Marcellus.

When he had recovered, he picked a stick from the ground and set off round the hole prodding it into the grass as he went. At a point he stopped and, as if talking in conversation to a friend, began kicking downwards.

The ground gave way; earth and roots tumbled into the hole. Now he took a few steps back. A loud shuffling noise and from the hole emerged an enormous boar, more ferocious in appearance than that on the banner of the XX.

He stood, stunned, for a moment. Then with a flick of his tail, off he raced into the woodland as fast as his cloven hooves could carry him.

CHAPTER TWELVE
ULLAN DUR

At that night's camp, on a rocky spur of land, Cal and the smaller of the dogs, whose name he told me was a word that meant 'fast' – I settled on Swift – went off to scout around. He left me with the big dog, Storm, and the task of getting a fire up and running. But when they got back things were pretty much in a mess; I'd built a useless mound of wood, too closely packed to catch light.

I was speechless with shame, but Cal only picked up a stick from the pile between index finger and thumb as if it were an object beyond contempt.

'What?' he joked in Latin. 'What?'

What indeed? And that night I was given my first lesson in building and lighting what the Britons call a smokeless fire, beside which we lay, wrapped in our blankets, he at one side of it, I at the other.

Despite its covering of bracken, the ground was incredibly hard, with what felt like ice seeping up from its core, so cold, in fact, that I lost all feeling in my body. In stark contrast, Cal seemed to me then to be dead to the world. Unable to follow his example, I sat up, pulled my blanket tightly round me and thrust my feet into the warm ashes at the fire's edge. Frigid moss soaked into the seat of my breeches, but that was beneath my backside. Above my head the night heavens stretched like an inky ocean, and sailing upon it were stars in their clusters; Orion, the Pleiades, Scorpius, Andromeda, Cepheus, Centaurus, Cassiopeia chained to her throne, Asterion and Chara held on their leashes by Boötes as they hunted the northern reaches for bears. I hadn't seen such a sky since I'd crossed the great desert to the temple all those years before. Peering up at its immense, stretching vastness, blotched over with cloud islands, I let my mind wander.

Where were we exactly? It had to be early November, so, taking the position of Thales into account, I tried to compare her position with how she'd be set in a Roman sky at this time of the year. I took up a stick and marked calculations in the pale fire ash. We were as far from Rome as it was from Thebes, at least; if a line were traced from one to the other, then extended in the opposite direction for an equal distance, this is roughly where Britain would be. My master's map had been wide of the mark, then, as I'd placed Island Britain a good bit further south.

I thought of what Marcus would say if he were able to see me now, sitting out of doors on that bitterly cold night, head shaven, clad in a pair of riotously coloured breeches, one somewhat crazed looking Briton asleep to my left, two huge monster dogs to my right. In my musings I let go of my stick; a flurry of sparks shot into the air, and with that Cal sprung up. I was yet to learn that on the trail a Briton never sleeps, well not completely. His eyes may have been shut but this only meant he was seeing with his ears being how they describe it.

One moment he was curled on the ground, the next looming over me, brandishing his sword. I must have looked more than somewhat alarmed. The dogs were on their feet now too, hackles raised in place of growling.

'Sorry,' I said, 'that was me.' Thinking, *this time I'm for it.*

But Cal seemed relieved more than anything else. He sat down beside me and dragged his pack towards him, out of which he pulled a leather flask and, opening the stopper, passed it to me.

Despite Marcus' best efforts, dainty glasses, or silver goblets of wine from our own estate, or a thimble full of warm grape-seed liquor was all I'd been used to till then. The liquid burnt my throat, and it took all my willpower to stop myself sputtering. But stop I did, and we drank the remainder of the ferociously strong liquid in silence, gazing up into the night. And, as if reading my mind, he raised his arm and pointed to the galaxy, winding her milky way from Sagittarius to Cassiopeia, as if to say, *what is the meaning of life and of that?*

The sky, the smell of wood smoke, the fizzle of the fire and Cal, and something in me changed; here I was, where the gods had chosen to place me, beneath a firmament not even the priests of Ra could have dreamt of, all thoughts of Marcus and my reasonable life spinning out of my head to join the whirling pools of light above me.

This was the moment my devotion to Cal and his island began, and what I now know was my rebirth.

We sat until the first hint of light touched the edge of the sky. And as the stars dissolved, we ate the last of our bread and dried meat, though my craving for food had simply dissolved; two days and a night had passed with only the bread from our packs and that mind-bending liquor passing my lips. During our first day's journey, I could have eaten my fingers, and as we progressed, my fingers and hands. But something inside me had changed and those overriding pleasures of the past such as eating were of no interest to me anymore.

During this too short space of time I found that if I spoke clearly, Cal was able to follow a fair deal of Latin, far beyond the base words I'd used until now ... 'what are these?' or 'foot' or 'sorry' ... in a mixture of his language and mine. We talked about many things, amongst which he told me that the hole with which we had so recently become acquainted had been set as a boar trap. Covered with branches, the animal would tumble into it and when dead would be pulled out through the exit, this being the hole into which we had fallen. The ingenuity of man never ceased to amaze me.

He asked about the land I came from and I told him what I could about Egypt that he might be able to understand. That it was a hot place with the river of life running through it, and trees that were different from those that grew here, that our temples weren't to be found in forests but instead were built of blocks of stone. And our gods? I held out my sunship and made an attempt to explain about Ra and his bark, and how each day he sailed across the sky from dawn until nightfall.

Next came questions about Rome. A vast city, I told him, filled with people, where every manner of thing took place. I felt it would be a step too far to try to describe the palaces to be found within its walls. Or the insulae with its dwelling places built one on top of the other.

He leaned towards me. 'They,' and now came a British word, followed by 'kill us.' And I knew it meant 'cannot'.

This was the moment I told him that I would do everything in my power to make sure it did not.

He looked at me with a soft and grateful expression and I knew he understood the hopelessness of their situation.

When first light whispered into the sky, we set off again. The land became rockier, the woodland was scattered and scant. It was frosty and we rode under bright skies. The wind whipped Cal's hair against his cloak. I saw how easily he supported his sword on his back, how straight he sat in his saddle.

Presently we came upon a brook rippling and gurgling over speckled pebbles. Here we dismounted and he performed two rituals. Kneeling beside it, he poured the contents of a leather pouch onto the surface of a rock. I thought it was flour. It wasn't though, it was lime. A little water from the brook, a little stirring around with a stick, and the gooey mess was applied to his scalp. And before it had time to dry, he drew his now white hair into spikes; one moment Cal of the starry midnight was in front of me, the next the demon who'd crashed his way into my dreams of the feast of Saturnalia back at the camp of dawn. My reaction to his metamorphosed state pleased him no end. He motioned for me to kneel beside him and stretching over he rubbed my stubbly head with the remainder of the gloop, lest, in my natural state, I might feel diminished as I hovered beside his new and stately being.

Standing now, he unfastened one of the thin golden bracelets clasped above his elbow, twisted it till it snapped, and dropped the two segments into the water. He pulled my sunship from its hiding place under my tunic. Was it to follow his bracelet? But no, pulling me beside him he pressed his elbows to his waist, extending his forearms, palms towards the sky, just as he'd done in the grove of skulls. And this time I copied along, joining him in thanksgiving for our safe passage, or so I imagined. I was learning, but not fast enough. It would take me a while to work out what lay behind the Britons' prayers, the fact that they never thanked their gods, only ever asked, and would be helped or not, depending on how Leu or Bel or Camul or Don might be inclined at that time. Sacrifices were made by way of a bribe, or as advanced payment, then forgotten and the deity would be contacted again only when the next problem cropped up.

The task completed, on we wandered, leading our horses, the dogs running out ahead of us.

As dusk settled in I was given the honour of doing what I'd made such a hash of the night before, namely lighting the fire that we'd built together. A proper fire, with flames that were permitted to flare up into the darkness. We were in hiding no longer.

'Now they will know we are here,' Cal said in his own language. I was getting used to it for he spoke even more than I did.

He appeared a short while later, a lone figure striding towards us. Cal stepped out to meet him and they stood beyond the fire, clasping left hands the way Britons do, talking in loud, cheerful voices. Unsure of what was expected of me, I got to my feet, took a step or two forward and found myself facing a new kind of man.

Smaller than any of the Britons I'd come across so far, he looked somewhat different. Of middle age he wore the same type of woollen breeches and cloak as they did but unlike those whom I'd come across so far, the strange thing about him was his eyebrows, or lack of them should I say; small blue circles were marked in their place. But I was in for a shock, for when he spoke it wasn't in the dialect to which I was becoming accustomed, but in an accent of someone born in the City; not like Petronius I hasten to add, but a real, blue-bloodied patrician.

'Good evening.'

'–ning,' I replied in utter amazement.

'My name is Ullan Dur,' he smiled. 'Welcome to the lands of Ciern. I hear you have joined us.'

And what did I say but a statement of the patently obvious. 'You speak Latin …'

To which he replied, in a confessional tone, 'I'm a bit out of practice, so bear with me won't you?' He studied me for a moment. 'You're Egyptian, I think.'

How could he know?

And seeing my puzzled expression he pointed at my sunship, which, since our libation at the stream, was still untangled from my tunic.

'I've never been there, I'm afraid, but I've heard much about it.' And with his words Cal looked at me with the same keen attention. 'So now you're here on our little island. It must be a bit of a shock, I imagine.'

'I like it very much, actually.' We might have been laundry maids passing the time of day as we laid out our washing by the fountain.

How could he sound so incredibly Roman? The only way I could account for this was that he'd been part of Petronius' shipwreck, … *there being some amongst them who decided to stay … just because they liked it here.*

'Cal tells me you're here to speak with Cartimand on High Caradoc's behalf. You'll know she's here with us at the moment … she came down from her stronghold in the north. She plans to join Rome, and she wants us to follow her. I am told that you may know of a way to prevent this, but you should recover from your journey before we speak any more about her.'

We sat by the fire eating food Ullan Dur had brought with him. It was very much better than anything I'd tasted on the farm, Petronius' crayfish apart – grainy bread, slices of some bird or other, soft curd cheese – and I set to eating with zeal.

Of course, he knew what I was thinking. 'You must be wondering about me but let me rectify matters. There's no need to tell you that I'm Roman, or should I say that once I was, but let me explain. I spent my childhood in Mediolanum. My father was an official who oversaw the distribution of grain. About twenty years ago he was charged with a crime he didn't commit.'

I'd been wrong about the shipwreck.

'When he was sentenced to death, he sent me here for protection. The Britons accepted me, I became a member of this tribe. In time, I was invited to be their leader, and I accepted … it was my little act of revenge. There are others here who are like me; by that I mean outcasts of the Empire, but now you've joined us, it's as if our presence has increased twentyfold.'

I felt free, then, to tell him my own story. That, as he could see I wasn't Roman, not in the true sense, and began with my life in the temple of Ra.

But before I went on, he stopped me. 'Are you permitted to tell me more about that?'

I didn't have much to tell, only that I'd been one of the young acolytes who read the stars.

'Was this for some religious purpose?'

'No, to follow the seasons and tell when the rains would come.'

'To escape them?'

'No, the opposite, our crops could only be sown if our great river flooded. If it didn't, there would be famine.'

He looked at me with keen interest. 'And this is where your amulet comes from?'

'We all wore them, it's called a sunship.'

'I'm honoured to know this,' he said. 'It's become something of a legend since it was hung in Nemeton, then taken away; none of the offerings have ever been removed from there until now.'

At this point I felt it better to say as little as possible on the subject, so after telling him that I didn't know much about why that had been, I moved back to the temple. I told him that a sign had come from the heavens telling the priests to abandon it, and when they fled that I had been bought by my master and taken to Rome.

'May I ask who he was?'

'His name is Publius Ostorius Scapula.'

He blew through his teeth. So, they'd heard about him even here.

'Yes,' I admitted, ashamed. Nothing to do with Publius but because now he, and more importantly Cal whom I'd hoped was still ignorant of my status, would know I was a slave.

'He was a good man,' I added. 'I learned a lot from him, and for that I shall always be grateful.'

'The gods have sent you to us,' he said next, which reassured me no end.

'And how, if you don't mind my asking, did you find yourself here in Britain? It's clear you're not an army man.'

And now came the point where I made, what was until then, the greatest decision of my life, where I sealed my fate forevermore. As a means of stalling for time, I'd asked Caradoc if I might join him. Now I knew that this was what I wanted to do; I had been granted two lives until now. This was my third. Just as he'd said the gods had set me on a new path, and I would follow it. And thus I sealed my fate.

'I was sent by my master to speak with Cartimand.'

'No, forgive me, I meant why were you sent from Rome?'

I smiled. 'To speak with Cartimand.'

He might have thought of many an answer to his question but this was the last one he could have imagined even had he been granted the gift of second sight. He stared at me, dumbstruck.

'It's hard for you to take this in, but I promise it's true.'

And whilst he was silent, I told him why. 'Just as you said, it's thought that she might be inclined to join Rome. And I was supposed to persuade her to do so.'

He took a moment. 'But how? And why you?'

I thought it too complicated to explain about Marcus' plan and so I continued with what was the truth, 'They said I'd get my orders when I reached the frontier but I didn't get that far. It's where they were taking me when I was captured.'

'Caradoc knows this?'

'No. I didn't want him to doubt me, I had to prove myself first. It was simply because I'd been with the legions that he sent me to tell her about Roman tactics. He thought it might convince her to stay with him, rather than joining the enemy.'

This was the first time I'd described Rome in this way.

'She wants us to join her, as I've said, but we will never do that.' He held my gaze, 'Apart from this, Cal tells me you have information that will help us greatly.'

'I think you must mean what I told Caradoc about the II Legion's plans.' I picked three sticks from the ground and set them down before us in the increasingly familiar shape of Leonitus' triangle. 'Here's Dun Camul,' and as before, I marked the spot with a stone. 'And here is the camp of the legion preparing to march against you.'

Ullan Dur looked up from the stick triangle. 'The camp of the Augusta,' he stated rather than asked.

'Yes,' I said, 'it is.'

'I know only a little about its commander, but he's our greatest fear.'

'Titus Flavius Vespasian,' and for once I remembered what Marcus had told me. 'You're right to fear him; they say he's the most dangerous of them all.'

'Do you know him?' Ullan Dur asked next.

And though I had watched as he spoke in the senate, that was all. 'I can't say I know him. My master does though.'

We talked for as long as I was able to form words, about the cohorts of the II, and anything else I was able to haul from the depths of my brain. Then I remembered, and with the last of my strength I asked about Petronius' Bantey … not gods or animals or spirits come to haunt us, their real name was the Atrebante, and they turned out, in fact, to be allies of Rome. The enemy, in other words.

'Their lands are placed close to ours.' He pointed to a spot on the triangle, and Leonitus' 'friendly country' sprang to mind, surrounded by its squiggles.

At this point I hadn't slept for a day and three quarters and was just about dead when we got to this subject. Every now and then I'd find myself dozing off, Petronius style, then jolting awake, embarrassed at what I felt must seem to my robust companions a horrible lack of self-discipline.

'I hear you had a bit of an adventure.'

I'd had so many of these from the moment I'd stepped off the boat, I wondered which one he meant.

'You rescued Cal from a boar trap.'

He had saved my dignity and so I said, 'He rescued me first.'

'They're meant to crash down into the pit, but Cal says he must have fallen in through the exit.'

He looked thoroughly amused at that turn of events. 'It's how legends are made I suppose.'

CHAPTER THIRTEEN
CARTIMANDUA

With the first glimmer of dawn, Ullan Dur stood and said, 'Let's go then, gentlemen.' No need to repeat his words in British as Cal was already strapping his sword to his back. I was only just awake.

The dogs kept to heel as leading our horses we set off across a swathe of undulating grassland and walked for some time before our destination came into sight, crouching on the horizon, white and gleaming, like some enormous sphinx. As we approached, I could make out earthen ramps spiralling round it in circles. The Dun of May which means the fortress on the plain, was high above us and we climbed the flat-topped hill by way of a steep pathway. I'd never seen white ground before, for that's what it was, brilliant and white like polished chalk. We pushed through the gates in the stone-walled defences as we climbed upwards, first one, then another, then another still, until we reached the summit.

I asked Ullan Dur what I thought was a sensible question; were these the gates of Ciern?

But 'No,' he told me, the term 'gate' simply referred to the entranceway leading from one god's lands to another's.

And Ciern, was he a god?

'Yes,' he said, 'he's something like Pan.'

At the summit, I gazed down over the ramparts and saw, in the early-winter sunshine, an undulating countryside stretching to the south. And there, I was told, was the sea, the very ocean I'd retched and quaked my way across not so very long before.

Though not in vast numbers, there were people around. They looked on in consternation as we passed, or should I say, as I passed, it being evident that men of such remarkable appearance as Cal with his spiked hair, and Ullan Dur of the circle-painted eyebrows, were of no particular interest to them. At this point a young boy hurried towards us and offered water from a flagon. I couldn't but help notice the carved ducks that decorated its handle.

The farm had been one thing, but here was a far more substantial community. On the grassy circle of the summit stood a group of circular houses built along much the same lines with wicker walls and thatch touching the ground. We entered the largest, which was set to one side. It took a while for my eyes to adjust from the dim of the tunnelled entranceway which led us indoors, but when they did, I saw a fire burning and iron lamps hanging from the rafters, their glow reflected by rows of polished shields ranged round the circle of the wall. As we entered, several men rose from their sitting positions and a horn was sounded. Soft to begin with, it reached a crescendo. From its serpent mouth held over the player's shoulder, its noise trembled and hung in the air.

Cal was motioned to take what I presumed to be the place of honour; he pulled my arm and made me sit beside him. Ullan Dur was to my left, and aware of the fact that I must have been feeling more than slightly intimidated by my surroundings, he leaned towards me and said, 'This house is known as the Hall of the Gates,' and he smiled ironically. 'Think of it as you would the Temple of Concord.'

I can't say that this information made me feel any less nervous.

First, we ate the usual meat fished out of a cauldron. The decorated edges of the iron frame from which it was suspended were fashioned to represent the heads of long-horned bulls. It was of much more interest to me than its contents. My one-time fixation, namely that of eating, was relegated to the nether regions of my mind, as I may have told you already. I'd traded my love of food for that of life itself.

The feasting had only just begun when Ullan Dur gestured that Cal should stand. And when he did, such was the silence cast upon the hall that a beetle could have been heard scuttling over the floor. As he opened his mouth to speak, the company lurched forward, intent upon hearing his every word. What these words were, I couldn't have guessed.

'He's explaining how he freed you from a Roman camp. That you saved his life. That you have pledged to help rid our lands of the Men of the Eagle.'

No word of the outpost garrison unit, or the fact that I had been with it. He had preserved my dignity, and I would forever be grateful to him for that.

They listened, enraptured, until the spell was broken by a young man who stood up, his shadow cast gigantic on the wall behind, to roar loud words which had a most unsettling effect upon me. Far from seeming concerned, however, Cal stood, unflinching, staring at his audience with unblinking eyes, then turned towards me and gestured that I should take my place beside him, which I did, but in a horribly feeble and embarrassed way. They must all have been thinking, *exceedingly strange behaviour. But what can you expect from such an odd-looking creature?*

And in a gesture, the memory of which I would carry with me during future months of forced exile, during nights when memory would lure me back to the lands of the Britons, and the best of my life only just started, Cal placed his arm round my shoulder and spoke again, but this time using words they all knew, for they mouthed them together in soft voices. At the time I took the mumbling to be some kind of oath and I was right but not until later would I be able to work out its meaning.

'Unless the sky falls, or the waves of the sea come over the forests,

we shall not give ground.'

When a rough silence had settled, Ullan Dur motioned us to follow him. Close to the door stood a woman, the likes of which I had not set eyes on before.

Small, with hair of a rich, deep brown and a cap of gold upon her head, she wore a green robe bound tightly round the upper part of her body, and circular brooches pinned to her shoulder. And then there were the marks on her face. On her forehead was what I recognised as the symbol of the waning moon, its lower peak looping down between her eyebrows. On one cheek the sun, and on the other the sign known to the Greeks as the Bear but which I now know, the Britons call The Steadfast One.

She lifted her right hand, on the back of which was a line drawn in brown which, to Britons is the symbol of the earth, with above a thicker one in blue which represents the sky.

She seemed too fragile to support the weight of the massive gold necklace clipped round her neck. I did not think she looked friendly.

Two men stood beside her, the most remarkable thing about them being their hair which, much like the little birdman's priests, was shaved in an arc from ear to ear, the unshaved portion hung to their waists. And like Ullan Dur, their eyebrows had been shaved, with small circles painted in their place. They were dressed in outstandingly plain clothes. Here before me stood the stuff of those wild tales and rumours whispered on the boat.

And though Quintus had made a muddled stab at explaining why Marcus had sent for me, in that short moment I solved the puzzle myself; why he had told me to bring my linen kilt and silk-fringed tunic, my kohl, and asked that I keep my hair plaited. If I, being as unlike a Roman as she, when we met her, I might be enough to tempt her to join them.

Ullan Dur talked to her briefly in their language but, turning to me, she replied in Latin and I knew right away; here was someone who did not tolerate weakness.

'You are sent from the east to deliver a message about our invaders. But if you have turned traitor against them, why should I believe what you tell me?'

If all those days spent with my master had taught me one thing it was that a hostile questioner requires a reply that will throw them off track.

'Because I'm not Roman.'

Her fixed expression told me that she was as adept at this kind of power game as he.

'I was a slave.'

Still her expression did not change, but there was a silence before she continued. 'If you were my slave, would you betray me so easily to my enemy?'

And here I thought of my master again. 'Yes,' I said,

'I would.'

Her lips moved slightly, another silence. 'So I should regard you as a danger?'

'Not necessarily. If you were a fair mistress, I would give my life to save you. If not, and the chance presented itself, I would be happy to turn traitor.'

'So Rome has not been a fair mistress?'

'No.' I held her gaze and hoped she wouldn't catch the conflict in my voice. 'She has not.'

She nodded to her right where Cal and Ullan Dur stood. 'They tell me you have come over to us.'

'Why should I not?' which was a fair question.

'What is this message?'

'You may not choose to hear it.' I tried to replicate my master's expression of boredom at this seemingly endless interrogation and thanked all the gods that it worked.

'I do.'

'Caradoc asked me what Rome's most successful tactic has turned out to be. I told him that it can be summed up in three words, and these words are, *divide and conquer*.'

It was clear that she knew what this meant but wanted to hear my explanation.

'If you allow the legions to divide your collective strength, they will defeat you. Stand together as a single force and you may have a chance to make them wonder if your island is worth the effort. Caesar eventually withdrew his legions, and Caligula's men picked seashells from the coast at Gaul in lieu of proper booty. It can be done.'

She answered without hesitation, '*May* and *can* are not words I like.'

To which I replied, 'I can't pretend you'd force them out, it wouldn't be a true appraisal. But if you let them proceed as they have until now, you will soon be their newest province.'

Marcus had sent for me to persuade her to join Rome, and there was I telling her why she shouldn't.

It was clear that she wasn't accustomed to facing someone not quaking in their boots, which she would certainly have succeeded in doing with the old Siva … but I was a new me now, and I spoke as many would not dare. Let her do what she wanted with me. I was past caring.

The next thing she said was intended to shock me into submission. 'If you're so keen on taking our side,' she said next, 'why don't you go back there and spy for us?'

Shamed by her question, Ullan Dur stepped forward and put his hand upon my shoulder. 'You have completed your task,' he said in a quiet voice, 'and we thank you.' And when she was gone, 'I beg you to forgive our guest. As I explained, she is the leader of very much larger tribe than ours. But what I did not tell you is that she seeks only glory and power. We are afraid that she'll throw in her hand with Rome and that will be the end for us all. But your words may have persuaded her to remain true.'

My answer surprised him. 'What if I were to take her up on her offer? Go back to the legion to which I was attached and send information back to you?'

The Britons were valiant, but Rome's might weighed heavily against them. I would do whatever I could to help them. Even if it meant returning to Rome.

He stood silent for a long time; I could see he was thinking. Then came his words, 'It is good of you to do this for us, we have been on our own until now. Oh, Caradoc has informers at the camp at Dunum but of course they are Britons and can only report what they pick up outside the walls. But you would be at the centre of things. We'll tell them about you and they will make contact. You can give them any message or warning and they will get it to Caradoc in the White Lands'

I didn't know that this was what his land was called.

'It is,' he said, 'and I would tell you why, but that is a tale too long to explain. Suffice to say that it's where the Catuvellauni are now. It's not too far from Dunum but too long a journey to travel there now. From what you have shown me the camp of the II is closer; if you agree, Cal will take you there. But how will you explain your sudden re-appearance, if they think you've been killed?'

'Oh I can take care of myself. I've witnessed Vespasian's performance in the senate; I know I can outfox him.'

'Then I will give you a Briton's warning, *when danger is all around, you must listen with your eyes and watch with your ears.*' And this is when I first heard that vividly graphic expression.

I told him I would and thought to add one last thing. 'My master has a son. He's here with the legions. His name is Marcus. I beg you if he's captured, please spare his life. He is my friend.'

He looked at me intently. 'I give you my word.'

That night I dreamt I was on a small island, surrounded by a lake. A voice was howling into the wind, telling the world that the great Pan was dead.

CHAPTER FOURTEEN
TO THE CAMP OF THE II AUGUSTA

With the onset of winter on that island had come a type of cold that men from the temperate lands of Noster can't even begin to imagine. And this was merely its start. Frost covered the ground with a coating of icy white. The ghost-like trees, their leafless silhouettes no longer black but silver now, looked as if they'd been etched against the blank of ground and sky where an opal sun, barely visible through the veil of mist hovered low on the horizon, more like a white moon than anything else. But as the day wore on, her light became, if not brighter then clearer as it touched the blue-tinged pools of shadows set between the tree trunks on either side of us. As Cal and I rode through that icy garden, I felt I could enter the mind of the first holy man who'd decided these forests were spiritual places, temples for the gods.

I was sick to my stomach at the thought of leaving him. The beauty made me even sadder.

When the time came for us to part, on a hill overlooking the distant oblong of the camp, I could barely force myself to look at his face. Is it destiny or chance that rules our lives? If chance, I might never see him again; if destiny then I knew I would. As I moved to go, he pushed Storm towards me with the flat of his foot. I caught the gist of what he said, 'Take the dog, for between the two of us it's you who'll need him most. When the time comes, he'll know how to lead you back to me.'

It took quite a while to reach the camp, which stood in a clearing cut into the forest. Trees had been felled in their hundreds, and logs and planks were stacked on either side of the track. There was smoke, and the clanging of hammers rang out. Funny to think I was walking across Leonatus' squiggles and crosses; a curious vision, a jabbing finger, 'friendly country' as he'd described it.

Perhaps it was the hum of men's voices, the reek of latrines mingled with leather, but as I got closer to Vespasian's camp, I was struck by a great wave of panic. Two months away from such a place, yet I had forgotten what chilling effect it had had upon me, the lookouts posted at forty-foot intervals and, inside, the rows of hut and tents, men playing knuckles or ludus; an atmosphere of hustle and bustle mixed with physical and emotional inertia. To the untrained eye it would have seemed no more than a palisaded rectangle covering a stretch of British flatland, but Rome was Rome, after all, and always would be Rome. Inside, her walls reigned 'civilisation', beyond them the world was held at bay.

Now in sight of the gate, above which fluttered the Capricorn standard of the II Augusta, Storm and I stopped.

A moment or two and a figure came striding towards us.

After being in the company of men even taller that I, or my own height, apart from Petronius and the tiny birdman, I wanted to laugh as I looked down at the diminutive guard who peered up at me from under the rim of his helmet, unable to believe his eyes. Or his ears.

'My name is Siva Ostorius,' I announced myself in my palatine Latin, 'and I'd like to speak with your commanding officer, if you'd be so kind.'

Still he peered, in total silence; had this place finally turned him stark staring mad?

'I'd be terribly grateful if you'd take me to him,' I prompted, to which he responded after long and awkward moments with a sideways jerk of his head, indicating that I should follow him round the rampart ditch. But to be fair to the poor chap, how was he to deal with this odd, dark, towering fellow? Who was I? And where in Dolicenus' name had I come from?

Walking through the main area of the camp, the guard some way in front, Storm sloping reluctantly by my side, I was met with looks of incredulity, accompanied, no doubt, by fingers forked behind backs. Strange this, since no one had looked at me twice when I'd been my old self, freedman's cap perched upon my head. Which made me think about Marcus.

'You don't have a junior tribune from the XX here, by any chance?' It was a long shot, but no harm in asking, after all Marcus did tend to pop up where you'd least expect him.

'No sir.' Now it was sir, in response, no doubt, to my accent, and he left me standing outside the leather curtain of a massive tent whilst he stepped forward to speak with some minion or other.

I was waved forward.

Titus Flavius Vespasian was broader, more neckless, than ever. He sat on a well-padded campstool, if stool you could call it, documents spread on the table beside him.

'Who have we here then?' he growled, half looking up.

'Siva Ostorius,' then I added, 'sir.'

'Is this some kind of joke?' A reference, I supposed, to the way I was dressed.

'No,' and again, 'sir.'

'And who is Siva,' and he snorted, 'Ostorius?'

I took a breath. 'Sir, I'm a freedman of the Scapula family.'

If he felt relief at my answer, he didn't show it. A slave … well then, there you had it, a subspecies who posed no threat whatsoever.

'And?' he drawled.

I launched into my well-rehearsed story, told him how I'd been travelling from base camp with the reserves to join my master, how we'd been set upon, how I'd been taken captive.

'Young Scapula is back in Camulodunum now. I'll send a carrier to tell him you're here and he can do what he wants about it,' meaning get me back there as fast as he could, and he turned his back on me.

I wondered how long it would take him to work out that I was of far more use to him here on his own patch, than I was to young Scapula of the XX. Storm and I had just started walking back out across the muddy area between the tents, following in the footsteps of the guard, who'd never again look upon me as a superior being and refer to me as 'sir', when we were summoned back.

Titus Flavius was on his feet now. He signalled for me to sit on the now vacant stool. Its padding was uncomfortably yielding beneath my buttocks which had become used to good solid ground during my time with the Britons.

'Freedman of Ostorius Scapula?'

'Yes, sir.'

I couldn't help thinking how much he resembled one of those overfed, sacred bulls back in Memphis as I watched him pacing up and down, up and down.

'You were taken prisoner, you say?'

'Yes, sir.'

'Taken prisoner, I see.' He stopped and glared at me for a moment before going back to his pacing.

'Taken prisoner, whilst all the others were butchered, now I wonder why that was.' I hated the way he was rubbing his chin between his thumb and forefinger. 'Do you have any idea why that was?'

Sitting, whilst he stood, was making me decidedly nervous. But he was clever; whilst I was a good head taller than he, he wasn't about to countenance looking up at someone of vastly inferior status and diminish his powers of interrogation.

I shifted to a half-truth now and told him that they'd taken me for a god.

'A god?' he said, feigning rapt fascination. 'I'm interested, freedman Scapula. Continue.'

Deciding to keep as close to the truth as was safe, I told him about my sunship, made the outrageous claim that it turned out to be like one worn by a British god.

'Being … captured … as you were, pray how did you manage to prize yourself from their grasp? If a god indeed they deemed you to be, surely they'd have kept you under wraps?'

He certainly was on his toes.

On I blundered, saying that I'd been hung in a cage.

'And you were worshipped, were you, in your cage?' Titus Flavius was known for his humour, a rare characteristic among generals; the men around him laughed.

Best to say nothing, I thought.

'You don't look like one who's suffered, freedman Scapula, not at all. You look as if you've been practising out on Mars Field, not cooped up in some cage for weeks on end.'

Pure invention, but here I claimed that I'd tricked the Britons into releasing me.

'Oh you did. I see. And how did you do that?'

And when I replied that this involved a rather long and complicated explanation, he fixed me with a smile. 'Oh pray don't concern yourself about time, freedman Scapula, I'm not rushing off to a dinner engagement,' laughter again, 'so why don't I just while away the hours listening to your good tale?'

Inspiration hit me, and using a vestige of what, after all, was the truth, I told him that illness had spread after my amulet had been hung from a tree in a place called Nemeton, how the British priests had been summoned.

'Not priests, Scapula. Druids.'

At this word, which till now I had only heard on the ship as the mariners talked in low voices about their power to raise the dead, a chill ran down my spine and the skin on my scalp seemed to shrink. I'd thought them wild tales of imagination but I had stood in front of them, had listened to their prayers, yet even though I had watched them carry fire had never thought to connect the Britons' holy men with those monstrous creatures. And to be fair, Petronius had never explained it, though that, indeed, was what they surely were. A flood of energy rushed through me for here beneath the mighty Vespasian, sat one who had taken part in the rituals of those very men he found so amusing.

Best to keep on talking, I thought. 'I told them that the amulet held strong magic, sir, that the presence of my god was angering theirs, that they should set me free.'

'How could you tell them anything if you didn't speak their language?'

By now I felt my brain would burst. Think Siva, think. 'Some amongst them understood enough Latin. It seems they used to trade with Rome.'

I stopped to see if I was making any headway here or whether I'd have to change tack. I could read nothing in his bovine expression.

'Simple as that was it? Where is it now then, this amulet?'

I pulled the sunship from between the layers of my tunic and showed him. Its copper sun circle, warm from my skin, needed a polish; the little carnelian ship was smudged with sweat and fingerprints, but still it played the part.

He barely glanced at it.

'I think, sir,' I ended up saying, 'it was all simply down to luck. That I was spared, I mean.'

'A substantial amount of luck, I would say. And the dog?'

My mind raced even faster. I told him he'd been bound up, ready for sacrifice, that I'd rescued him, which I hoped would ring true since Romans themselves were forever offering some poor animal to the gods. Dogs were their favourite.

'Well what a story. Egyptian talismans, a Druid dog, a cage.' Laughter again. 'If my men were to catch wind of such tales, I'd have a mutiny on my hands. You can't be allowed to roam out amongst them, their minds are filled with enough crazy notions.'

He resumed his pacing. 'But, freedman Scapula, one thing's for sure, if I had authority over you, I'd crucify you here and now. That wouldn't do much for morale, though. At least I don't think so.'

A moment's pause. 'But now I come to think on it, I'm not so sure. There hasn't been much in the way of fun here since we dug camp. Maybe a good execution ... some entertainment ...?'

At this he turned his gaze upon those around him, inviting his poor men to support his sham misgivings. They struggled to retain their iron demeanour.

'Luck, Scapula, and luck again. Lucky that you're not under my jurisdiction, for if you were I'd have you out there pinned to a cross.' He stopped his pacing. 'Do you know what I think? I think you've joined them, come down here to spy.'

Oh no, indeed the sons of Rome hadn't conquered the world as poor unsuspecting souls. But razor sharp though their minds might be, I hadn't spent all that time taking notes for my master without having learned how to turn any argument to my favour.

'If this is what you think, sir, then nothing I say will change your mind. I'll go back to Dunum.' I did my best to look ill at ease, which wasn't so terribly difficult, considering the situation at hand. 'And from there my master is bound to deport me.'

Knowing Romans as I did, I was pretty sure of my tactics. What he presumed he heard me say was, 'I'll own up to anything you want, as long as it gets me back to the City; comfort, feasts, baths, the races ...'

A slight hesitation and then the words, 'I'll tell you what I'm going to do, freedman Scapula. I'm going to place you under guard until I've had sufficient time to mull this whole thing over. If, and I'm not saying I believe a word of your preposterous claim, if I deem you to be of more help to me here than back at base, I might very well decide to keep you with me.'

And he made that familiar gesture, prerogative of the senatorial classes and Romans such as he. *Take him away*, he motioned, *take him away*.

They put me in a lock-up, with no space to move more than half a step to either side. The cold was indescribable and it occurred to me that had the little birdman hung me in the cage I'd taken such pains to describe to Titus Flavius in weather like this, I'd have lasted less than an hour. But I belonged to Cal's world now, and to remind myself of my new status I ran my hand across my shaven head; the old me might have risen to the surface when targeted by the penetrating interrogations of Titus Flavius Vespasian but, that apart, I was changed forever.

I crouched in that lock-up and thought about Cal. He'd be there on the hillside, not so very far away, dug in with Swift, the embers of a smokeless fire glowing warm beside him. I knew what he'd have eaten, a wedge of barley bread and the last of the bacon ribs. With no Storm to keep her in check, Swift would be left to her own devices, scampering out to catch squirrels and small nocturnal creatures.

I longed to be sitting beside him as I'd done so many times before now, hoping that he wouldn't be able to read the truth in my eyes. As far as he was concerned, I was his friend, no more than that.

Storm was tied up somewhere by the storehouse. I asked if he'd caused any trouble.

'Not as far as I know, he hasn't,' said one of the guards. Incredible, really, since by all rights he should have bitten off a couple of hands by now. I could only put his good behaviour down to a bout of stultifying bewilderment.

The guards? Well, all that interested them as far as the painted tribes were concerned were tales of the absurd, and the more outrageous the better: 'Is it true they can live beneath water, that they're really not human but ravens and crows, that their singing has power to waken the dead?'

But sensationalism appealed to Titus Flavius not a whit, more's the pity, he wanted facts, and I was taken back to face him day after day.

'Now, freedman Scapula, I wonder if you'd humour me

a little longer. Please do tell me something about this tribe of yours. No, let me put that another way, about the tribe that took you captive. Ah, yes?'

'I really can't say sir, and naturally they couldn't understand me. Shall I tell you what they looked like?'

'No need, dear chap, no need. Huge, hairy, painted monsters, all of them, unless your lot were any different. And if that's the case, why I'd be pleased to have a description.'

'No, sir, that just about sums them up.'

'And Caratacus, what can you tell me about him?'

Unaware then that this was the name Rome had chosen for Caradoc, he could see I was genuinely puzzled. 'The name means nothing to me, my lord,' I said, which was the first real thing I'd told him.

Titus Flavius' eyes bored into mine, like hot brands.

'Did you travel from south or from west?'

'I was trying to follow a map I had seen. The II's camp was marked upon it, but I was stumbling around, really, without much knowledge of where I was going. It was simply luck that I ended up here.'

'Luck,' he said, 'now haven't I heard that word before?'

There was nothing else for it, I'd have to give him something to get his teeth into. He knew where I'd come from, so why not just say it so.

'I'd hate to give you false information but since the map turned out to be right, it must have been from the north, sir. Then I went east.'

'Why not simply go east to your own camp?'

Frantic scrabbling about in my mind, I replied, 'It wasn't marked upon it. I didn't know where it was. But I did have a fair idea of where yours is, sir, so that's why I took that direction.'

'How many were in the tribe?' he asked next, jumping from one subject to the next, intent on keeping me off-balance.

'It was a small one, not many.' I thought of Ruadon's farm, dividing by ten the number of men gathered there, hoping to put him off the scent. 'A couple of hundred, no more than that.'

'How do you know it was small?'

I had never lost a game of tabula; he was good, but not as good as me.

'I suppose I was expecting a huge throng of people, sir. The sailors on the boat that took me from Ostia spoke about *great hordes of Britons.*'

'So they're all small groups, are they?'

'I really can't say. I was only with that one lot, but something tells me they might be quite typical of the sections of tribes.'

'Oh yes, and what makes you think that?'

'Well sir, they seemed wealthy, and I assumed that they wouldn't lack men for want of being able to afford them.'

'Wealthy? What do you mean wealthy?'

'Well, dripping with gold, sir. Something tells me they're pretty representative of the Britons as a whole.' As soon as I'd said it, I could have ripped my tongue out. But surely, he'd seen their gold for himself.

'Anything in particular?' Now he was paying attention.

'Not really,' I said, trying to underplay my blunder, 'just the usual stuff.'

And so it turned out, the camp of the II Augusta was not a place where I'd be allowed to pick up even the tiniest scrap of information. On my sixth day there Titus Flavius said, 'I'm sending you back to base. And when you get there, you can entertain young Ostorius with your anecdotes.'

CHAPTER FIFTEEN
BACK TO ROME

We left with the snow. I'd never seen such a thing before; tiny white flakes sailed down from a sky the shade of a moth's wing, but as we rode along the forest trail it started to fall in earnest, the snowflakes growing larger and larger, covering everything about us in a gossamer mantle.

It took two days, riding flat out with a brigade of auxilia, Storm bounding in front of us, tongue lolling, to get from the camp of the II to that of the XX. I rode up front with their captain, glad of my ankle-length breeches, feeling sorry for the rest of the company whose knee-length army issue versions meant their shins shone blue with cold.

Crossing that frigid white landscape heading eastwards, I felt great sadness not being with Cal. If we'd been together, I'd have asked many questions. What were these lines of wooden stakes sticking out of the icy marshland? What were these great hummocks that looked like tiny snow-covered pyramids built on a ridge of high ground? What was the name of this wide, slow-moving river snaking and twisting out into the distance. We crossed from its south bank to its north by way of a makeshift pontoon, only just constructed by a corps of engineers attached to the Augusta, leaving our horses behind, picking up fresh mounts on the other side.

Here we made our most comfortable stop of the journey, crouched over fires with a contingent of re-enlisted veterans drinking a warm onion brew from their mess-tins and eating seed cakes, before pushing on, eastwards this time, into flatter land filled with herds of young stags with antlers like those of the eerie Samhain drummer.

On our second evening we reached the camp at Dunum. I'd spent a day at most in the place before I'd set off with Leonatus and his men barely two months earlier. I couldn't believe how much it had changed; new walls had been built, the ways were marked out and barrack blocks stood neatly in rows. The old palisade, an enormous structure by any layman's reckoning, had been heightened and widened, and even more new gate towers were under construction. And now, instead of the Capricorn Standard, above the gates of the II Augusta hung the boar version of the XX Victrix.

We dismounted at the principal gate. I let our captain do the talking. He'd turned out to be not such a bad chap after all; being in the company of someone who'd fallen into enemy hands had been quite the novelty for him, to say nothing of his men. The previous night, after we'd trenched ourselves in, he'd asked the inevitable questions. He came from Thrace, I could tell by his accent.

'Big men, those Britons,' he stated the obvious.

I said that, yes, they were.

'How come you're still alive then?'

'Luck, I suppose,' I said, half expecting the poor man to come up with, *now, haven't I heard that word before.*

Perhaps I should have been fabricating a pattern of misinformation about the Britons, describing them as the half-human barbarians of the tales that had done the rounds on the boat, afraid of nothing, out to slaughter as many of our own good boys as possible. But I couldn't bring myself to demean my fellow Catuvellauni by lying about qualities they didn't possess. No I couldn't do that yet, though I'd have to start soon.

To my horror, Storm was led away; it seemed that dogs had to be kept in the kennels.

'Take care of him!' I shouted after the legionary who led him away. He turned with a quizzical expression, surely a dog as enormous as this was well equipped to take care of himself. And so, without my new companion, I was escorted to Quintus' office, and there he was at his table, just as before.

A wild expression washed over his face; it was as though he were seeing a dead man dancing. He tried to stand but overturned his stool and went sprawling.

'Quintus,' and now I was pulling him to his feet.

He stood in a daze, trying to take it all in; hair even shorter than his, coloured breeches covered in mud and shoulders twice the size they'd been when last he'd seen me.

'By the immortal gods,' said he.

And though not to quite the extent as I had, the camp was changed too; building work was still underway and now it was beginning to look a great deal more like a fortress. Bathed in the brand-new bathhouse, and just as before wrapped in a blanket, my legs uncomfortably bare, new army issue hobnails on my feet, I was back where I'd been when my new life had started and, as before, I was ready to eat with an ecstatic Quintus. Is it not peculiar that my memories of Britain are of bitter cold and misery only when I think back to those times spent in camp? Or maybe the weather was as perishing back in enemy territory, but out there, with Cal, I'd been too ensconced in my joy at being with him to notice.

That night was cold. The fire basket was small and a second had to be called for. The snow wasn't lying anything as deeply as it had been further inland, which meant, in fact, that here it was even colder. An icy wind with sharp and frozen teeth blew in from the ocean. It whistled between the few remaining tents and the rows of brand-new barrack blocks, biting deep into everyone's bones.

'Come on then.' Quintus leaned towards me. He looked fit to burst had he been forced to wait a moment longer and sat, entranced, as I recounted my story … which, thanks to my travelling companions had to be all round the place by now. I trundled through it much as I had with Vespasian; the camp at dawn, the attack, the blood, the gore, my capture, the cage. I said nothing about Nemeton, or the branches hung with skulls and gold, only that I had been freed, thanks to my sunship, which they thought was a god, being released close to the camp of the Augusta, interrogated by the man himself.

He stared at me, appalled.

At this point, I thought it best to tell him that he'd all but accused me of throwing my cap in with the Britons, of being sent back to spy.

A smile broke through Quintus' mask of horror. He said reassuringly, 'Oh don't mind Titus Flavius, his bark, you know, and all that. But I have to say,' he shook his head, 'I simply can't believe it. Did he remember you though, do you think? You've been in the Senate House enough.'

'I don't know, he didn't let on.'

'Oh to be fair now, I could hardly recognise you myself, you're not the pretty boy you were back in the City.'

'I'll take that as a compliment. But I ask you, me, spying, and for that wretched lot of barbarians?' There, I'd said it.

By now I knew that Marcus hadn't returned from his posting up on the frontier; he'd been sent from there with a crack unit by way of Calleva, to somewhere called the bowed river.

Leonatus' voice crashed into my mind. *It's in Calleva, friendly country.*

'Calleva,' I butted in. 'Where's that?'

A 'Petronius, *you worry me sometimes, you do*, look' washed over Quintus' face.

'Should I know?' I asked.

'But, Siva, you've just come from there … from the camp of the II. I think I may have told you before.'

'Oh yes.' I tried to avoid the fact. 'Lost for days, staggering in through the gates of Camp Augusta to be met by a smiling guard, *Welcome to Calleva*, you think he said? *Do step this way if you'd be so kind.* I knew it was the II's camp, I couldn't have cared if it was in a place called Crustumerium.'

Quintus laughed, but I knew he was mightily relieved to have someone even less soldierly with him now.

'It's in friendly country you say?'

'Yes, in Atrebante lands. They're our allies, you know.'

Them Bantey, Petronius had called them.

And when I made no answer, Quintus went on, 'The only good Britons around.' I did my best at smiling. 'I'll get a message out to Marcus; tell him you've appeared intact. He knows what happened, poor chap.' He didn't have to say anymore. 'He had a run in with him too.'

I presumed he meant Marcus had a run in with Vespasian; I didn't doubt it.

'He'll be fine, I'm sure. Trouble with him is he couldn't care less, right or wrong, he stands his ground.'

'Stubborn?' I laughed. 'Pig-headed? Arrogant?'

'Titus Flavius wanted him seconded to his own frontier troops; your darling master just plain refused.'

'Good show, Marcus.'

'Always the bride, never the bridesmaid,' chortled Quintus, more at his joke than anything else.

But I knew what he meant.

The second fire basket arrived at this point. Glowing hot, the juniors carried it on outstretched arms, protected by oversized leather gauntlets. But now that we had one each, our faces got scorched whilst our backs remained blocks of ice.

Quintus ran out, brought them back and the baskets were shifted. One stood in front of us now, and one behind. Lucky for me, though he wasn't much of a soldier, he had his priorities right.

'Caius would never have let him go off on a jaunt like that,' continued he, toasting his feet. I knew he had been the last prefect. 'But Plautius, well, he's a different kettle of fish, and you know even better than I do how Marcus gets round men like him. His plan sounded reasonable enough at the time, I was there when he set it all out. But after he was gone and it was too late to fetch him back, he began to have second thoughts. *Perhaps it wasn't prudent to send young Scapula on such a hazardous mission. I hope we haven't seen the last of him.* Least that's what he said. I've been worried.'

Worried was one thing, I was struck with dread; whilst there wasn't much Marcus didn't know about fighting, he was only trained in the Roman way. What if he ran into Cal and his men, what then?

I tried to turn my thoughts away from Marcus and any fate crouched, ready for the attack, one of Fabius' stock phrases coming to mind, *all lap of the gods stuff now, my sweet.* But whose gods? That was the question.

And trying to brush his fears away, 'But of course we haven't. And when he gets back, he'll be decorated for outstanding gallantry.'

Despite Vespasian's sceptic observations, luck was with me still, for much though I wanted to see him, had I been in his camp when Marcus arrived, there'd have been no need to send me back to Dunum, and Dunum was where I had to be.

Only now did I realise that I'd made no mention of Storm. I tried to sound flippant. '… a dog. I'd picked him up on the way. No one would think about attacking me with him around.'

That night I bedded down in the tribunes' slave's quarter. Thanks to Quintus I'd been given permission to stay there; I did, after all, belong to their world and he knew how much easier I'd find them to be around than a bunch of Marcus' fellow officers. 'I'm not going to spoil it, but you're going to get a big surprise.'

I'd only just stepped over the threshold, was pulling off my muddy breeches, when I heard a voice behind me.

'Oh my word, is it you after all? What a turn up for the books,' and who was there but Quintus' freedman, the very last person I could have dreamt of coming across in that dump of a place. 'I got here last month. Just after you left.'

But though to Polydorus, Dunum must have seemed an especially horrid version of Hades, he hadn't allowed circumstances to get in his way. By the look of things, it was business as usual. Once Quintus had told me that back in the City, he'd rise early to have time to himself; he'd needed this precious hour or so to bathe, curl his hair, apply a pinch of rouge to his cheeks, manicure his nails and read a little. The result was perfection, a well-tended mind and body, though the latter was beginning to show signs of wear. Being Athenian, his Greek was dauntingly refined, as was his Latin and he spoke Hebrew and Aramaic, having spent some considerable time in Judea with his master's father some years before.

'My, oh my, I can barely find words.'

Just as well for I could imagine what he was thinking ... a ghastly apparition stood there in front of his eyes; shorn hair and wearing such hideous clothes; an old, ripped army issue cloak with nothing underneath it save my half-on, half-off mud-caked breeches. He'd rushed through the door of the slave quarter having heard a rumour ... a peculiar looking dark-skinned 'Briton' had just arrived, and what do you know, he'd been dining with Quintus Paulinus.

'Give them here and I'll put them on the fire.'

He was referring to said breeches. But I'd never allow them to be burned.

'Oh thanks, but d'you know, I'm going to hold onto them as a kind of memento, for once my hair grows back and my body turns to flab, who'll ever believe me when I tell the tale of what I've been through?' And I proceeded to recount the very same story I had less than an hour before.

He sat down on the camp bed and listened open mouthed. And when my tale had come to its end, 'How in the name of Phlegyas you endured it is beyond me,' he said, more astounded than pitying. 'This place is bad enough, never mind the wilderness beyond. But I don't need to say how happy I am that you did.' A flicker of amusement crossed his face. 'It would seem that Marcus has a rival now.'

When he left me, I unrolled my mattress and stuffed my breeches inside it, praying to Cal's god that it wouldn't be too long before I'd be putting them back on again.

Stripped of my breeches, I'd been handed a pile of fresh tunics, a soft kidskin one amongst them. And along with a new waterproof cloak, apart from my hair, or lack of it, I was a remodelled version of my old self. I sat amongst a collection of slaves who'd come along to goggle at '... him ... you know ... the one who was captured.'

I was drinking a bowl of sweet, scalded wine, steamy and rich with aromatic herbs, trying to look relieved at being out of my warm, barbarian breeches. To add to this, I was fretting about Storm, here was I cocooned in luxury whilst he was imprisoned out in some freezing yard.

But I had to push him out of my mind, I was on a mission. Over the next stretch of time, I'd *listen with my eyes, and watch with my ears*, glean chunks of vital information from the very slaves with whom I was lodging. Their quarters were the place to be; if you wanted to know what was going on anywhere within the vast stretches of the Empire you only needed to ask one of those silent creatures who stood, invisible, on the sidelines, as matters pertaining to the conquered world were discussed all around them.

This was my first campaign, if it could be called that, but they were all veterans of some past war or other. It was evident, however, that to a man, they thought Britain the worst place they'd been. They pulled their ten or so layers of cloaks tightly around them. 'I mind it enough when it's warm, but this ...'

'It's probably a bad idea to talk to me,' I said straight off, putting my plan into action, 'about anything from a military point of view, I mean, not whilst I'm still under suspicion.'

'Oh for goodness sake, what else is there to talk about in army camp?'

And now Polydorus asked the first question. 'It's true then, about your ordeal?'

Of course he knew it was but had taken it upon himself to play the talebearer.

'You of all people, but how could you have borne it? How simply horrendous.'

I adopted a stoic expression.

'Are they as monstrous as we're told?'

'Oh yes.'

'Dear gods.'

'Indeed.'

'We've seen some of them, they look like beings from Tartarus.'

'I know.'

'They do pile victims in cages, then, and set them up in flames?'

'Oh yes. I've seen cagefuls of people. The screaming, the smells of roasting flesh, I still can't bear to sleep at night, the image will haunt me forever.'

'We've left a little lamp by your bed; you can keep it burning throughout the dark hours.'

Dear Polydorus, I felt guilty spinning my lies, but I had to keep up the pretence, even in the slave quarter, one wrong word and I'd be out on the parade ground, fastened to a cross.

That first night, back in Dunum I should, I suppose, have been formulating my next plan, asking questions, listening carefully to the answers, but I was too weary even for sleep. Instead I lay on my mattress, wallowing in a serious bout of soul-sickness, inebriated still with memories of Cal. I fell into a kind of half wakened, half-dreaming state, and the dreams I dreamt were of him.

I saw the laughter in his eyes. But his body was cut and dripping with blood.

CHAPTER SIXTEEN
TIBERIUS CLAUDIUS COGIDUBNUS

Storm had been rescued. I thanked the gods and Polydorus, who had gone to the kennels with an order written by himself and stamped with Quintus' seal. I hoped it wouldn't be a problem for him. 'Dear boy,' he had tutted, 'don't you think my master has enough to contend with ... salaries, food lists, inventories of those ghastly weapons, I'm relieving him of inconsequential trivialities, like having to do it himself.'

The officers' slaves fell in love with Storm and insisted on keeping him with them though an animal in barracks was against all rules. If the poor dog had been confused back at Camp Augusta, he was even more so now. I'd an inkling of what was going on inside that canine head of his; these people were friends of his master's peculiar Dark Stranger, but they looked more like Romans to him. So, though in normal times he'd have growled and bared his teeth, he let them rub him down with laundered towels and feed him the choicest titbits. I wondered what Cal would have said about that, since British dogs were never indoors, even on the coldest of nights. What could I do but give in and hope that their kindness wouldn't turn him into some oversized lapdog.

But what was I doing fretting about Storm, I asked myself,

the thought having struck me that by the time we'd both had a share of this kind of treatment we'd be the most perfectly suited of companions.

The perishing winds whipping in from the ocean had eased up, and snow was falling in earnest. The place looked less like a military stronghold and more like a vast building site. Since no work could be done in such weather, hundreds of restless men were confined to barracks. A gang of auxilia had been set the task of clearing the dugout channel upon which a permanent pavement would be laid when the weather took a turn for the better. They scraped away with their shovels, metal against the frozen earth, making a noise that grated my teeth, stacking icy mountains against the walls of the barrack huts. The snow kept on falling, however, which meant that an hour or so later the same area had to be cleared all over again.

I was standing by the headquarters, thinking, unassailable though the camp of the XX was, it only took a British snowstorm to grind it to a halt.

The situation here was pretty much the same as it had been at Ruadon's farm, despite the fact that new barrack blocks were being put up at speed, the number of incoming men – legionaries, auxilia, artisans – far exceeded available quarters. The sleeping quarters had been doubled, the cause of much grumbling, whilst the lowest of the lower ranks and the few centurions who preferred chilly privacy to overcrowded warmth were billeted in a tent village, tacked onto the back of the hospital block, spilling out in imprecise rows.

Everyone looked miserable.

Amidst the half-finished barracks and piles of paving stones, three buildings were more or less completed; the governor's house, with, next to it, the headquarters, and since Romans tend to get their priorities right, towards the line of the northern palisade, the proper centurions' bathhouse where I had bathed the night before.

Great effort had gone into getting the warm and cold baths up and running, but it could have been worse since the main elements required, namely water and timber, were in plentiful supply. Day and night, Polydorus had told me, the furnace-room belched out pipe loads of scorching heat which boiled enough to thaw hundreds of frozen bodies on a daily basis.

The bathhouse was where I spent my first few days, luxuriating in an atmosphere of balmy despair, thinking of Cal and, somewhat more significantly, spying. Here, without making any great effort, I could eavesdrop to my heart's content. Most of the lower ranks of the XX were old campaigners, which meant they were experts; there was nothing they liked better than laying bets as to what their commanders were likely to get up to next.

I learned about the separate cohort's strength and weaknesses, the attitude of the auxilia, the characters of those in charge – who was considered a walkover, who a tyrant.

One early afternoon, someone they referred to as 'he' or 'him' was the topic of conversation.

'... big handsome bloke all the same.'

'... weirdo, if you ask me.'

'... must be rolling in it.'

'... wouldn't trust him as far as I could throw him.'

'Who are they talking about?' I asked one of the bath-slaves. From the three who'd been there when I'd first arrived, their number had grown to around twenty, and even then, they were so overworked they'd hardly a moment to stop.

'King or some such. Didn't see him then when he came in?'

I hurried back to the quarters to hear what Polydorus had to say on the subject of 'him'. 'He', it seemed, went by the name of Tiberius Claudius Cogidubnus … I seemed to have heard that name before; I racked my brain but couldn't remember where. As luck would have it, he was still in the camp, having lunch with the governor.

I left Storm lying beside my mattress, knowing he'd be on it the moment I shut the door behind me, and huddled in my cloak, slipped and slithered my way along the icy track towards the governor's house. As I approached it, a booming centurion's voice giving marching orders – 'Right. Right. Right.' – told me something was happening. I turned to the little band of snow-clearers hunched on the path beside it, blowing their fingers and with, 'Looks like you could do with a hand,' took one of the older chap's shovels. The poor fellow looked flummoxed as he stood back and let me get on with it. I broke into the next portion of snow and started piling. Three months before and I'd have been the one standing back.

The sound of hobnails on frozen ground got louder; the unit of guards came closer, and past us they marched, a towering figure in their midst.

He was a Briton, no mistaking; white of skin and grey flecked hair which he wore wild and bushy. Round his neck was clasped a mighty torc , the bosses of which, in a token gesture towards the Imperial City, were crafted in eagles' heads of such prominence as to ensure they'd never escape a Roman's eye or his approval.

In his features, his white skin and wild hair, he was a Briton. With his torc, a Briton making some slight mark of respect towards Mother Rome. In his toga, however, which he carried expertly, his bearing was rather like Ullan Dur's accent, patrician through and through. Had I seen a man like that anywhere other than Dunum, I'd have found him utterly fascinating. But as it was, the moment I clapped eyes upon him I knew he was trouble.

'That fellow, who is he?'

I was back in Quintus' hut where the two fire baskets were making little headway against the draughts of frigid air gusting through the gaps in the stitched leather seams of his door. Defeated by the perishing cold he was preparing to move back into the barrack-block with other junior officers. He was in a dismal state. I knew all he wanted was to magic himself back across the sea to his beloved Stabiae where, if only his father were not still alive, he'd be able to concentrate on his books and his gardening, with a little fishing thrown in for good measure.

But he hadn't been listening. He kicked his kit bag across the floor. It landed outside in the snow. 'By Castor, Siva, how do those Britons survive it here, winter after poxing winter? Who, in their right mind would choose a place like this to live? Leave them to it, that's what I say, and let's go home the lot of us.'

He was beside himself, having been forced to relinquish his small slice of privacy. Tonight he'd be warm with the rest of his friends, but the snoring, the high jinks, the losing great fortunes at dice only to be accused of being tight-fisted when you run out of cash, the same old stories, over and over, the constantly being surrounded by it all.

'The minute the cold loosens up, I'll be back, just you see … What was that you were saying?'

'The big Briton.'

'Oh him, Cogidubnus. Bit of an oddball. Story goes he was fostered in Rome as a youngster, the rest you'll have to find out for yourself. Ask him, why don't you, next time you see him. Then tell me, you know how much I like a good story.'

'I take it he's a leader, something of that sort?'

'King of one of the tribes around here. But names,' he scratched his head, 'I should have them off pat by now. Hang on though,' and now he was rummaging through great piles of documents and tablets strewn over the table. His eyesight which had always been poor was getting worse. All I could do was sit still and wait until such time as he came up with an answer confirming what I'd long since managed to work out for myself.

'Yes now, here we have it. There are two main tribes allied to us. One, the Atrebante of Cogidubnus, king of the Regni, Atrebante lands having been ceded over to him for services rendered, the other being the Iceni of Prasa, Prasa …'

'… tog?' I guessed correctly as it turned out.

'Yes, that's it.'

Now was the time to ask, 'And what about the woman Cartimand?' Hoping to cover my blunder, I quickly changed her name to its Roman version, and lest I made another one, quickly added, 'since I didn't get to meet her?' Not only had I become the greatest ever teller of untruths, but could do so without the slightest flicker of deception.

'Ye gods Siva, don't let's start bothering about her, she's hundreds of miles away to the north.'

And, trying to delve deeper, 'Don't you think it's interesting, a woman in charge and all that?'

'Not anymore. Since the day I got here all I've seen of British women have been enormous Amazons, towering above me.' He started looking fed up again. 'Thing is, you see, I can't be bothered anymore. It's all too tedious for words. This tribe, that tribe, this lot on her side, that lot against us, and all with ridiculous names. Why can't I simply resign myself to it, play it for the game it is, be more like Marcus. But I don't suppose I want that either, not really. I couldn't care less about Cartimandua, Cogidubnus and the like. Forget about me, you're the authority, you're the one who's been living amongst them. One thing though, I'll feel a lot happier when spring comes and that bunch along the southern coast are reined in. Once Titus Flavius has done that, we'll be able to breathe more easily.'

And following his kitbag, he plunged out into the snow.

My worst fear had come to pass … It would happen, after all, when winter had ended.

So this was it. I struggled to think but think I would have to. I sat down on Quintus' camp stool and forcing the memory of Leonatus' triangle to focus clearly in my mind, I pulled one of his blank tablets towards me and from the best of my memory marked towards the mid point where Vespasian's camp had been, and May, from where I had returned at its western edge. Dunum came next. We'd travelled, through what he'd called 'friendly country'. The baseline, which had meant nothing to me then, ran along what I now knew was the coast. If the other two angles added up to ninety degrees, I stabbed the wax with Quintus' stylus, this was where the gates of Ciern must be.

I calculated again; thirty miles marching per day. mayby three days, but there were no roads which added, perhaps, another two days.

So, just as Leonatus had predicted, his next campaign would take place in Ullan Dur's land. I sniffed around everywhere I could think of, the bathhouse, of course, down by the quartermaster's stores, the stables and eventually heard from one of the auxilia, keen to flaunt his knowledge, that a plan was indeed in the hatching; once the worst of winter was over the cohorts of the II would set off in a diagonal direction to the foot of the triangle, with the intention of annihilating the western tribes.

Until that moment I'd been firmly stuck in the present but now I would have to start thinking in advance. I still had hope. If Vespasian thought defeat would be a simple exercise for his troops, he'd be in for a shock. The massed warriors of May were a force to be reckoned with. But even if I were able to translate this to any of Caradoc's spies I knew he could never make his men understand the nature of the disciplined ranks of the legion they'd be facing. *Dear gods, Petronius*, I could but hope that he'd do a good enough job in explaining it all, for if he did he might just be able to help Ullan Dur cause enough damage to turn Rome around.

Back in the slave quarters I slumped on my mattress. Nothing there was 'regulation', bedding was bulked up with torn linen rags, pillows filled with ducks' down, lamps with the finest double-filtered oil. We all wore caps whilst we slept, not freedman's style but of soft lambs' wool, with ear flaps and Persian-style socks on our feet. As there was no one to see what they got up to, they got up to as much as they possibly could.

That little bed would have been a paradise had it not been for Storm who, now freed from his prison, was stretched out beside me, taking up more than his fair share of space, and the fact that my mind was in fervid turmoil. There was no time to spare; I should be getting a message out to Caradoc, warning of what was in store for Ullan Dur and his men.

But none of his spies able to take a message to the White

Lands had introduced themselves to me yet. I put this down to the fact that until the snow eased up, the only Britons permitted into camp were those who carried goods through the gates from the pack-carts coming up from the port.

Plans dashed in and out of my mind, and when I was at the end of my tether, my thoughts turned to Cal and the last thing he'd said to me, *When the time comes, he'll know how to lead you back to me.* What about slipping away, and letting Storm do as he'd told me, in other words lead our way back to him? But it would take about ten times as long as it had on horseback … and would we ever make it? The forest trails, which had been dangerous enough even when I was with him, were bound to defeat me. But if I thought it would help change disaster at the hands of Titus Flavius into triumph for the Durotriges …

Then I began to think sensibly. Heading back to Cal, though I longed to do just that, wouldn't help him or the Britons at all. This was merely the earliest stages as far as campaigning was concerned, and ever greater plans would be hatched in the months to come. If I stayed put, nose to the ground, I'd be able to root out all kinds of stuff, not simply what Titus Flavius was scheming up on the short term, but how his plans might be thwarted.

That state of desperation which shuts off my normal train of thought has on a few occasions been responsible for producing inspirational flashes of genius. And so it came to me that night; lying in my turmoil, weighing up once and weighing up again the choices set before me, should I go or should I stay, *When the time comes, he'll know how to lead you back to me.* If he could do that, why was I needed?

Storm would take the news. I'd set him off in a generally

westward direction and, pray Mercury, that unencumbered by the bumbling presence of his master's new friend, doubtless a novice in the art of following a trail, he'd make it back to Cal very quickly indeed. A few feet of snow would be nothing to him.

But how could he carry a message? Then it struck me, my sunship. All kinds of things had been stored in its hollow; disks of perfume in the temple and later in Rome, along with love notes and betting slips passed to me at the races, one of Asselina's earrings ... why not a message? My burning relief turned to ice, however, as one of Petronius' exasperatingly relevant facts came to mind; the Britons didn't read and despite his fair use of Latin perhaps not even Caradoc. I cursed the fact that I couldn't direct Storm to May and Ullan Dur ... he'd only go to where Cal was. I thought hard; the only one amongst those out there in the White Lands with a smattering of knowledge as far as reading was concerned, would be the little man himself. He'd be able to write his name, along, perhaps, with those of his friends. He might even have known how to inscribe the title of his patron god, and when he was young, he'd have marked the walls beside his local tavern with gladiator captions. But that would be all.

The solution, then ... I'd draw my message in pictures on a scrap of cloth from one of my tunics, using as few words as necessary. Storm gazed at me reproachfully as I pushed him aside and got up from our mattress. I looked around me, what could I use as a quill? I settled on a pair of tweezers and used them to mix a spoonful of water with soot that had gathered under my fire basket. Task completed, I sat in a corner and by the light of Polydorus' lamp, dipped the tweezers into my 'ink' and marked a square upon the linen, within its centre Lego II

AUG, which I hoped even Petronius would recognise as being the camp of the Augusta surrounded by its stockade. Just to make certain there'd be no mistake, I placed a little stick figure and a little stick figure dog entering through the main watchtower gate. There, that should do it. Next, I marked out a hill with spiralling ramparts and marked the letters DURO but hoped the message was clear even without its title. Back up to the Roman camp again, I sketched Vespasian wearing his helmet, beside which I added the Capricorn standard for good effect. The message might be lost on the Britons but not Petronius.

Satisfied, I took up my sooty tweezers again and from the Capricorn standard beside the camp, drew an arrow to the hill. The message was clear; Vespasian's II Legion would attack the Durotriges, just as we'd thought. Pleased with my work and emboldened now, I added some further information, drawing snow clouds and beside it a sun … when winter was over. For once, the cold and snow might serve them very well.

And so it was that I wound the sunship round his neck and clipped it firmly.

We shuffled round the walls, and in an unfinished section which still had its old palisade I found a space. And though it seemed to be too small, he amazed me by wriggling through it. I was sure he'd be reluctant, but he was raring to go.

'I wish you well, my friend,' I whispered after him as he bounded off, a dark grey shape against the virgin white snow.

Back in the slave quarters, grief reigned supreme when I told Polydorus that Storm had escaped through a hole in the palisade.

'But why would he leave us?'

What could I say but, 'He was a wild dog and wild

creatures will always want to be free.'

'But how will he manage? What if he dies out there in the snow?'

Dear gods, I said to myself, *then all would be lost*, but, just as so many times before, I couldn't allow myself to start thinking like this.

CHAPTER SEVENTEEN
THE SPINNER OF FATE

Plate upon plate, dish upon dish was set out before his esteemed guests. Petronius would have fallen into a drooling swoon at the sight of it; pickled walnuts, elvers glistening in aspic, stuffed mushrooms, wafer-thin slices of ham drizzled black with truffle oil, crumbly edged vegetable tarts, balls of green-flecked savoury cheese, and in the centre of it all something that looked, amazingly enough, like a salted blowfish, its flesh scored into a diamond shape. Slaves ran back and forth between table and kitchen.

But let me explain why I'm able to describe such a scene.

Two weeks had passed since I'd set Storm back to Cal with his message. They'd know that the legion of the II Augusta would soon be setting out for May. And, by now, Ullan Dur would know too. I thanked the gods that this was the main topic of conversation amongst the men, that, so far, nothing else of any great consequence had cropped up. The snow was falling less thickly and in this short lull in which it had all but disappeared, the first pack-carts appeared and with them a boy who caught my eye as I stood watching by the gates. He pretended to stumble and pushed his barrow in my direction, his ploy performed with such expertise, not even the gruffest of the quartermasters could have thought it other than genuine.

I pushed it back, he picked himself up and rubbed his knees, I bent over him as if in concern, which meant our faces were hidden.

'I send many days ago one message to Caradoc,' I whispered, half in Latin, half in British. Not yet knowing how to use a past participle in his language, I hoped he would understand and was relieved that he seemed to. Yet to learn the word for nothing, I added, 'Not ... more now.'

He whispered back, 'Thank you.'

All this having taken no time at all, he returned to work pushing his barrow.

Next came my first big piece of luck.

Since I had first arrived in his camp, even after my release from Vespasian's clutches, the governor had paid little to no interest in me. I had been captured; now I was free and that was all there was to it. But something happened that alerted him to the fact that perhaps he should have been more interested in Marcus Ostorius' freedman and his stay with the Britons. I was summoned to headquarters, where standing in front of the great man it soon became clear that though he had changed his mind about my usefulness, his view on my status remained the same; I was a slave and there was an end to it. This was the first time I'd been in the esteemed presence of Plautius. He spoke to me in a slow measured voice, as if I were someone of a childish level of intelligence.

'I'm sending you with Tribune Maxentius to the lands of a man called Tiberius Claudius Cogidubnus.' Pause. 'He is a leader of an allied tribe.' Pause again. 'As you have been with the savages for some time, it follows that you must know something of their language and habits.' Pause. 'When you get there, I want you to observe and listen to anything said or done that seems wrong or suspicious.' A shorter pause now; he could see I was following his every word. 'Cogidubnus will have no idea who you are, other than a minion. Stand apart in the shadows, see what you can pick up.'

And that was all.

This was an astonishing turn of fate; I thanked every god I could think of and had to force my demeanour into one of unhappy resignation.

The journey would take two days.

We'd set off the following morning, riding southwest. By now the image of Leonatus' triangle was branded into my brain. Dunum was halfway down the right slant and Quintus had told me that Cogidubnus' villa was somewhere along the southern coast, in other words, on its bottom line. This meant we would be travelling cross-country ... Leonatus' jabbing finger ... through the newly conquered lands then into what he'd described as friendly country.

As Maxentius was known to be the most terrifying of the three junior tribunes, his first words to me had fairly lifted my spirits. He'd made the usual military greeting to one of a lower order, or in my case, none at all.

'I'm told you're a freedman of the Scapula household.' A nifty way of avoiding any reference to the fact that I'd been, and in fact still was, their slave.

'Yes sir, you're right.'

He smiled. 'Don't look so worried, I know Marcus well. He's a good chap, if not slightly impetuous, if I may be forgiven for saying it.'

I'm sure he'd regard your opinion as a compliment, sir.'

'You came here to join him?'

I smiled in return. 'Not so much *came* as was summoned.'

'And when you did, he was gone?'

'Well, what can you do, sir?'

'Oh no sirs, at least until we're close to snooping ears. You were with the outpost unit when it was attacked and taken prisoner.'

This was a statement, but also a question.

'Yes.' It felt most awkward not ending my answer with *sir*.

'You've become quite a legend … you survived.'

'Not due to any skill on my part, if you don't mind me saying, it was more to do with the fact that I don't look much like your regular citizen. They simply took pity on me.' Where was this nonsense coming from? Surely my imagination had been set alight since joining the ranks of the painted people.

*

As far as our journey was concerned, the normal system applied. We were accompanied by a fifty-man auxilia unit and some kind of weapon called a manuballista which Quintus informed me would put paid to even the largest group of Britons foolish enough to attack us. My heart stopped as I watched it being loaded onto its wagon.

We made our way down-country, first through the newly conquered lands … though farmland destroyed by the militia. Everything had been put to the torch, fields, patches of woodland, homesteads and houses. Every now and then we'd catch a glimpse of the unfortunates who'd been unable to escape to the safety of lands still outside the clutches of Rome;

here an old woman leading a desperately thin cow on a rope, there a boy with an armful of tinder. As we passed along the way, I sensed the tribune's consternation. There were no great throngs of natives huddling, overawed, by the wayside. Unusual this, for wasn't it normally the case that subdued peoples would gather to gape at their conquerors as they cantered by on well-groomed horses, cuirasses shining, banners fluttering in the wind?

I applauded the surly attitude of those forsaken tribes, though their defiance was bound to grate on Plautius when Maxentius made his report. As far as our governor was concerned, the Britons were no more than a bunch of uncultured rowdies who should have been grateful for their deliverance into Rome's hands, for only she would free them from their barbarian state.

But the defeated tribes were the victors that day … it was impossible to appear so imposing, so magnificent, with no one there to see them.

Soon, however, as we left the lands of the vanquished and rode into Leonatus' 'friendly country' which belonged to a people long allied to Rome, a people who had put up, or who had been able to put up no resistance, we might as well have passed from night into day. Here, under its covering of patchy melting snow, fields lay in neat, tilled strips, waiting for the warmth of spring which even now, seemed to be making some small mark on the land. The farmsteads looked well cared for, the animals fat from their winter feeding and the people, much to Maxentius' relief, came down from their fields to watch us pass along the way.

Under the protection of the governor's elite squadron, we'd been able to forge ahead with speed, riding flat out since the dawn of the day before with only one stop, and after the mandatory ditch digging, assembling of tents, bread making, etcetera, we'd risen the following morning and set off on our way before light. Lying that night in a tent with seven others, I'd forced myself to perform an act of great suffering, but I hadn't been doing that at all. I was a Briton now and the hard, frozen ground didn't bother me at all.

As dusk closed in, we approached Cogidubnus' estate. I'd lived in the legions' world for long enough to be unsurprised that Maxentius didn't pause to wash the mud from his face before heading on. It showed a kind of manly power; riding at speed, the unit under his control covering the miles from Dunum in record time; a counter against our host's mighty bearing.

The troops had settled in a half mile or so before we inched our way along a cinder path that crunched beneath our horses' hooves. We were thankful that their shoes had been attached for those last few yards of our journey. By 'we' I mean Maxentius, his bodyguards and me. We clattered over a wooden bridge and the dark shape of a building rose before us, flares hung from its walls to left and right, their flames whipping wildly as they danced to the music of the wind gusting in from the sea. From what I could see of Cogidubnus' house, it seemed eccentric as the man himself.

I suppose I'd imagined quite a different kind of place, a fortified mansion at least. But it turned out to be what looked like a collection of tumbledown outhouses clustered haphazardly under a crumbling roof. Built of wood, it followed the straight lines of the Roman oblong rather than British circles.

Servants stood waiting to take charge our horses, and after dismounting we were led through the timbered colonnade of a courtyard, around which statues of Venus, Pluto and the like were ranged, imported, no doubt, from the City herself.

Here our host stood to greet his eminent guest. He looked much as he had before; in his toga Roman as could be whilst his hair, moustache and giant torc proclaimed him to be utterly British.

He saluted. Maxentius bent his head slightly.

Cogidubnus gave his greetings in a Latin as patrician as his choice of dress. He was a bluff character, certainly, but hearing him speak for the first time, his modulated tone made me think that perhaps I had somewhat misjudged him; a conclusion so contrary to the perceived perception it could have been made only by a fellow foreigner … in other words me.

Through the entranceway, with pillars carved in wood in place of marble, that familiar smell, a mix of wood and resin, soot and straw, hung in the air, making me think of Ruadon's farm. We followed him along a warren of narrow passages, with what I can only describe as open cubicles on our left, their plaster walls painted with cupids and wreaths of flowers. The top of my head all but skimmed its ceiling, as did Cogidubnus'. Maxentius didn't have that problem.

We entered a dimly lit hall, with plastered walls supported by a grid of timbers, at the end of which a fire burned, its light reflecting against the polished planks of the floor, and in its warm draft silver lamps suspended from the rafters swayed gently to and fro. On the wall beside us, gigantic gilt-tipped horns from some long dead animal jutted towards us, like spears.

And here, as in the courtyard, the furnishings simple but fabulously valuable belonged to Rome, but a Rome so very long past as to make an antiquarian's eyes grow wide in his head. The couches, which had survived from the time of Augustus, or so I felt, were set out in proper order. The tables in front of them seemed to belong to a time older still, whilst to their right stood a glass fishbowl, red gold shapes moving languorously within whilst, to their left, a short-skirted Diana ran motionless on her podium, clasping her bow to her breast.

Maxentius made a polite comment about the villa. Cogidubnus thanked him. 'But,' he pronounced, 'all this is soon to be gone. I'm hatching plans to build a palace in its place, you see.'

To the uninitiated, the expression on Maxentius' face could have been interpreted as one of mild interest though it was obvious to his retinue that he found the big Briton as much of a joke as they did. He might be the enemy, but nonetheless I had to smile along with them, disguise being the prime tool, is it not?

I stood in the shadows as instructed.

'My secretary will take notes regarding points of interest,' Maxentius explained. As this sounded quite plausible, it left no cause for suspicion.

The conversation returned to the subject of the intended palace.

'How simply splendid. Though it will be difficult to lay one's hands on building material, I imagine.' It was clear that Maxentius was warming him up for some request or other.

Desperate to miss not a word, I took a step forward.

Cogidubnus' response came more quickly than I'd imagined.

'Yes, at the moment that's true. However, once Durotrige lands just out to the east have fallen,' I could hardly bear to think of it, 'we'll have access to the stone quarries your engineers have discovered, be able to start on the temple in Dunum and my own little project. In the meantime I'm handing over a stretch of land to the legions. You intend to set up a military depot, or so I've heard. No objection to that, no objection to that whatsoever.'

'So very kind,' murmured Maxentius, when in fact what he meant was, *you can't possibly think that Governor Plautius requires your permission to requisition any property he thinks fit.*

Once he and Maxentius were settled on their couches and their shoes removed, and water and towels had been offered for the washing of hands, Cogidubnus presented his wife and daughters to his esteemed guest.

Small and dark, they seemed more Roman than British. They stood before them for the briefest of moments, enough time to exchange a pleasantry or two; his wife's family were Etruscan, she was pleased to explain. And as I watched her, I could tell that far from being an embarrassment to her, she was proud of her husband; there was a certain expression in her eyes which only happy women possess. The older daughter was a beauty by any standard, with hair cut round her shoulders in the style of the wigs worn in Egypt, and for a moment my memory took me back and I saw again the white-clothed priests with their scarab necklets walking through the pillars of Amun. But audience over, rather than following her mother and sister out of the door through which they'd entered, she walked in my direction. And passing me, as her gaze met mine, I saw Cal's eyes, the same pale green of warm sea shallows, but where his were bright and laughing, hers were cool as a cat's beneath her dark brows.

'Dangerous,' I thought.

The food kept coming, great plates of the stuff; the tableware, beautiful as any I'd seen was removed to be set out again, and again; pearl-studded silver, glass, saltcellars, golden picks for extracting flesh from crayfish claws, which made me think of Petronius. Servants were everywhere to be seen, laying down yet more plates and, between courses, offering bowls for washing of fingers and fresh towels for the drying of them.

How often had I stood on the sidelines, impatient, hovering, my mind adrift far from the business at hand? Now, though, I was listening intently.

During the first phase of eating, the conversation centred on plans for the eventual layout of New Camulodunum. At the next plate-spreading, they were onto more serious business, Durotriges and such like, Cogidubnus being of the opinion that Vespasian's task was fairly straightforward. I smiled to myself.

'But I have little idea of when this might be.'

'Ah then, let me enlighten you.' Maxentius was taking a great deal of pleasure in informing his inferior. 'He has drawn up plans to invade in the forthcoming weeks. The enemy will expect us to wait till the snows have entirely gone. But his legion has fought in far colder places.'

My blood ran cold, my message had told them they'd strike when winter had ended. I had been wrong. Worse than that, I had given them false information. I tried to console myself, but I couldn't. Head spinning, I forced my attention back to what Maxentius was saying.

'Now the time has come to put words into action. We can rely upon you?' He paused for a moment. 'For clarity's sake I refer to our treaty, agreed when you met with the governor. Part of this states that Rome will supply you with grain. In return ...'

Cogidubnus flipped his hand as if swatting a fly. 'No need

to remind me, Tribune Maxentius. I am on board. The other part of the bargain was that I will supply you with spies. I have them ready; they've been well instructed; they know what to do.'

I thanked the gods for helping Storm to deliver my warning. Everything I had stated on that scrap of linen would have given them a head start. They were alerted, and luck was with us; Cogidubnus was only just setting his spies out, which meant less time for information to be gathered.

The last spreading of dishes, and other matters came to light, our host waxing lyrical about how, in his opinion, the country should be split.

Did he wish to disparage what Maxentius had just told him, or did he mean it? 'Forget the east, it won't be much trouble at least for the moment, concentrate on the west and central lands. Get them settled into the Empire, reward those who help, come down hard on the others. Once they were secure, why then and only then, should they even start to think about moving their forces beyond the Bowed River.'

I stored that name in mind ... it couldn't be the Tamesis. According to Leonatus our ships were plying their way along it already, and it had been marked well below Dunum on his triangle. Maxentius listened indulgently, what a barbarian could tell Rome about invasion tactics could be written on a minim coin.

'And Cartimandua?' Maxentius was referring to her the very way Quintus had.

'Oh, she'll make a fair enough ally. We'll meet her soon enough.'

Just then I heard a whispered 'pssst'. I peered behind me into the dark of the passage, saw nothing and was about to turn my attention back to the conversation when I heard it again – 'pssst ... pssst' – and, as my eyes adjusted to the gloom, I saw her, Cogidubnus' daughter, lurking behind the folds of a curtain, trying to hide herself from all but me. And now, flap, flap, flap, signalling that I should turn around again, so's not to draw attention to her hovering there in the shadows.

I did, but took a step back, then another, until I felt at a safe enough distance to hear what she wanted to say without others hearing, and as I did, she stepped out from the shadows, took my hand and placed a large, flat object against my palm, fixing my fingertips, one by one, around its smooth shape. And before I could whisper a word, she was hurrying down the passageway.

I kept my fist closed until I was back in my place, but when I opened my hand, I had to blink several times over for there on my palm, plain as day, was my sunship. So stunned was I it took a moment to conquer my shock ... *what in dear heaven?*

With clumsy fingers I pulled a scrap of parchment from its disk; when unfolded, it read, in Latin:

'We need to talk. Come down to the cliff edge when you can get away. Follow the track leading left.'

Hot and cold ran through my veins.

The eating continued, things were discussed, important things to which I should have been paying attention, but a heavy cloud was shifting inside me. The worst, what was the worst this could mean? The worst was that something had happened to Storm. Polydorius' words crashed into my mind, *what if he dies out there on the snow?* The worst was that my message, flawed though it was, hadn't reached Cal, that Caradoc knew nothing about Vespasian's plans to strike, the worst was that Plautius knew I was a traitor, had been brought along on purpose so they could see what my next step would be. But surely this was too much to contemplate, for if I'd been rumbled, they'd have had me strung up long before now.

And what about Cogidubnus' daughter? Was it some kind of plan? Would I seal my guilt by following her orders? But if I didn't meet her, would I relinquish all hope of ever knowing how she'd got hold of the sunship? There was nothing else for it, I'd have to take the chance.

When the eating finished and I managed to steal away, I found the night had resolved to help me, grey and starless as she was. Wrapped in my dark military cloak, I lowered myself from a window onto the ground below; it was either this or making my way past the guards at the entrance. The rest was relatively simple; I followed the path towards the sea, my footsteps drowned out by the screaming wind. But once I got as close to the cliff edge as I dared – I knew it was the edge for I heard waves crashing below – and saw the track stretching out on either side of me, I stood for a moment thinking. There was every chance that if I turned to the left, and the east, as instructed, I'd walk into a trap. Why shouldn't I go to the right instead? I pictured the triangle. I was standing on its bottom line, still in friendly country. To my right lay Leonatus' 'unknown territories'. But they weren't so very unknown to me, so why not go that way? For if I did, I'd have a chance of reaching May.

So that's how it all came about, simple really, one moment I was standing in a part of the world claimed by Rome, the next stepping out of it, walking into the wind towards the west. And when I got there, I'd only have to pronounce Ullan Dur's name and I'd be taken to him. Then, pray Jupiter, someone would get me home, which was no longer some specific place in my mind, like the house on the Quirinal, but wherever Cal happened to be.

I was still a stranger to the forest trail, the flint path by the ocean, the hurdled bogs and marshes. That may have been, but I'd travelled across vast continents, on horseback, in carriages, on foot, both as a free citizen of some far-off land and as a servant of the Empire, and no great harm had befallen me yet, added to the fact that I was Catuvellauni now, and what was a few days walk along the cliff path to someone like me?

As the pale-green slash of dawn rose over the edge of the ocean, on that first morning of my expedition, I curled myself up in a hollow, and only a sense of euphoria at the thought of seeing Cal again prevented me from tumbling into sleep.

It soon became clear that my journey would take far longer than I'd first supposed. On my second morning, I found myself looking across a wide estuary and realised there was nothing else for it but to follow its frosty bank inland to a point where the water, shored up by a beaver's lodge, was shallow enough to wade across, which added more time to my journey.

This was the first time I'd travelled cross-country unaccompanied, and it gave me great satisfaction to discover that I could just about manage to fend for myself. During these first days, I set a couple of traps, as Cal had taught me, and caught fat birds on both occasions. I was overjoyed when lying on my chest on a riverbank, I felt the cold, hard belly of the grayling swimming over my fingers and whipped the thrashing, slippery fish onto the bank.

I was alone, but not lonely for the land was my companion. Walking through a copse of trees, I noticed the branches around me were tipped with the merest suggestion of buds. Pools and slow-moving streams were filled with frogs in their hundreds slithering and slipping over each other. In these streams too, waded grey, long-legged birds, like ibis, and treading across the melting grassland, a warm, sweet smell came up from the earth.

The coastline of the southern edge of Britain is dramatic, spectacular, and it was clear that many feet had trodden along its edge. And though travellers chose to avoid such paths in those dangerous times, I could tell that only a matter of months before it had been a busy thoroughfare, linking the lands of other gods to those of May.

Up there then, on those cliffs, looking out towards the horizon, to a point where the bruise-coloured sky dipped into the ocean, I thought of Cal.

I closed my eyes and remembered how he had looked the day we'd parted on the hill beside Vespasian's camp, the hood of his cloak pushed away from his face, his pale copper hair, his golden cuffs and torc, the Whisperer strapped to his back. Where was he now, what was he doing? Would I ever see him again? My spirit would break if I didn't.

On the morning of my fourth day I settled down to sleep, listening to the sea birds cawing not so very high above me. But when I woke, my dream lingered still, as undissolved dreams often do, and as I looked out from behind the window of that dream, I saw a vision of Storm, running out ahead of me, I was on the cliff road no longer but travelling north instead. I knew this for in my half-dream I saw the shadow of the sun cast out in front of me.

'North, go north,' a voice inside my head whispered softly, so north I went.

Since leaving the White Lands and those of the Durotriges, my instincts, hunches and the like had just about gone, and I'd blamed this on Dunum itself. Army camp discipline leaves nothing to chance, decisions in such places are made only after the weighing up of relevant pieces of information. But out on the cliffs that morning there was nothing to guide me, save my instinct and my dream of Storm. So, trusting them both, off I set again, this time with the sun to my right. In those days I knew nothing of shape-changers or the like, the name given by the Britons to those who assume the appearance of another, human or unhuman, and who, in these changed forms perform both good and evil. That morning, then, was it Ciern who led me to safety by donning the guise of Storm and entering my dreams?

That 'dream Storm' led me inland, away from the coast, and after walking a good mile or so I found myself enveloped by the same penetrating rain that had fallen the day I'd set off for the border with Leonatus' little unit all those months and lifetimes before.

The rain was one thing, but then came claps of thunder, which at first seemed pretty far off; sheets of light ripped through the charcoal curtain of the sky. The rain turned to downpour and I peered into the murky mists ahead, looking for some shelter, even a spread of bushes, but could make out nothing save a vast, treeless moor. The shape of a hill loomed in front of me and I started my way up it, giving thanks to the god of army issue cloaks. Yet the kidskin tunic I wore beneath it stopped just short of my knees, and the wind, which had changed direction by this time, attacked me from the east, tearing at my legs until they became so numb and raw that after moments walking against its force, there was not the slightest of feeling left in them. By now I could barely see an arm's length in front of me. But even though I was struck by misery beyond imagining and paroxysms of fear, what wouldn't I give to go back in time, to have that tempestuous morning again and all that was to come.

Later, in praise-songs dedicated to my journey, they claimed I didn't falter. But of course I did. That morning, as I realised I was lost and at the mercy of the gods, I reached the stage where I could climb no further and knew I was beaten. I sank to my knees on the drenched and sopping earth and committed myself to the elements. Hungry, frozen, soaked to the skin and bereft of hope, I lay down and buried my face in the sodden ground and I can't say to which spirit I prayed, one deep within me, I suppose, created in the likeness of Cal. What would he have done if he'd been me? A drop or two of rain wouldn't have held him back.

How long did I lie there, huddled up, dying? Hours, perhaps, or days? I gave myself up to the gods but instead they sent warmth. It seeped into my body. I came back to life. The rain had stopped. I rolled onto my back, opened my eyes, and saw above me the sun committing battle with clouds that were fairly scudding across the sky. My body ached from frozen muscles, numb joints; my knees were so swollen I thought they'd never straighten but slowly, slowly I forced myself up, and, standing now, I saw the hand.

CHAPTER EIGHTEEN
GOD OF THE HUNT

A hand it was, a giant hand, cut into the chalky ground beside me, a thumb and one, two, three, four fingers of the one carved into the hillside who'd led me to safety. And all this time I'd been lying on his palm.

I was hungry, tired, wet and lost no longer. I stepped from his etched thumb, walked along the line of his forearm to his shoulder and onto the chalk curves of his face, where I encountered two round eyes, two startled eyebrows and a triangle of a mouth. Upon his head stretched antlers, high as his body, like branches of giant trees. I walked round his head, round his shoulder, and now was standing on the chest of a god, looking down upon his enormous phallus.

There I stood and, finding my voice had returned, whispered my thanks into the wind.

Just as the sun sailed out from behind the largest of the clouds, I looked out across the plain and saw them riding towards me.

There were two of them. I stood, arms wide, to show that I carried no weapons.

The younger man approached first, and as he did the consternation melted from his face. Thank all the gods, he recognised me.

'Greetings,' I said in their language and heard my voice, puny and strangled from the damp and cold of my journey.

He smiled. What's more, he remembered my name. 'Stranger,' he exclaimed, clasping me to him, despite the fact that I was soaking wet and so filthy I could smell myself.

I must have looked as exhausted as I felt, for they insisted that I took one of the horses. The young chap whose horse it was seemed happy to walk, leading the way across the plain to May and up the winding pathway.

Once in the fortress, I was taken past the same central roundhouse where Cal had addressed the gathering, from which emanated the greatest of noise; no doubt about it, a feast was still in full swing. I was glad that I wasn't invited to join it, but instead was led to a squat low hut behind it, inside which a fire blazed, its flames licking up and over an andiron set on the centre of the floor. A moment and Ullan Dur appeared at the door, his face filled with alarm. 'Siva,' he said, 'what dear gods are you doing here?'

I stumbled over my words. 'I've come with news. The II is about to attack …'

'But we know.'

'What?'

'We know.'

I looked at him, in consternation.

'Cal came. He told us.'

'Cal …' and after a moments silence, 'he was here?'

'You've just missed him. He had to turn round and go back to the White Lands. Trouble is brewing close by.' And as I listened, I heard words that made no sense. 'He brought news that Vespasian is set to march against us. That they'll strike when winter has ended.'

And where I should have measured my answer, told him as calmly as I was able that I had got my timing wrong, I blurted out, 'I'm afraid I have very bad news, they're not waiting till spring. They'll be here soon.'

This was a blow, but his Roman sense of self-discipline prevented him from reacting with fear. 'I will rally the men and though it will be earlier than we thought we shall be ready.'

There passed a moment of gloomy silence before it struck me, I looked at him in utter confusion; how did Cal know about all this?

And now it was Ullan Dur's turn to look confused. 'But you were the one who told him. You sent a message.'

He stood looking into my eyes. Then he clasped my wrist and asked, 'Siva, are you quite well?'

'Yes,' I said, but I was more than quite well. I was ecstatic. Great floods of relief coursed through me, dousing my fear that without my message Cal might have thought that once safely returned to the legions, I'd simply abandoned them. What I was hearing now meant that the sunship had reached him after all, despite the fact that Cogidubnus' daughter had presented me with proof that it hadn't. I was simply mystified.

'His dog brought it to him,' Ullan Dur continued, as if telling me something I didn't know. 'It was folded inside your amulet.' Seeing my astonished face, and fearing I didn't believe him, he added, 'It was tied round his neck.'

'But ...' I pulled the sunship from beneath my sodden tunic. 'Cogidubnus' daughter had it ... She gave it to me.'

He leant towards me, his expression changed, and I listened to words that made no sense at all

'Don't you know ... the Lady Claudia is with us?'

'With us?'

He nodded.

'Against her father?'

'Yes.'

'But why?'

'I'll explain, but first you must eat.'

It took all of two minutes to gulp down a cup of beer and the contents of a bowl of stew. They brought another, which I took a little more time to devour, along with a pair of breeches and a woollen cloak. Where my old army one was good for rain, this one was good for cold, and I was ready to listen.

'I said I would tell you what I know, but I'm afraid it's very little. They say she's in love with a Briton ... we don't know who ... and this is the reason she joined us. But how did she manage to give it to you?'

I told him how Vespasian had sent me back to the camp of the XX, of my journey with Maxentius to Cogidubnus' house, how, as someone who'd lived amongst the Britons for some time, I'd been sent with him to pick up anything he said that I might find suspicious. How she'd waited in the shadows and pressed the sunship into my hand when no one was looking.

'Why did she have it?'

'The first thing Cal did after he gave us your message was send a boy to take it to her and ask her to get it back to you. Of all our allies, she is the nearest. It's strange she didn't explain this.'

'There was no time. I didn't know what to think, only that Storm had been caught and the message hadn't reached you. But I'm glad that my misunderstanding sent me here to you now. I listened to every word Cogidubnus said and that's why I know about the attack.'

Ullan Dur sat for a moment, then blew his cheeks. 'How long do we have?'

'I'm sorry, I don't know, but I'd start preparing as if it were soon.'

I could imagine the discipline in the Roman ranks, the preparations for the fight and once on the march, the camps with their trenches, guards posted whilst the men took it in turns to stretch out in their tents for an hour or so. If even as few as two cohorts had remained at their camp, it would still mean more than four thousand men. Four thousand men on the march towards May, digging themselves into their ditches, eating lightly, conserving their strength.

'One other thing, Cogidubnus spoke about the many spies he's set amongst you.'

He laughed. 'He thinks they're on his side, but he's wrong, they're on ours. You might remember I told you that many have joined us … his daughter is the most important of them all.'

I thought of the gracious way she had greeted Maxentius, smiling and bowing her head as if deemed unworthy to be in the presence of a greater being.

Ullan Dur broke into my thoughts. 'You've done a very great deal for us, Siva, and we are eternally grateful. But here is the question, will you go back to the legion?'

I told him I would.

He squeezed my arm. 'Then you must sleep. And when you're rested enough, we'll help you get back to the Lady Claudia, and from there she'll take you back to Dunum. One of our boys will start you on your way.'

Only now did it strike me, what would I say to Maxentius; how would I explain my mysterious absence?'

'She'll know what to do.'

But before he left me, he lowered his voice and whispered, 'We have both lived within the bounds of the Empire and understand it well enough to know that Britain cannot win. At least not outright. But we can make the cohorts' lives such a misery that they will come to regret the day they ever launched their ships from Gaul. We are a small band, but now you have joined us and we may be able to turn the tide, if only for now.'

Ominous words which set my mind spinning. I lay down on my blankets and thought of Cal. The fact that I'd missed him by less than a day filled me with a thudding melancholy. And now I was heading back to Cogidubnus' place, my misery such that I didn't care what might happen to me next.

It wasn't until the next morning that I thought to ask about the figure hewn into the chalk on the hillside; I told him I'd fallen asleep on his hand.

'Ciern,' said he. 'You may remember I told you that he's much like Pan. A god of the wild, but he's also a god of the hunt.'

I thought of his towering antlers in place of Pan's curling horns.

'He's the one who looks over us. And it seems he looked over you too.'

I left early. The frozen dawn seemed fitting for such sorrow. My young travelling companion stood beside us. It was clear he was keen to be off; the sooner we were on our way, the sooner he'd be back. As we were going on foot, we carried small packs; mine held a knife, some food, dry flints and, last but not least, my kidskin tunic, wrapped inside my army cloak. My new woollen version was lighter and would be easier to walk in. Before I set foot into Roman territory, I'd have to change back into those constituents of my old uniform. In the meantime, all that would expose me as a foreigner was the colour of my skin and my hobnails.

As I stood with the men at the foot of May, gripping forearms and slapping backs, the young lad interrupted.

'Look,' he pointed.

Half a dozen pairs of eyes followed his finger.

And there it was, a dark shape darting across the flat land towards us.

'Is that not one of Cal's dogs?' or words to that effect, someone said. I could just about pick up the words.

There passed a silent, heart-stopping moment as we stood waiting, sure that we'd see him next. But we didn't.

Smaller and paler than Storm, it was Swift. I bellowed her name into the wind, one of the big warriors beside me helping me along with his whistles. But neither shouts nor whistles were needed as she bounded towards us, tongue lolling. She came straight at me, all but knocking me off my feet. She was frantic; I'd never seen her like this before.

'What's up, my girl.' And though I said this in Latin, it was clear that though unlike Storm we hadn't spent much time together, she understood me every bit as well as she did the others speaking in their British. She caught the fabric of my cloak by now and was pulling me in the direction from which she'd appeared.

'Easy, easy. I'm coming. I'm coming.'

'Don't be crazy,' a voice behind me said, in British, 'it's south you must go. Forget the dog.'

'Look,' I said, 'I'm going with her. Get me a horse. Come on. Quick.'

They glanced around at each other, not knowing what to do. One of the swordsmiths with un-limed hair spoke now. 'You can't go east,' he said, 'Danger's there. If Cal is harmed then you will be too. Why not just go on south, as planned?

That's what he'd want.'

'I'm sure you're right, but it's not what I want. Look I'm going with her, horse or no horse.' Was this gentle Siva speaking?

I started out across the plain, casting aside my pack as I went.

Ullan Dur came after me. He picked up my pack and thrust it into my hands. 'We'll give you a horse, of course we will.' He squeezed my arm, understanding the extent of my agony. 'But we can't let the boy go, he might not come back and, well, he's needed here.'

I felt myself shaking as I set out and was worried too about Swift. She was exhausted, I could tell. She'd stopped at May only long enough to lap from a puddle and swallow a slice of meat, closely followed by another, thrown at him by the boy who'd led my horse down the Dun. I tried to set a steady pace, but she wouldn't let up; she raced out in front of me, urging me on.

Behind us a weeping sky pressed her tear-stained cheek upon May.

CHAPTER NINETEEN
THE GREAT PAN IS DEAD

How a fine-boned cavalry mount would have tackled that grooved and rutted forest track I can't imagine; a fall, a broken fetlock, with the rider left to finish his journey on foot. While it's true that, judged against the noble animals bred in the region of Aquilea, British horses seemed small, unpromising, they were wonderfully suited to their island's terrain, able to canter for hours across the stoniest, rockiest ground.

We travelled all day, and only as the sun sank low in the sky did Swift lessen her pace and I knew we were approaching the end of our journey. Round the track and to the right, she stopped by the forest's edge and there she stood, shivering from her nose to the tip of her tail, the faintest growl trembling in her throat. I dismounted and tied the horse's reins to a branch loosely enough to let her drink from the stream beside it.

Silence hung in the air, no sound, save that of the wind in the branches and Swift's soft growling as she stood head down, nose forward.

I stood peering into the dark of the forest, trying to think what to do. Whatever was in there was voiceless, silent; a very great terror welled up inside me.

Perhaps it was that same, intuitive voice – the one I'd heard down by the cliffs near Cogidubnus' place – that spoke to me then. It told me to move forward, and quickly. But what to do with Swift? If I obeyed the voice and pushed into the forest, I'd have to move on feet of air. Swift was in such a demented state, I couldn't be sure what she would do next, but I couldn't leave her behind. I took the knife from my pack and cutting a thong from the horse's rein, tied it round her neck.

We must have gone a good quarter mile, Swift pulling me along in a state of desperation, and at a point where I could see a faint light ahead, she stopped, and I heard it ... a creak ... creak ... creak, like the ropes of a swing swaying back and forth.

'Stay,' I motioned, and stay she did, shoulders forward, though ready to launch herself forward if need be.

Clutching the knife, I crept towards the sound, step by silent step, the shush of wind in the treetops muffling the crack of twigs beneath my feet.

I was upon him before I saw him and stopped in my tracks just in time. I can't say what made me hold back, for it wasn't a man of the legions I saw in front of me as I'd thought it would be, but a Briton. *One of us*, was my immediate thought, but a cold reluctance prevented me from reaching out to greet him; those uncanny, intuitive powers of mine.

I halted mid-stride and looked out from the shadows.

He stood no more than ten arm-lengths' away. With his blue cloak, his silvery hair and golden cuffs, he could have been Catuvellauni had it not been for the fact that in front of him hung Cal, upside down, like a carcase on a butcher's hook. Side to side, side to side his body swung, a limp and flaccid figure suspended from that tree of execution by a binding tied round his ankle; a line of muscle stretched from his rigid leg, through his torso to his shoulder. His arms dangled down, his unbound leg curving out from his knee and the tips of his spiked hair trailing on the ground. His body, painted as intricately as that of any of the warriors back in May, but into his flesh a hundred or so little cuts had been nicked, and rivulets of blood trickled over his skin, plopping onto the ground. Beneath him lay Storm, his neck cut to the bone, to the right the Whisperer just out of his reach.

The shock would hit me later. But as I stood staring, I might have been seeing through the eyes of another; a dead and dripping Cal was strung up in front of me, yet there I was, calmly regarding the scene as if I were a participant in one of my own brands of dreams, as though I were not Siva, and all this was not real.

Time stopped; no shushing in the treetops, no creaking of rope, no noise of breath or sound of heartbeat, until the thing slammed into me. It battered through my chest, and so violent was the force of it that an involuntary roar blasted from my throat, my heartbeat returned, a rush of heat seared through me, a sensation, startling in its newness, which would, in time, become recognisable as an old friend.

Its blast pitched me out of the shadows, tumbling the towering back-turned figure in front of me to the ground, giving me time to seize the Whisperer, lift it above his head and, as the blue-cloaked Briton rose from his knees, to crash the impossibly heavy blade down upon his head. Only then did I discover the skill required to slice through a neck with one motion as I'd seen Cal do the morning he'd spun the poor trumpeter's head into the air as though it were a wooden ball and he a juggler in the circus of Tarquinius Priscus.

In shameful contrast, however, my blow only stunned, for the figure was on his knees now, not dead but reeling. Down the Whisperer crashed again, pulverising his skull; a mess of bone and brain oozed out of the red, pulsating cavity. I forced my arms up one last time and thrust them downwards. The solid bulk of the Briton moved forward slowly; his body reached a halfway point and slumped to the ground.

A pumping started in my ears, but through it I heard a new sound and a second figure came charging towards me. It could not have been me; I know that it was the new force inside me. One moment the knife was in my hand, the next whizzing through the air into the running man's neck. And, just as suddenly as it had come, the power flew away from me, leaving numbness in place of its strength.

I stood in front of Cal's dripping body and pulled him up, supporting his weight as I tried to cut through the binding, my shaking arms grasping tight his slippery torso. He was dead, so why did I care that he wouldn't thump down onto the bloody ground? But I cared deeply. The whole thing was beyond a nightmare task, not only was I shuddering and trembling, but my feet slipped and slid on that carpet of wet, squelching redness. It took long lifetimes as I kept on with my frantic sawing when at last it was cut, Cal slumped onto my shoulder. I carried him away from the tree and as I laid him down, drops of rain started to fall on his face. I heard a voice call 'Swift,' it must have been mine. She came leaping towards me and whined and whimpered over Storm's crumpled body. I knelt beside him and touched his face, my tears, which I'd mistaken for raindrops, smearing his blood a mess of watery pink, and imagined him with Ullan Dur, arriving at the fort the sober-clad person he'd so recently become and leaving his old self, painted and ready for battle.

His lips were parted making me think of how often I'd seen them smile. That smile might be dead now, but I'd carry it with me forever.

Unbidden, the Prayer of Anubis came to me, 'You are born again, you live again. You are born again, you live again.'

I'd take him away from this fearful place, but not till tomorrow. Tomorrow we'd set off on our last journey together, to where I didn't know.

I wrapped him in the woollen cloak and lay beside him.

With the first glimmer of dawn, I felt his skin warm against mine. And as I had throughout the night, I placed my fingers on his neck; his pulse was stronger now. And it was then that the birdsong began. First one piped out a warbling hymn and soon the place was ablaze with music. And my heart was singing because Cal had come back to me. But there was no time for sentiment, his life was in my hands; only I could save him.

Leaving Swift lying against him, I pulled the dead Britons further into the forest then lit a smokeless fire, and hearing the rush of a stream, followed its sound which led me back towards the forest's edge; a little further and I found my horse patiently standing where I'd left her. I led her to a place where the stream flowed more gently and as she drank and cropped the grass, I unstrapped my pack and took from it the circle of bread, some meat left over from the feast and a small drinking bowl which I filled with water.

I took off my woollen cloak; it was soft and warm where my waterproof one was cold and clammy, and wrapped it round Cal. I would wear my old one, a decision that would save our lives.

Two days and two nights passed in that forest, Cal slowly coming back to life. I forced him to drink and, when he had strength enough, to eat, first a few crumbs of the bread, but on the second day I guddled a fish. And all this time I searched my brain trying to set out a plan, my first problem being where I should take him … the choices were few to non-existent. Not back to May: the II would be upon it at any moment. What about the White Lands? With the cohorts attacking in the west, would the east be less of a risk? And then there was the south and Claudia Cogidubnus. But could I trust her? I knew only what Ullan Dur had told me about her, but living with Romans half my life, I was justified in feeling that he might be mistaken. One thing was certain, however, we had to get away from this place. I'd learned enough by now to know that it wouldn't be long before Cal's executioners returned to look for their missing comrades.

I buried Storm under an oak tree, scattering acorns over her grave. And after I had spoken his name, and offered up his soul to Ra, I led the horse close to where Cal was lying, and locking my arms around him, balanced him against my legs as I pulled my British tunic over his head, then set to with the breeches; my old prissy sense of decorum meant that I couldn't let him stay naked even if under my new woollen cloak. And though he helped as much as he could, grasping my shoulder as I pushed him up onto the horse's back, it was hard work, I can tell you.

And so it was that we left that place of execution, Cal half sitting, half slumped upon the horse's neck, Swift padding stealthily beside us, I, wearing my waterproof cloak with the Whisperer strapped to my back.

East it would have to be.

It was morning and we made our way onward, towards a watery sun. When Cal became too tired, or it was evident he was in pain, I'd sit in front of him and he'd collapse against me.

Swift stayed close to the horse's hooves, looking up at us for reassurance every now and again. With our supplies gone, we were reduced to eating what she could catch. She brought us a hare and two dormice. Knowing they were considered holy of holies, I skinned the hare out of Cal's sight. To regain his strength he had to eat, and that was all there was about it.

It started to drizzle. We kept to the forest's edge for shelter. Standing under the dripping leaves, my voice sounded hollow as I answered Cal in my stilted British. He had found strength to ask where we were going. 'Not far now.' Lying to him was more than I could bear.

A little after what I perceived to be noon, we heard a vague sound, like the beating of drums. I say 'we' but I mean only Swift and I, Cal was incapable of hearing anything. I pulled our horse further into the forest; with the sudden jolt he slipped to one side but managed to right himself. Swift followed, silently. I stood, hardly daring to breathe. What I had mistaken as a drumbeat turned into the sound of marching feet. Above it a voice marked the pace, Right. Right. Right. Not auxilia then for there was no sound of horses. I reckoned it stopped about thirty paces away. A few moments of heart-stopping silence and now, too close for comfort, came the scuffle of hobnails. They'd sent out scouts, no doubt about it. If I had been Marcus, I'd have known what was bound to come next. But I wasn't, and I didn't ... until it began.

It came in the form of a whizzing ballista ball, crashing down through the branches. Then another ... and another. The barking of orders. Plainly, their scouts had caught sight of us; they weren't taking any chances.

Signalling at Swift to 'Stay' I ran to the forest's edge and peered out through the tree trunks. A little way off stood a unit of troops, their captain held a flag. Somewhere not too far behind him, his detachment waited for orders. When he raised it, the ballista would start firing again.

My instincts flashed into action. For the umpteenth time, I thanked the gods for granting me inspiration, along with my army issue cloak and hobnails.

Praying that he wouldn't give the signal just yet, I ran back, and with Swift by my side, led the horse into open ground, where tempering my step and taking my cue from Marcus' swagger, I sauntered towards them, arm outstretched in salute.

Incredulous looks. Swords pulled from their sheaths. This was the point where the captain should signal attack. But my cloak, my hobnails; I was Roman, wasn't I?

'Salve,' I greeted in an imperious tone.

The captain stepped towards me. 'Mars' balls,' he said, 'who are you?' He spoke with a northern accent and was young enough to be hoodwinked. Both facts put me slightly more at ease.

'My name is Siva Ostorius. I am at your service. sir.'

'By heck,' he said next, 'you were almost a gonner.'

'And may I present my comrade at arms. We are making our way back to the king's palace.'

Palace was it … Ye gods. 'What king?'

'Tiberius Claudius Cogidubnus.' And, not wishing to infer that his understanding of local facts was scant to non-existent, I added, 'You will know to whom I am referring.'

'Aye.' But it was clear that he didn't.

Now his stare rested upon Cal, slumped upon the horse's neck.

'This gentleman is one of our spies. He was set upon by some wretched Catuvellauni. Left for dead.'

It was plain he'd believed me at first, but now he began to wonder.

A moment's reflection. 'And what's your part in all this?'

'It is a long story but I will tell it if you have time.'

He took a step towards us. 'Tell it, but quick.'

'I was with an outpost garrison unit. We came across him hung from a tree. I recognised him and volunteered to take him back to headquarters. I wonder if you would be kind enough to let me know how far it is to the coast, at a walking pace.'

It was plain that he didn't have any idea. In place of an answer, he jutted his thumb at Cal. 'Still alive then?'

'Very much so.'

How long could this conversation go on? To put an end to it, I heightened my voice. 'Not so far to go then, sir. If you permit us, we'll be off. The sooner we get going, and all that stuff ...' and grasping the horse's reins, led it and its precious load past his gaping men. Many a sight they had seen on their numerous tours of duty, but this, most certainly, was the strangest.

I looked back and thanked them; I hadn't been sure where to take Cal, but I did now.

CHAPTER TWENTY
HAIL MY BROTHER AND FAREWELL

It was night by the time we got there. The drizzle had stopped, and I thanked Luna that just when we needed her, she and her celestial companions appeared from behind the ceiling of cloud. Her light shone brightly enough on the cliff path to find a safe place … a shelter of trees behind which I left Cal. I felt that he understood when I told him I'd be back soon and, as all he wanted to do was sleep, I thought it safer to leave him on the horse; she was by far more comfortable than the sodden ground. There was no need to tell Swift to stand guard and bite the balls off anyone who chanced to come near. I took the Whisperer with me.

As it turned out, it couldn't have been easier to get back into Cogidubnus' dilapidated villa. I simply scaled a wooden fence, then its tumbledown wall. A few bored looking sentries were posted at the front and back of the building but no one else was about.

I scrambled through an unbarred window and found myself in a cellar. The man who can afford any number of guards must think himself well protected, and until that night I'd have thought so myself. But inside the house, every one of them was dozing in some corner or other and I simply walked up the somewhat shaky, timber staircase to what might be described as the atrium. I must have passed through here with Maxentius, but it was plain that I hadn't been paying attention. I scanned the space and tried to make out where I was, and now, praise Risus, came the sound of laughter. Following it, step by creaking step across the floor, I found myself in the same passage where Claudia – now I knew her name – had curled my fingertips around the sunship. Illuminated by the hanging lanterns, a scene was set out before me; this time she was alone with her mother and sister picking at sweetmeats set out on a tray. Time passed. A tightness gripped my throat. What about Cal, down there by the cliff path. How long could he live without help?

'Calm,' I told myself. 'Keep calm.'

But I had to endure only one more moment of suffering, for now she stood, and pulling a shawl round her shoulders, kissed her mother and came towards me. Here was my chance, but her sister called out and ran after her, forcing me to step back into the dark and let them pass. I watched as they crossed the atrium. Surely their slave girls would appear, but they continued alone, and I had to remind myself that though this place was wrapped in the guise of Rome, it wasn't. They turned down a corridor at its far end and, keeping to the shadows, I crept after them and watched as her sister disappeared into one room, she into another. This was my chance; only now did I think about the next part of my plan, namely, what if I were caught?

I pushed away the thought, parted its curtained doorway and stepped in. It seemed the gods were with me for she stood on a stool by her window, looking out at the moon, and so couldn't see me behind her. I'd have to act now.

Clasping my hand over her mouth, I whispered, 'Don't scream. I'm not going to hurt you.'

I let go, and she turned round, gulping.

If I'd imagined Claudia Cogidubnus to be a docile, polite little lady, I was in for a shock. She lunged out, raking my face with her nails, but when she saw who I was she hissed up at me, 'Are you entirely out of your mind?' and stretching up, she pushed her face close to mine. 'It's not enough that you disappear like,' she snapped her fingers, 'that. Oh no, you sneak back in the middle of the night. Don't you know what they'll do if they find you here? String you up by your balls, that's what.' This from the lips of that gracious, Roman maiden. 'I suppose …' But before she could say anymore, I clasped my hand back over her mouth, which had the desired effect.

'Will you listen? I've come from May with a wounded man. My horse is outside the fence and he is upon it.' I took my hand from her mouth. 'If you don't come with me now, he'll be dead before we get to him.'

And though my words made an impact, she shushed up at me, and now it was her turn to press her hand against my mouth. 'How did you get in?' which struck me as an odd response.

I readjusted my thoughts. 'From the cellar.'

'Well go back and wait for me there.'

So I did.

After what seemed an interminable time, she appeared at the end of the crypt-like space, a ghostly shape bathed in the light of the earthen lamps she held in either hand, their flames winking out in the dark, a cover from her bed around her shoulders. By now I was frantic.

'I left him on the cliff path. We have to go … this minute.'

She put her finger to her lips and flapped at me to follow her. At the far end of the cellar were two broken ladders balanced against a wall.

'Move them aside,' she ordered. And when I followed her instruction, I saw they'd been hiding a gaping crack running down it, its bottom half had crumbled away leaving a gap wide enough to squeeze through. She handed me one of the lamps and I followed her into the gusting wind, where an elderly man stood as if waiting.

'Appolinaris is my servant,' she informed me. 'He will know what to do.' And without further introduction, she waved her hand. 'Go on then, we'll follow you.'

We reached the horse. I thanked the gods that my worst fears had come to nothing for Cal was still slumped on its neck. Appolinaris might have been old but he was strong. Placing his lamp on the ground, he helped me take him down and lay him on the ground, where he knelt over him. Claudia stood silent, her own lamp shone upon Cal's face and it was as if she had been struck by a lightning bolt, stepping back in what could only be a state of utter shock.

A few moments passed before Appolinaris said in Latin, 'He has lost a great deal of blood, but he might live.'

'Might' was not the word I wanted to hear.

He spoke again. 'I told my boys to come and find us. I'll need their help to get your friend indoors where I can tend to him.'

I turned to Claudia. 'Is that safe?'

She didn't reply but stood staring as if with unseeing eyes. I would have tried to comfort her but there was no time to say more, for three figures appeared, running towards our flickering lamps.

Appolinaris' boys seemed to know what they were doing; almost as though they had done it before, that this was not a new thing for them. They unfolded blankets which they'd been carrying and rolled Cal on top of them. But before they lifted him, I took the sunship from my neck and put it on his; all I could do now, for him and for me, was pray that his own gods would protect him, but if they could not, that Anpu would take him safely on his journey into night. The movement stirred him; he looked up at me through half-closed eyes and said something softly. I couldn't understand his words.

But Appolinaris did. 'He said, he thanks you.'

And with that, he disappeared from the shelter of the trees, his boys behind him gripping the corners of the blankets.

And though my soul was frozen, I found my voice and whispered into the searing wind, 'Hail my brother ... and farewell.'

Swift took a few steps after him. It ripped my heart even more open for I had to call her back.

There was no time for sentiment, however. Claudia's voice was no longer the forceful one of before ... where that had been curt and ferocious this one was shaky and weak. 'Go back to the cellar.'

It pulled me out of my shock. But I needed a moment to recover enough to answer. Mistaking my silence, she shook me, and repeating her words she added, 'Stay beside the broken wall. Don't go in. I'll meet you there.'

I held up my lamp to answer her and saw that her face was wet with tears. I traced my finger across her cheek and, taking a moment before I left her, made my way back along the cliff path, the Whisperer in my hand, Swift at my heels, a great trepidation filling my soul. One moment Cal had been with me, the next he was gone. The words he *may* live overwhelmed me, for surely, they meant he *may not*. I stopped and gazed up at the stars and asked, 'Will I ever see you again?'

And though my strength was all but gone, and I was filled with a very great sorrow, I forced myself to keep on going; across the fence, the wall and round by the way I had come. At that very moment the moon chose to disappear behind clouds, which was a blessing as only an owl could have seen us, but this was a hinderance too, as without her guidance, it took some time to find the meeting place.

As if in lamentation, the wind screamed around us. I hunkered down and waited, Swift pressing herself tight against me. 'Don't worry,' I said to her, but more to myself, 'he'll be back to his old self in no time.'

She gazed up at me and it was as if her doleful expression said, *I don't believe you at all.*

It seemed too long a time before I heard a shuffle of footsteps, and there she was.

'Come,' she beckoned and for the second time that night I followed behind her flickering lamp as she led me down a rocky path to a dark and blustery pinnacle of cliff, Swift treading cautiously behind us. When we reached its foot, she clasped my wrist and guided me slowly, slowly, until we came to a gaping hole cut into a bank of ferns and bracken. She scrambled through it, I followed her and we were out of the blasting wind, which had reached crescendo point.

'We're safe now.'

We sat down on the leaf-strewn earth, and now it was her turn to say, 'Listen. My men have taken ... your friend ... to a safe place. When he is well enough, they'll get him back to the White Lands, for that's where he came from. You know that already, though, don't you?'

I nodded.

'This is what will happen now. You'll stay here until you're recovered and rested. And then we'll get you back to the legion.'

'But how?'

'There's no time to talk about all that now, I have to go. You'll be safe here. A boy will bring you food and clothes. I'll come tomorrow and tell you then.'

'And what about Swift? She can't come with me.' Hearing her name, she pricked up her ears and gazed at me in anticipation.

'The boy will take her,' and, with that she stepped back out into the wind.

I had lost Cal, and now I'd lose Swift. I knelt beside her and took her in my arms. My only consolation was that if he did live, she would be there for him and they'd travel back to the White Lands together.

Too long a time passed before a boy appeared with a bucket of water, a woollen tunic and food. I thanked him and said a few words of greeting but it was clear that he didn't understand, and so I did my best to say them in British, which made him smile.

He pointed at Swift.

I nodded but sensing something of my sadness at parting from her, he smiled again and, holding a slice of meat towards her, said a word I did know. 'Hello.'

I should tell him her name. I scoured my brain to remember what her British one was, to no avail so I said 'Swift'.

He tried it out – 'Sueft' – which was pretty near perfect. But she was too busy wolfing down the meat to worry about pronunciations.

When the last morsel was gone, he threaded a string around her neck and off they went into the night. I was thankful that she hadn't turned to cast her sorrowful eyes upon me.

It was only when I forced myself to look at the bread and chicken legs that I realised I was starving, and following Swift's example just about swallowed them down in one, doing the same with the bread. I managed to pull my new tunic over my old one and drink the contents of a stone bottle – very good wine indeed. I then drank a great deal of the water, washed my face and arms with the rest, and stretching out on the leafy ground laid the Whisperer beside me. I thanked Hypnos for casting me adrift upon a void of sleep; my spirit had fled and I was dreaming of Cal.

He was in a carriage with Fabius, travelling along the Via Patricius.

CHAPTER TWENTY-ONE
THE BADGERS' SETT

So deep was my sleep that I woke only when I heard a voice above me.

I opened my eyes; a beautiful face peered down at me. 'You look more human now,' and the hideous reality came flooding back.

I struggled to sit. It felt as if an enormous mallet had smashed my bones into pulp, along with which my mouth felt akin to the floor of a pigeon coop. A moment battling with my voice before I managed, 'I slept.'

'I'm not surprised.' She didn't sound it. 'I put a little something in your wine.'

She placed a parcel on the ground. I watched as she opened it and took out a slice of oiled bread and bowl of meatballs. And as I set upon them with gusto, she said, 'My mother and sister have gone with my father to look at the place where he's building his villa. Least where he wants to build it if Rome will allow him. It will take some time to get there and back, so we can talk for a little.'

This was the first time I'd seen her in daylight. I studied her while I ate; my dream had reminded me how white British skin was, so white as to be almost translucent, but her hair, black and cut round her shoulders, wasn't British at all. She wore a checkered cloak, but her laced shoes were of a fashion back in the city. Her puffy eyes and swollen face told me she'd been crying again. I wanted to comfort her but she was Roman, and I was still enough of one to know about decorum.

'My friend … How is he?' All I had in the world depended on what she would say.

'He's gone now. They took him to a secret place. Even I don't know where it is. Oh, I know roughly but I could never find it, even with a description of where to go. And I can't go to many places.'

I hadn't peed for a very long time. This was the first time I'd ever had to ask permission. 'Would you mind; I have to relieve myself.'

But she only said, 'Watch you don't fall down into the sea.'

I returned without mishap and she let me eat before she asked her first question; I knew what it was going to be.

'So, who are you? You don't look like a Roman … and why have you chosen to help us?'

'My name is Siva. I am … I was … a slave of the Scapula family, though I might have been described as more of a freedman. And I don't look like one because I'm not.'

'What are you then?' I was somewhat relieved that her fierceness had returned.

In the vain hope of softening her with a smile, I kept it simple. 'Egypt.'

'Oh.' I could tell that she didn't know much about there, but she wasn't about to admit it. 'And what is someone from Egypt doing dressed as you are?' She meant in army uniform.

'I was with the legions.'

This shook her. 'They told me you were on our side. How can you be both things at once?'

I tried to smile again, but her expression stayed fixed in its glowering glory. No doubt about it, she was wary of me.

'My master's here. He sent for me to join him. But when I arrived, I was captured.' I told her about the outpost garrison unit. The attack. The fact that I was saved by my amulet. 'The one I sent with the message.'

'What is it anyway?'

This set me off track. 'It's called a sunship.'

'Why?'

And so I told her about the god Amun Ra who sails his ship across the heavens. 'It carries the sun from the moment it rises until it sinks into the night.'

This little story succeeded where I had struggled. She smiled.

'Do you know anything about this new god?'

Which flummoxed me; I shook my head.

'I thought it might be a sign that you belonged to his sect. They have fish symbols, and fishermen, and ships have something to do with that, do they not?'

I had no idea what she was talking about.

'They worship in secret,' she said, as if to prompt my memory, but I was still none the wiser and she left it at that.

'So how did it save you?'

I told her about the camp in the forest. How I'd been captured. I couldn't continue without saying his name; I gave him his real one, 'By Calgac.'

At this she shrank back as if she'd been struck and I felt that she had stopped listening. Sensing a chilly change in the atmosphere I did my best to avoid her old surly gaze; a moment's pause but all she said was, 'It's a wonder you're still alive.'

I thought it best to plough on, telling her how we'd come face to face that early morning, how he'd spared me because I was wearing it, about the skull-hung clearing, and what had happened there, how I had reached out and plucked the golden ball from the tree … of how he'd taken me to Ruadon's farm, my time spent with his tribe and its leader, a man named Caradoc. How I became one of them. This drew her out of her stupor.

'Rome calls him Caratacus,' she said. 'He's the only one they fear.' Vespasian's voice rose up in my mind; *and Caratacus, what can you tell me about him?* I thanked the gods that until this moment I had known him only as Caradoc and forced my mind back to what she was saying. 'But if you liked it so much with him there,' and her suddenly petulant voice gave me an inkling of what was behind it, 'why did you go back to the legions?'

'To spy,' I said. 'To spy.' And I told her that it was when I'd learned about Vespasian's plan to attack, that I'd sent Cal a message in my sunship warning of what was to come. And that night when I came to her father's house with Maxentius and she put it into my hand, how I'd thought it couldn't have reached him, and so had set off to tell them what was about to take place. That only then had I discovered that she was on their side.

This seemed to mollify her. 'One of their boys brought it to me, but that was all. They must have known that you'd be with those who were coming to visit my father. They didn't tell me who you were. Why didn't you come to meet me?' This she said in an accusing tone.

'I didn't know you were with us. I thought it was a trap.'

She seemed to accept this in good grace, and I continued with my story; telling her how when I was set to return to her Swift had appeared and led me to Cal hung on the tree.

At this point in my story, she shrunk back into her dismal state and where I might have asked if she knew who he was, her expression told me it was best to steer clear of that subject.

'The man who did it … I killed him.'

These are the words that won her over. She stared at me, wide-eyed, and after a while she smiled. 'I'm glad you did.'

'Who was he? And why hang him on a tree? Why cut him all over like that?'

'It's an old way of punishment,' she said, 'and as far as who he was, we are three factions, those who fight against Rome, those who are its allies, and those yet undecided. The tribes who wish to join the Empire hate those who don't.'

'Ullan Dur sent me to you. I was to ask you to get me back to the XX but when I found him, I didn't know if it was the right thing to do. Perhaps I should have tried to take him to the White Lands but when it became clear that he wouldn't make it that far, I brought him here. You were the only one I knew who could help him. Now it's your turn to tell me why you're on the Briton's side.'

She took a long time to answer. 'They're my people. I can't turn against them, even for the sake of my father. I know we can never beat the legions, but we must go down fighting.'

'Then we both belong to one camp but have joined the other.' I was trying to find common ground.

'You must think me strange to be working against him.'

'No stranger than you must think I am.'

'He's not a bad man … he simply thinks he's on the right

side. He was fostered in Rome as a child, alongside future kings of lands incorporated into the Empire.'

I knew this to be something that vassal kings did with their sons to show their allegiance to the emperor. If they turned against the City, their son would be killed.

'He was given a Roman education, swam in the great baths, visited the games, and ate his food whilst stretched out upon a silken couch. He was captivated, completely and absolutely, by everything Roman. But he wasn't Roman, he was the type they call barbarian, and a barbarian Briton to boot. Don't think I'm excusing him, for I'm not, I'm only trying to explain. *Like it or not*, he says, by way of excusing himself, *their victory is a foregone conclusion, so why not simply bend the knee from the start and save a whole lot of bloodshed.* I don't agree, but that's what he thinks ... *Go calmly, welcome Rome and all will be well in the end.*'

And though she pretended not to mind that her father was considered a traitor by men such as Caradoc, I could tell that she did. She understood only too well that rather than the exotic hybrid he imagined himself to be, to men of the City he was a mere mongrel, expendable once he'd served his purpose, given them what they wanted. Once he'd done that, they'd take his lands, every last part of his old domain, and his new one too.

'If he's lucky, they might leave him our house by the Tiber.' It was close to the temple of Portunus, she said, and wasn't grand enough for snatching.

'After all this time... After all these hours at the foot of his tutor back in the City, he understands them not a jot.'

'Can't you make him see sense?'

'What do you think I've been doing all this time, sitting back and nodding my head?' she snapped.

Which confirmed what had dawned on me a fair time before; I'd have to tread more carefully if I wanted to keep on the right side of Claudia Cogidubnus, and so I said, rather tentatively, 'But he's not alone, is he? There are other tribes who want to join Rome.'

'Hold him up as a shining example of what we all might aspire to becoming, you mean, half one thing, half the other. All those who don't know the truth place me in that category. But, you see, where my father's a Briton by birth but thinks of himself as a Roman, I, who at least can claim to be Roman, no thanks to my mother,' I thought of the small dark woman standing in front of Maxentius, 'consider myself wholly and absolutely British.'

But, despite her claims, just listening to her, I could sense something intrinsically Roman glimmering through her Britishness, her clarity of vision, her strength of purpose, her self-confidence – stubborn, headstrong, defiant, being the words that sprang to my mind. Rather like Marcus, in fact.

She gripped my arm. 'But look,' she said, 'we don't have time to talk about such things ... we have to get you back to the legion. It seems you're the only one who can help us.'

I was not inclined to ask what she meant by 'seems', and forcing myself to ignore the barb went on to ask how on earth was she going to do that. I couldn't saunter back as if nothing had happened. Where had I been all this time? They'd execute me as a deserter. No, even worse.

'Don't you imagine,' she said, 'that I've thought of all that? But they won't and I'll tell you why. You'll take them a message, sealed with my father's stamp, to make them believe what you tell them is true, that after your tribune met with my father, after you reported back to ... him ...'

'He's called Maxentius.'

'Maxentius … you went down to the cliffs to gather your thoughts. You were set upon by men from another tribe, those who are enemies of Rome. They mustn't suspect that anyone here is working against my father, they must believe that they're all faithful to him. They knocked you unconscious, pulled you off the path and left you for dead. The guards didn't find you until the next evening. By then your unit had left. When I waited on the cliffs that night and you didn't come, it was the worst thing that could have happened. I couldn't make sense of it. So this story didn't come fresh from my mind, it's one of the things I thought might have happened.'

'By your father's men?'

'Most are with him, some are not. But Rome mustn't know this; they must believe that everyone here is to be trusted.'

'What was Maxentius' reaction when I disappeared?'

'I don't know. You'll have to ask him.' She could quickly change back to her glib and brusque manner. 'But, let me tell you, this is what will happen now. Someone will come for you at first light. Be ready to go with him. He's one of my father's men, but one of us too. He speaks Latin so if you should bump into troops, he'll simply tell them he's taking one of their spies – namely you – to report back to base what information he's rooted out here. And if you come across any of us, he'll tell them the truth. Your tunic's too clean,' she said next. 'Where's your old one?'

'Under this.'

'Change them round then.'

I felt I was back in the temple, she the Grand Oracle, I the quivering novice.

'It's better I go now, but I'll come to Dunum as soon as I can. And as far as the dog is concerned,' she changed this to

Swift, 'we'll take good care of her. Don't worry about leaving her, she's forgotten you already.'

I supposed this was to make me feel better, but it had the opposite effect.

I thanked her.

'No, you're one of us now.' She stood and took a few steps towards the mouth of what I can only describe as the cave. But before she left, I had to ask her, 'What is this place?'

We think it's an old badgers' sett. It's a secret place for those who're on our side to meet. It's been used for a long time. A priest lived here some time ago'

'A druid?' And then I said, 'A wisdom carrier?'

'Yes.'

'Why would he want to do that?'

'It's what they like.'

'All by himself? Ye gods.'

I thought of the oracle again; she had contact with no one apart from those seeking guidance, even her acolytes, like me, but at least she knew we were there, to say nothing of the fact that she lived in a luxurious temple. And Egypt; well, Egypt was warm.

That night I dreamt I was back there. The sun rose upon the horizon. Someone appeared beside me. I knew it was Cal. But when I turned, he was gone.

CHAPTER TWENTY-TWO
THE OSIRIS MOON

The giant who appeared at the edge of the dawn had no need to wake me; after my dream, I'd been lying in torment, thinking of Cal.

He was oldish, big and moustachioed with the smiling eyes of the British warrior; it was time to go.

I strapped the Whisperer to my back and he motioned that I should follow him. We walked along the cliff path until we reached a group of men standing behind a fully packed cart, harnessed by two ponies. A young boy sat at the reins.

Romans are accustomed to every kind of man – black, white, brown short, medium-sized, tall, fat, thin – but not the Britons. They stared at me and it was as if they wanted to rip their eyes out in consternation.

I took the Whisperer from my back and, hoping what Claudia had told me was right, that he would understand, I said in Latin, 'Would you keep this, and get it back to me at the end of all this?'

He took the blade with the ease of a man who'd handled weapons like this all his life. 'Nice,' was all he said as he buried it under the bulging sacks piled up in the cart and motioned that I should get in beside them. And when I did, he said, 'I'm sorry but we must make this look real,' and producing a knife and telling me that I should keep still, plunged it into my leg. Ye gods, the pain. He then nicked my forehead and cheek after which he bound my leg and rubbed what, too soon I realised was salt into the brand-new cuts on my face.

Stepping back to admire his handywork, there could be no mistaking it; now I looked like a man who'd been caught by the enemy. And with that my moustachioed saviour led the cart forward. There was no going back; I was in the hand of the gods.

Would I ever know if Cal was still with us in this world, or if he was not? I tried to force him from my mind, there was no place for wild emotion; I was on a mission and I had to start thinking like him.

For the first few miles, we kept to the cliff path. Things were changing, however. No longer were those tracks and trails the empty places of my outward journey with Maxentius. We were travelling away from the forthcoming battles, and so it seemed was the rest of the world.

We made our way up-country, through the bleak conquered lands.

Just as the early morning light expanded into day, we entered the wide ones of the east; I knew this for the land ranged into vast tracks of moor, edged by deep swathes of forest. We'd see a little group, bedraggled and miserable, huddled round a fire by the wayside, or hear a noise, and round the distant bend, a herd of cattle would lumber past us, young girls whipping them along as fast as their weary legs could carry them.

There were Romans about too, or should I say men of the auxilia, Thracians, Pannonians, Gauls, Macedonians, setting to in their work parties, or guarding groups of surveyors, planning their roads out already. We trundled beside one still under construction. Its surface cut a high, straight scar through the tender green of its surroundings. And as we travelled further east we passed yet more gangs of men piling their stakes and shovels into carts, finished their labour for the day, ready to make their way back to their marching camps; a bite to eat, and if weariness didn't lay claim to them first, a game or two of knucklebones.

Poor blighters.

Once again, I gave thanks for my army issue cloak ... and with my dark skin I looked even less British than I had Roman. But British I was. My softness was gone. I was proud of the covering of muscle on my body, on my legs, on my forearms and I smiled at the thought of what I'd been before. In place of lily-livered Siva was one of them, and though I'd never be a match for even the youngest of a tribe, I'd be more than able to hold my own against any man of the legions who cared to take me on.

The movement of displaced people or blocks of marching troops slowed us down but we barely stopped. The first day was easy going, but on the second the heavens opened and it didn't take long for dry land to turn into what more resembled a marsh. The cart squelched through it but every so often a wheel would get stuck and we'd have to unharness the ponies and push it through the quagmire, not helped by my cut and festering leg.

On the late afternoon of the third we reached Dunum. It wasn't really so long since I'd set off with Maxentius but during the short time I'd been away, the camp of the XX had become a real Little Rome. The old palisade, an enormous structure by any layman's reckoning, had been heightened and widened even further. Archers stared down at us from new, even taller crossed towers at either side of the gate; they had a menacingly permanent look about them.

The big Briton, whose name by now I knew was Pran, drove the cart as close to them as he could without having arrows shot through our necks. He slapped me on my back and, making great show of my limp, I stepped down into the mud. By now my bandaged leg was encased in crusted blood, the wounds on my face oozing slime.

The gate opened; a guard stepped out. I had done this twice by now and was a dab hand.

First came my 'Salve' then, 'It is I, Siva Ostorius.'

The guard looked up at the watchmen. One of them nodded and I was led in, and along a partially dry path to Maxentius' quarters.

'Ye gods,' he said, and rose from his table when he saw me.

I won't go over our short conversation, suffice to say that I spun him my tale, or should I say Claudia's tale and handed over the message designed to save me. He did no more than scan it, which was reassuring for it meant he believed me without pouring over every last word. Or any word at all for that matter.

'I'm sorry freedman Ostorius.' He thought for a moment, and ever the military man added, 'Even in that place! It's a lesson. They're everywhere. I'm glad you're back in one piece. I wouldn't have liked to tell Marcus, had there been a different outcome.'

'I'm to blame.' I used some stoic philosophy here. 'I shouldn't have gone wandering out by myself. I endangered the unit and am ready for punishment.'

'Oh come now, Marcus can do so if he feels it is fit. But as I've said, I'm only glad you're alive. Let us talk more about Cogidubnus when you've been to the bathhouse. A physician and good rub down, that's what you need now.'

Marcus' popularity had come to my aid once again. Everyone loved him, but not quite as much as I did myself.

He called for his slave, entirely ignorant of the fact that by now Cinthus and I knew each other more than well. Had I been his tutor, I'd have given him top marks for his reaction upon seeing me. A ghost come back to life … and for the second time in as many months. But we slaves are a strange species, are we not, belonging as we do to a secret life? Where those who live in the normal world would exclaim or show delight in seeing me, he knew better. The less our masters understood about us, the better. But as an entirely blank expression would seem implausible even for him, he gave a formal smile.

'Siva Ostorius is returned to us,' Maxentius informed, though this observation hardly needed announcing.

'I am most glad to see you.'

'Take him to our bathhouse, will you and after that have his wounds looked at by the physician. Then get him something to eat.'

By 'our bathhouse' he meant the one used by the upper ranks, which was a relief as it would keep me away from the regulars who'd insist upon hearing my story. Of course I would have repeated the one I'd just told Maxentius, but I didn't have strength to join in their hilarious banter.

Only when Cinthus and I were halfway along the log-corded path did we feel it safe to whisper.

He: 'By Janus, Siva, where have you been?'

I: 'You almost had a heart attack.'

He: 'Wait till Polydorus sees you. We'll have to get a chair ready.'

I'd reel out the story I'd just spun to his master. 'I'll tell you what happened but …' and before I could add that he must keep it to himself, he turned an invisible key to his lips.

As we entered the bathhouse, I was grateful to see only a couple of others stretched out on the benches, but even so, we kept our guard. Cinthus helped me strip off my filthy tunics, and unfastened my hobnails – they'd done incredibly well, considering they'd been off my feet only once during the long days' past, taking me all the way to May, and back – and now I stood in the scooped-out area whilst he poured ladle upon ladle of tepid water over my muddy and filth-covered body. Whilst performing this much appreciated task, the wound on my leg opened, turning the muddy water to pink. He whispered, 'Sacred gods.'

A stinging balm put paid to that, the bleeding stopped and now came the hot pool.

And though lifetimes before it had been Fabius' little bathhouse, set in the garden of his villa, out on the Via Tusculanum I'd dreamt about; the star-spattered dome of its roof, the coloured tiles, the lemon trees in their earthen pots, ranged along the pillared walls, the linen towels, the perfumed oils, the chatter of finches in their cages, the woven sandals by the step, worn once then cast away. But I'd have traded a thousand such dreams for this one reality, which seemed to me then the greatest devised by man: the water trickling over my skin, the roughness of the stone beneath my feet, the slightly acrid smell of chalky water, the pungent heat of the place in contrast to the drizzly out of doors. And stepping into the bath, lying back in the warmth, feeling the chill dissolve from my shoulders, from my legs and feet, from my arms. What sumptuous indulgence. I lay there for a long time, until I heard snoring, and peering through the cloud of misty steam I saw Cinthus, asleep by the stove, head slumped, mouth wide open.

The physician appeared and looked me over, an infusion of some sort, more stinging balm, 'You'll live to see another day.' Not quite knowing if he was jesting with me, I could only suppose that my wounds were but nothing compared to those he usually had to deal with.

A soft massage, then came food; chickpeas and ham, and I and my body were restored. My emotions, however, were close to the surface. I would have to batten them down.

'Now that's more like it.' Maxentius said when I returned, waving me forward to sit with him.

'We spoke briefly about Cogidubnus. You said you felt we could trust him. What makes you so sure? And do you have anything to add? We didn't have time to speak at length before you performed your disappearing act.'

'Well, sir.' My 'sir' had returned. 'It's obvious that he craves power. And who better to get it from than Rome. He has the choice to be either the leader of a small British tribe or part of the Empire. He has ambition.'

'But it might be thwarted. Not all those under his command support him, as proven by your case. He may end up having a fair number of his men doing battle against us. Where do their loyalties lie, I wonder.'

We were getting too close for comfort. 'I can only say that I'm sure that those who attacked me belonged to an enemy tribe. After my encounter, he gave orders that they should be found and executed. But of course this may not have been possible. But it does prove that he comes down hard on those who act against him … from what I've seen, those of his own tribe regard him as their protector. He's strong and will lead them to glory.' Even I was amazed at the speedily devised tactics I'd picked up from my master.

'Those enemy tribes you talk of are naught but a hotbed of rebellion against us … and against him too.' And on he went for a very long time on the subject.

And it was here that I was struck with a flash of genius.

'May I add something of my own feelings, sir?'

He nodded his assent.

'They're enemies of Rome, and I would fight alongside the legions for this reason alone. But I have developed a deep hatred for them; they've attacked me twice now but I'm still alive. My personal loathing has given me,' on I went … etcetera … etcetera. 'And when I was recovering in Cogidubnus' house I realised that I understood very much more of their language than I had realised.' Here I went on with some nonsense, which of course being Roman he would take as granted. 'It's not like Latin sir, it's basic and as I speak our own plus Hindu, Greek, Egyptian, Syriac, it's easy for me. I can now say, with no hesitation that I can easily interpret on your behalf. And I don't care if they kill me the next time … I can't stand by without doing my duty.'

I could only hope that Maxentius' path wouldn't cross with Cogidubnus' any time soon. I thought about Claudia too. And what of the men back at May?

The day had started well; I'd been helping Quintus with his accounts. But it wasn't till evening had passed when the answer arrived with a messenger unit. May had been obliterated. Ullan

Dur and his warriors were dead, his people forced north.

I couldn't let anyone witness my shock and so, using the need to stretch my legs, I excused myself and walked out into the night to be alone. A little way along the path I stood by the armament store and made a silent prayer. The moon had risen by now, a full round moon, what is known in Egypt as an Osiris moon. Osiris, who brought death but regeneration too, even to those who had been defeated.

'The youngest of the gods was my father,
I am Osiris, who conducted a large and numerous army
as far as thedeserts of India,
and travelled over the greatest part of the world,
and visited the streams of the Isted and the remotest shores of the ocean
diffusing benevolence to all the inhabitants of the world.'

We'd be reborn; we would travel along the star corridor. But I wasn't comforted by such a thought for I had lived in the marble City and knew what reality was. And now I found my heart was breaking.

With the message had come the first load of booty: torcs, arm cuffs, rings, anklets, belt buckles, horse trappings, all to be melted down and rendered into bars. Beyond their value in gold, these items were of no interest to the legion. By our commander's way of thinking, a ring, dreamt up from the shapes of two swirling serpents, was of far more use stamped into coins bearing the head of our esteemed emperor, even though there were millions upon millions of them changing hands every day.

And what of Cal? When his face came into my mind, I would chase his image away … it was the only way I could survive. At night I'd lie brooding about how it had been with him. I'd see him again at the camp by the forest's edge, or striding in front of me, his skin so white against the smudged grey of the sky. I thought of how he'd looked that long day past, when we'd parted near Vespasian's camp, his expression tough and tender at the same time. I felt his arm across my shoulder, its dry warmth against it. I felt the power of him, lifting my arms to strike the traitor blue cloak, once then again.

I kept my hair shorn and spent long hours in the exercise yard. And when the evening torches were lit, I'd sit with the men of the ranks, playing ludus and talking about home, wherever that might be for them. I had a feeling, however, that once back there, they'd do the same about Britain.

It was too dangerous to ask Quintus of plans to come next, this being information restricted to those of the upper ranks. And though he and I felt a very great affinity towards one another, he was part of that esteemed body and he knew what the rules were. Beside the few hours I spent alongside him, helping him with odds and ends of this and of that, my time was my own, and so I would walk round the square of the wall, or down towards the mess hall, listening for snippets of news that might give me some inadvertent clues as to where the legion planned to strike next.

CHAPTER TWENTY-THREE
A VISITOR

After two weeks of abject misery, I was told to report to Maxentius.

He sat in the same position he had during our last conversation. The only thing changed about the scene set out in front of me was a small figure sitting where I had before. A woman, which seemed entirely strange, with what looked to all intents and purposes, a British bodyguard standing behind her.

'Ah, freedman Siva. You have a visitor.'

She turned and I all but fell on the ground in shock.

'The Lady Cogidubnus. Well, I will let you speak for yourself, my lady.'

She pushed back her hood. Her hair had grown longer. I caught a glimpse of tiny bell earrings, a golden brooch was pinned to her cloak and her cheeks were smudged with cinnabar. Something stirred within my heart and I knew that it was entirely due to our link with Cal.

'My father sent me to ask how you are. He is most sorry about what happened.'

I gave a little bow and keeping my language as formal as I would when conversing with patrician women back in the City, said, 'I am well, my lady.'

'Oh, he will be most glad to hear it.' She turned back to Maxentius. 'As I have explained, our family has a small estate in the area.' She might have been talking about one set in the hills above Rome. 'If ever you feel like a change from camp life, please do visit. We have a vineyard and an orchard. And we have a very good cook.'

She rose from her seat. 'I will go now, but before I do, much though it is good to see you again, and fully recovered, the purpose of my visit was to return this to you.'

She clicked her fingers, the bodyguard stepped forward. He smiled conspiratorially as he held towards me an object wrapped in red cloth. I knew what it was.

She gave me time to gather my thoughts.

'As I you might know, my father sent his men to scour the ground where you were attacked. They found it close to where you'd been lying. It seems they were more intent on murder than robbery.'

I unwrapped the cloth and there was the sunship.

The smallest shooting star of hope skimmed through my dark despair. It lasted no more than a heartbeat, however, before its light was snuffed for now it struck me; if Cal were alive surely he would have kept it. Only if he wasn't would they return it to me. A shuddering bleakness filled my soul and the world was muted.

'What is it, we wondered?' Of course she knew, but talking about trifling matters could be a distraction from the case at hand.

'It's Egyptian, my lady.'

She feigned surprise at this. 'And you're from that land?' An easy question.

'I am.' An easy answer.

'Oh dear,' she turned her lips down; I hoped that only I could see that her eyes were shining. 'You must hate it here. So cold, so wet, so filled with barbarians.' But slaves are not permitted to give their opinions, which got me off the hook.

Now it was Maxentius' turn. But rather than admit that he longed to get back to the City, 'It has its problems,' he replied.

He flicked his fingers; one of his guards stepped forward. 'Escort the lady back to her carriage.' And turning to Claudia, 'I thank you for coming; I hope this won't be the last time we meet.'

He stood and gave a little bow as she rose from her chair.

'I leave in a very few days, so I don't think we shall this time.' Information meant for me. 'But you may return to my father's lands before too much time has passed.'

'I pray that I am given the chance, my lady.' And with that she and her bodyguard departed, Maxentius' escorting them to his door, a few respectful steps behind them.

Propriety demanded that I couldn't walk with a highborn lady, and so I hung back, but saw through the leather flaps of the door that she turned her head to look at me.

'I've a feeling that she was happy to have a reason to see you,' chuckled Maxentius.

I did my best at chuckling back. But a tinge of longing deep inside me let me know that what until now I had suspected ... I had started to fall in love with her.

My sunship was with me again, but surely it meant that the worst of my nightmares had become real. Cal was dead. Or was he alive? I was desperate to read the message that would surely be folded inside it ... yet I wasn't.

Forcing my reluctant fingers, I opened the sun disc, I

unrolled the small piece of parchment, and read

Find a way to come to me. I must leave by the nones. I counted forward; two weeks' time. A diagram told me how to get there. The camp was a square, and behind it a snaking line which I took to be a river, with a star marked on the opposite bank. *I have set my boys to watch for you. They will see you as you approach.*

If he were alive, she'd have told me. But maybe she wouldn't. I asked myself, was it torture or a reprieve that her note told me nothing. I closed my eyes; no longer could I form a picture of his face in my mind. I could see him walking in front of me, see his arms, the way his shoulders were set, I could describe the colour of his hair. And I knew that he carried laughter in his eyes. But I couldn't see his face.

'Just once,' I asked the gods as I lay awake, 'just let me see him once more.'

But they weren't listening.

*

I had to get to Claudia, and I had to get to her fast. I knew that her snaking line of river was on the edge of a field behind the southern gate. This was the place the auxilia set their horses free to wander, leading them there at the end of the day. Perhaps this was the very way to get me through the gates.

At the stable block I set my sight upon a small thin fellow unharnessing his mount.

I approached him and smiled in a friendly manner. 'How are they holding up, and have you lost many?'

He didn't seem to mind me looming over him.

'Do you know,' he said, 'you're the first one who's asked that. You're interested in horses, I take it.'

'I am. Very much.' I hoped I wouldn't have to prove it.

'To answer your question … yes, they're doing pretty well, and two hundred and forty-six, over the time since we got here.'

I was shocked, and he saw it.

'But we can't think of that,' he said next, 'or we'd never have strength to go on.'

'Just terrible,' was all I could think to say, but I meant it.

'I'm taking her down to the river. We do it when we're not on patrol, first thing in the morning and late afternoon. Come if you want.' Fortuna was certainly with me.

We walked by the edge of the palisade and out through the gate; it was late afternoon by now and they had been opened for the purpose. I'd only have to ask if I might accompany him tomorrow and the rest would be simple.

Until now, the closed gates had blocked out the view beyond them, but now a scene unfolded, with groups of men and horses scattered along a riverbank.

'It's shallow so it's safe for them to go in, it's good for their feet.'

As I've said, I had come here to check out the river and look for a way to get across it, but even if this turned out to be impossible, I'd come here again for it was a magical place; I'd never seen water meadows before, which is what the field turned out to be – weedy and grassy, and partly submerged under still pools. As we approached the small herd of horses, it was impossible to tell if they were walking in the river or on the land beside it.

By now a plan had formed in my mind, but before I could do anything about it my auxilia pointed. The same guard who had escorted Claudia out of my presence was marching his purposeful way towards us. Maxentius had sent for me again.

CHAPTER TWENTY-FOUR
ICENI

This time he was bent over his table, studying something. When he signalled that I should join him I saw it was a tablet of a type with which I was exceedingly familiar.

'The governor is taking me off up-country to talk with a people on the frontier. Our spies have an idea that they might be persuaded to join us. He wanted to do the job himself but I persuaded him otherwise. I suggested that I go with him and bring you along in place of those damned Gaulish translators. He agreed, but insists we take at least one of them. But that's not so bad; he can interpret and leave you to do as you did with Cogidubnus, keep your ear to the ground and look out for anything suspicious. It's a day's ride to reach the edge of their lands, and there will be less risk for you now; you've had enough frights to stick to the rules. It's a short enough journey. You'll return with him the following day. I will go north to the frontier.'

I thanked the gods that I would get there and back in time to meet Claudia. I was desperate to hear what she knew about Cal, but only if she quietened my anguish and told me he was alive. But maybe it was better not to know for then I'd still have hope.

'When do we leave, sir?' I wondered if he would tell me to cease calling him 'sir', but it was clear such trifles weren't topmost in his mind; he seemed somewhat troubled.

'At dawn.'

'May I ask who you're talking with?'

'A tribe,' he said. 'A tribe. I can't imagine they differ from any of the others we've encountered. They're called the Iceni. Their chief goes by the name Prasatog.' And again I thought of one of my conversations with Quintus. 'As I said, you'll return with the governor, I will head north to speak with another lot.'

I tried to sound nonchalant. 'And who are they, I only ask for safety's sake?' I didn't have a clue what I could possibly mean by this, but I needed to know and had to soften my query. I added, 'sir?'

'The Brigante. Their leader's a harridan by all accounts. But one thing's certain, she won't get the better of me.'

Rome has a goddess of delusion and folly, who leads men down the path of ruin. But at least he hadn't asked me to join him.

On that journey north, with Plautius' eagle, I felt even worse than I had when riding through the forsaken lands on the way to meet Cogidubnus, for then my army issue waterproof cloak had covered my shame. Now, however, I was kitted out in full regalia, breastplate, baldric and helmet with a buckler strapped to my arm. An auxilia of Rome was I, for all the world to see. Add to this the fact that I was sick to my stomach until it struck me; I was on a mission and might end up helping the Britons more than ever I had done before.

Keep your head, Siva, I said to myself, *and this could work out spectacularly well.*

This was the first time I'd ridden out with a proper military unit; the one I'd been part of before was a detachment of fifty men at most. Now however there were at least five times that number. Was this because we were heading to the border of relatively unknown territory or was it to display to our possible allies that Rome was not to be crossed. Holding your seat on an army horse was a tricky business in places like Britain. Though good fast-travellers on firm, cobbled roads they weren't cut out for wading through waterlogged terrain or picking their feet across boulder-strewn country. Sturdy little British ones would have got us there in half the time.

We went by the coast through flat, windswept land, an iron-grey sea stretching out to our right, and we were there. The Iceni capital was larger than I'd expected; its houses were set in neat, compact circles. A welcoming party came out to meet us, their musicians playing low notes on their serpent-headed horns, a melancholy memory of the feast at May.

Being inside a chieftain's roundhouse this time with both Plautius and Maxentius their bodyguards and various other lackeys was a thoroughly unpleasant experience. The Britons sat on the floor in their usual cross-legged way; Plautius had his camp stool brought in. Maxentius and I stood behind him. Prasatog spoke good Latin, which meant there was no need to use the services of the Gallic interpreter. But his wife was a different matter. She made it clear she'd prefer to be roasted alive than foul her mouth with the language of the invader. I listened closely, with hopes of catching her name but could only make out something that sounded like Bud Icca.

I could tell that the Iceni chief was a thinker, a man modelled along the lines of Caradoc. Less ostentatiously dressed than his wife, his gold was restricted to his torc, his hair was dark and cut short. With the type of silent power that carries great dignity, he handled his guests beautifully, giving the impression of agreeing with everything Plautius said without actually saying or doing anything that could later be presented as evidence against him. A masterly performance. And I'd thought I understood these people, thought they'd be outsmarted, not because I'd imagined the likes of Plautius were more intelligent, or abler, but simply because until then I'd have described the Britons as guileless, forthright and unaffected.

At the end of discussions, Prasatog made his gift to the governor, and it was at this point I came to understand just how artful he was. The wooden boxes were edged with fine, beaten gold and inlaid with coloured carbuncles. It took two men to carry each one, which were filled, not with precious metals fashioned by master-smiths, but with coin, exactly the kind of offering to quench the Roman thirst for booty.

Until that moment, I'd sought to regard myself as British. Now I knew I was.

Forcing my face to adopt an expression of gravest solemnity, I followed Maxentius and the governor back to camp and there I told them him that Prasatog was to be trusted, but of course, to my joy, now I knew he was not.

'And his wife?' Plautius seemed more interested in her than her husband.

'She seemed pretty stupid to me, sir, if you don't mind me saying.' This being exactly the opposite to what I had witnessed.

'What else are you here for?' he scoffed.

He gave me a disdainful look, as if he thought me beyond his contempt and I started to worry that he didn't quite trust me, or could it simply be that I was a slave. But how could I know that to get me away from the increasingly irascible governor, Maxentius had decided to save me.

An unusually bright sun was rising in the east. Our camp had been dismantled and we were ready to return to base. Only four days had passed since Claudia had brought her message. I would get back in plenty of time to cross the river and give her my news. But my relief didn't last long. I was with the governor's troops waiting to head back south when Maxentius put his rescue plan into action. 'On second thought, freedman Ostorius,' he shouted across the snorting of horses and muddling hubbub, 'you're coming with me.'

Which could be worse, missing my chance to meet Claudia for I longed to see her, or facing up to Cartimand, this time with him?

The first thought filled me with bitter dismay. Facing up to Cartimand once more was in a different league. *But wait*, I said to myself as I tried to digest this new and hellish turn of events, *she was the one who'd challenged me to return to Rome. Why wouldn't she think I was simply doing the job she'd suggested.*

The guides had arrived and the governor, his small but proficient detachment of bodyguards and the double unit of turma to which I'd been attached were ready to head out of Iceni territory and continue their way back through friendly country; the remainder of the unit, a hundred and sixty auxilia to which I now was attached, along with the Gaul who whom it seemed was coming along too, all in the charge of Maxentius being detailed for the onward journey. We were leading our horses into formation when we heard it, the faint but unmistakable blast of the cornu and a moment later we saw them a mile or so out to the east; the glinting body-armour, their mounts, much too large to be British, the sense of order; men of the legions, no doubt about it, picking their way across the banks set amongst the flooded marshland

A mile, half a mile, and now we could make out their standard bearer in his lion skin to the fore, holding aloft the red and gold bull standard of a detachment of what I now knew belonged to the IX.

I gazed out over the heads of the men in front of me and watched whilst the little company drew to a halt and their officer dismounted.

Plautius raised his arm and our own standard bearer ran out, words were exchanged and the signal 'Stand Firm' was given. Stand firm we could just about cope with, though the wind whipping in from the ocean was numbing our legs to such an extent that had orders been changed to 'Mount and Head On' I don't know what any of us could have done about it.

Now their young captain pulled off his helmet and, ye gods, I had to blink twice, for Marcus was striding towards us. He looked more than a little shambolic, the leather straps of his cuirass were slashed and some were missing, his hair was filthy and he needed a shave. His stolid and somewhat detached expression was gone, holding within it instead a look of extreme satisfaction, like that of a small boy who's won an egg and spoon race.

Helmet tucked under his arm, he stopped in front of Plautius and saluted, and pressing his right hand to his heart announced himself in a clear and loud voice, 'Marcus Ostorius, sir, temporarily assigned to the IX.'

Plautius cut him short. 'You bring news?'

'No, sir, we're heading southwest to join commander

Vespasian, we saw you as we came down and thought to ask if we could be of assistance.'

'Good man. Good man. But no need at all.'

But as he made the signal to mount and move on, it was evident that our governor had been struck by a transient thought. 'Ostorius.'

'Yes sir?'

'I've got someone here who might be of interest to you.'

He motioned the front row of troops to move a little and there I was, standing to attention, gripping tight my horse's reins.

Marcus took one step, then another, and as I saluted, he seemed to shrink.

Decorum being what it is in Roman society, and army life above all else, a sense of what is and what is not acceptable dictated that as he was my master and I his slave, it was down to him to speak first. 'But ... Siva,' was all he managed to summon.

The eyes of the entire company were upon us now.

'Sir.' I stood to attention

Later he told me that what he'd really wanted to say was, *Vulcan's iron balls, my friend, but what in the world has happened to you?*

Instead, however, he had to make do with, 'How pleased I am to see you after all this time.'

And mustering his last vestige of self-control, he turned his attention back to Plautius. 'Sir.'

'Speak up, we haven't all day.'

'Sir, I was wondering ... or should I say I am wondering. Yes, that's it, I am wondering.'

'Spit it out, man.'

'I was only thinking that perhaps, well maybe you would permit me to have a word with my freedman?'

The governor's voice boomed towards us, 'If you must, but we're heading off tribune Scapula, we don't have time to hang about until you've finished your chit-chat.' Luckily he spied one of the scouts from IX and dismounting, signalled him forward. Here was someone he could interrogate as to what was going on up there beyond the frontier; the Land of Horror as Leonatus had called it. A happy chance as this would give us more time.

We saluted, and Marcus led me a little way off and when Plautius and his unit were out of sight, we sat on a pile of debris left from the camp.

His expression changed from that of self-congratulation to one of utter humility. 'Siva ... The gods have saved me. I was desperate. I couldn't eat or sleep until I got the god-sent message that you were alive.'

I couldn't lie, he'd know I was and so I picked my words carefully. 'I thought about you every day until I got back to the XX and Quintus told me he'd sent word to you.'

'How in the name of all that is sacred, did you survive?'

I would have to tread carefully here, after all these years together he could read me like a book ... only tell him what's true. *Truth is easily forgotten, lies easily recalled.*

'I'm sure it sounds much worse than it was; at first I was terrified, but they didn't harm me.' *Quick, get on to the next part.* 'In fact, it was one of their fighters who took me back, to Vespasian's camp.'

'Thanks be that I knew it before I turned up. There I was, just arrived, all eager and raring to go, and what d'you think his first words to me were?' He did a very good impression of Titus

Flavius' drawl. *Your slave came here Ostorius, some several days ago. The one who was lost with the scouts. Simply walked out of the wilds and presented himself to us.* I thought he'd gone stark staring bonkers.'

'He took a violent dislike to me; accused me of spying for the Britons.'

'Yes, he told me. *A menacing looking individual* was how he described you. I scratched my head and tried to work it out. *Sir, that can't be Siva,* I told him, he's an elegant person, quiet, gentle, refined. *Oh it was him alright,* he said, *but he'd left all his elegance, gentleness and refinement behind him in the forest.*' He laughed and rubbed his hand across my shorn head. 'But now I can see how he might have got that impression.'

And here his tone changed. 'I'm sorry Siva, I should never have asked you to come here, but I didn't know they'd send me up-country and by the time I did it was too late, you were on the ship already. I thought you'd be safe with the auxilia.'

'Quintus said it was something to do with Cartimand …' I corrected myself, '… Cartimandua,' hoping he hadn't noticed.

'That's right. There was no way to get through to her but I knew if we won her over, she'd open the unknown lands to us. It's wild up there. You think the southern tribes are bad but they're nothing in comparison. The Brigante are somewhere in between. North of her they're untouched by Rome whereas many in the south have a history with us. The greatest difference between them and us is their mystic ways. And appearance. They look upon us as completely alien. I brought you for your beauty, and forgive me for saying this, Siva, for your appearance. If I presented you as part of Rome it might have led them to believe there are other aspects to us.'

'You mean I was strange enough for her to relate to me. Strange and odd.'

I let him sweat for a moment. 'Oh, um, well,' until I could bear it no longer. I burst into laughter and he followed suit.

'Well, I can't complain, it worked for me anyway; my appearance, I mean.' I had to make this sound genuine. 'They'd never seen anyone like me. I think I terrified them a little.'

Here came the question I dreaded. 'Why didn't they kill you with the rest, though I'm most happy they didn't?'

'They're a superstitious people, but I'm sure you know it. I imagine they thought that if they did there would be consequences related to some foreign god or other. After they saw my sunship, I mean.'

'And now you're doing what I had planned in the first place, but in a completely different guise.'

'Not really, it's Maxentius' job to soften them up. I'm just here to tell anything I might find suspicious ... spending a miniscule amount of time with the tribes makes them think I'm able to work it all out.'

'Be careful of her.' He looked at me intently. 'She's clever, not one to be underestimated, but I'm sure you'd have seen it right away. You don't look like your old, clever self but it's clear you are inside. But I should go now and get the men ready.'

It broke my heart to think that he was heading off to join Vespasian.

We got to our feet, but before we made our farewells, he gave me a sorry look. 'I would hug you, but it isn't quite form.'

And as we strode back to the troops, where he adopted an air of indifference, and keeping a business-like look on his face said in a low voice, 'I should be back in Dunum in a few weeks, but in the meantime, take care, old chap, I don't ever want to go through that again.'

I was becoming fairly satisfied with my new equestrian skills as I'd managed to keep up with the tempered members of the auxilia. Even they seemed relatively impressed.

'Thought you said you hadn't much riding experience,' this from a cavalry officer who spoke to me in Greek, grasping the chance to use his own language, 'but you're doing not badly at all.'

We were on the move again, keeping to the coast, where the salty air and marsh grasses were whipped around us by the wind. My thoughts were only of Marcus. The fire in his eyes had burned brighter than ever; he'd become even more passionate about the soldier's life. This 'rebel' country was where he belonged, here on the windswept marshes. To him, as to me, Rome was a world away.

A camp was made, and at daybreak we struck out again. A thick mist hung around us like a silky screen of frozen breath and soon our armour, our equipment, our weapons were covered in a film of shiny dampness; the surface of my leather knee breeches, my metal studs and buckles looked as if they were sweating cold tears. I remembered Petronius had told me that the thing the Britons feared most was that the sky would tumble down and crush them. Crossing the stone-planted plain with Cal and that day, too, it had seemed as if the heavens themselves had engulfed us in a cloud of frigid white, making it all but impossible to see as much as an arm span in front of us.

For several miles on we led our increasingly skittish horses. With every new sound, the whirring as a lapwing launched itself from the grass in front of us, or the crack of pebbles tumbling over the shelf of the cliffs, they strained their necks and pulled on their reins. Only with careful cajoling were we able to tempt them to pick their fine-legged way along a hard-packed path of sand, the mist tumbled away and the glinting swell of the ocean was beside us, a stretch of silver, its dunes sculpted by the winds, desolate and beautiful.

Sad to say that towards noon we turned away from the ocean and headed inland, leaving its surf-crashing presence behind us.

'Now that,' said the Iberian trooper beside me, 'I didn't like one little bit. If we'd been set upon back there in that mist we'd have been cut to pieces and our body parts cast into the waves before we could have done a thing about it.'

Presently, however, the ground firmed up, and the land became more undulating with craggy outcrops of rocks.

On our second evening, we reached the boundary ridges and our own guides, and the young boy who'd been sent out on a pony to keep us on course, led us across the border into Brigante country and towards a mound much like that of May. I recognised its sphinx-like outline far off in the distance.

'Not another bloody dun,' grumbled the Iberian. 'Sick of them I am.'

With the setting of the sun, the customary camp was dug. I was mightily relieved we'd made it this far unmolested; for though we were a unit of two hundred plus, just as the Iberian had put it, nothing would have been easier for a handful of Britons than the moving down of even a relatively large group like ours.

CHAPTER TWENTY-FIVE
BRIGANTE

When the guards were in place, Maxentius summoned me to his tent.

'So what happens now?'

Had Marcus been witness to such an event, the notion of his gentle slave being an authority on anything even vaguely related to military goings on would have baffled him entirely.

'I'm guessing here, sir. They might send out a welcoming party.'

And I was right. When darkness had closed in and a thousand stars were twinkling in the firmament above us, a guard gave the signal, and as we looked out over our ditches it seemed that a handful had detached itself from the galaxy to begin a silent drifting towards us. But as they approached across the plain, they turned into a pattern of torches.

When they stopped a little way in front of our camp it was evident there was nothing tamed about these chaps. No Roman edict had reached as far north as this, prohibiting a war-like demeanour, and relinquishing of arms. Or, if it had, they would have ignored it. They stood, huge men, hair limed in spikes, moustaches trailing onto their chests, wearing their multicoloured cloaks and breeches. In the light cast by the torches, the glint of gold shone out like bright fishes, caught in a net. Bedecked with it, they were. But I had a feeling that this wouldn't be even a tenth of what each man possessed.

Maxentius stepped forward, and though he must have felt decidedly small beside those giants, he wasn't about to have his status judged alongside his height. He was Roman, after all, and they nothing more than a bunch of savages.

Now it was down to our Gaul, a large chap with bright red hair pulled sideways in a thick braid, and almost as fearsome looking as them. The men eyeballed him, he eyeballed back.

'I'm to tell you that here is the delegation come up from Dun Camul to speak with your queen Cartimandua, in the name of our great emperor, Claudius Tiberius Drusus Nero.'

A look of amusement crept into the Britons' eyes. What else could we have been?

Maxentius turned to me. 'Why do they laugh?'

That's not laughing, I wanted to say, *you'll know all about it when they start doing that,* but had to settle instead for, 'I really don't know, sir.'

The torches flickered in the wind; an owl hooted, a bad omen for Maxentius but a good enough one for the Britons.

And now we were striding through a muddy, marshy field of reeds towards the dun; its outline loomed out of the darkness as we approached. First, we hit a stone path, but then the slurping noise made by our hobnails changed as we started along a wooden walkway. A few steps led to a bridge, covered by a roof but open to the elements on either side. Here I looked down, expecting to see water beneath us, but there was only a deep escarpment, rather like a fortress ditch.

Under the roofed walkway and out at the other end, the hobnails of the auxilia in front of me sparked as the path changed back to stone and puddles. We reached a gate. It was opened and we were inside, being led between the type of circular houses, their wattle walls and reed-stacked roofs achingly familiar to me.

On entering the Brigante hall, I was seized with a heart-rending sense of nostalgia. A fire blazed in the centre of the floor and shields with their skins of hammered bronze were ranged round the wall. Cartimand's men sat cross-legged in its circle.

The lady herself stood before us. Her appearance might have surprised Maxentius' bodyguards, but it didn't seem to have much effect upon him ... or the Gaul for that matter. And though I had the advantage of having been in her company before, I couldn't help but gaze at her unworldly appearance a little longer than I should have.

Despite my regalia, she recognised me straight away – how could she not? – and looked at me with distaste. I knew what was running through her head; was I here as the spy I'd agreed to become, or had I scuttled back into the flabby arms of Mother Rome just as she'd suspected?

What should I do? For yet another of the countless times since I'd left him, I thought about what my master would say and *Nothing* came the answer.

Maxentius sat himself upon the high campstool which his adjutant had carried in behind us as though it were a curule chair and he, Titus Larcius reincarnate, dictator absolute. Perched a good head higher than his audience he was no doubt feeling a great deal happier at the prospect of addressing the gathered assembly. I stood beside the Gaul. I may have been able to understand only a little of what she was about to say, but at least I could get the gist of it. And if I felt that gist was a reliable rendering, it would be valuable information to pass on to Claudia. My task, as well as being a counter to the man beside me was to pick up anything suspicious. I'd have to come up with anything at all that might seem of enough importance to keep hold of my value to Maxentius.

We were offered the usual un-watered wine of the customarily fine quality; the Brigante had, so far at least, managed to avoid the ravages of the invasion.

There was silence while the Gaul uttered once more all the proclamations he'd become so used to mouthing, ad nauseum, during the time he'd spent with the XX, all those long words about Rome and Claudius Tiberius Drusus Nero, God and Emperor absolute.

And, deigning not to utter so much as a word in the enemy's language, she spoke in a low, assured tone, and slowly enough to be translated with ease. 'I welcome you to my sixteen lands, the sixteen lands of my people, the High Ones. You Romans have come here as conquerors and now, with many of the southern territories lying vanquished in your hands, you plan to push west, into the lands now held by Caradoc.' So he and his men had moved west. I could but pray that Cal was with them 'If we battle against him, he will win. If we battle against you, you will win. To the north, beyond our sixteen lands, are those of the ...' Here she names three of what I took to be tribes. 'Should the war reach their borders they will join forces with Caradoc. Do you understand me, men of Rome?'

It seemed to me that her words were well translated, that the Gaul was to be trusted.

'Yes, yes, we understand. Now get on with it.' Or at least that's what Maxentius' lazy gesture was meant to imply.

'You will know that we Brigante are willing to ally ourselves to you.'

'In return for what?' He used language this time.

'That you leave my lands intact, that I will be free to lead my people, that Rome will hold me in esteem.'

Her request seemed rational, tantalisingly acceptable. And accepted it surely would be. But could it be true that just like Claudia's father, Cartimandua was incapable of recognising that any treaty drawn up between Rome and a small and still unvanquished domain placed on the frontier of her newest province would signify nothing, nothing at all? Rome would agree, her request would be upheld, but only until her Brigante were no longer of service to the invaders. Her lands would be used as a buffer between the tribes to the north and Caradoc's faction, now to the west; and, as ever, Rome would take advantage of the newly recruited subjects' lack of insight regarding the manner in which the masters of the Empire chose to operate, encouraging hostilities between her sixteen tribes and all the others. And then, when Rome had her hands on what she wanted, when it was all over, the legions would move in and Cartimand's dominion would be reduced to the lowly standing of a protectorate.

She was bound to know all this though, wasn't she?

I looked at her warriors, big men, fighting men. Did she have their backing? Were they in agreement? What did they think about what she'd just said?

Maxentius spoke. He thanked the lady Cartimandua for her offer, that if accepted, agreements would be set out, like this and like that. For me a simple pax would have been enough. But here, as I had so many times before, I found myself witnessing that characteristically Roman stratagem; it could never be simply a case of putting one's name to a treaty. Oh no, a little something of one's own had to be added, a requirement devised to put the other side at a disadvantage. So instead of saying, *Oh yes please, that's exactly what we came for*, he made a great show of pondering, as if he were wrestling with the pros and cons of the argument.

This was designed to unsettle her; she'd left herself nothing to barter with now the bartering had begun. But to give her her due, she made a first-rate job of concealing any sense of unease she must have been feeling, burying it in a guise of haughty disdain.

'On one condition.' Maxentius was on his feet now, pacing round the circle, the leather straps of his cuirass creaking in the stop-breathed silence. 'You talk of the rebel tribes. We require that you play your part in disarming them, the consequence of which will prove your allegiance to Rome.'

Impossible, her look implied.

'These are the governor's wishes. Unless you do just that, the cohorts of the IX and XIV will enter your lands and you will be forced to surrender.'

He was talking nonsense, of course he was. This was a spur of the moment addition. Put them at a disadvantage, make them beg; barbarians couldn't be allowed to wield the upper hand, couldn't issue terms to Rome. Only Rome could do that. Thus can a whole mighty nation be manipulated, the many by the few. But Maxentius had left himself a fair bit of leeway. If she agreed, well what a coup! If, however, she was unable to serve them up what they wanted, she'd be bound to plead with them to reconsider her original offer, and after a lot of humming and hawing that's just what he'd do. Whichever way it turned out, Rome had everything to gain.

Or so he thought, I wasn't so sure.

Cartimandua spoke again, and again the Gaul turned to her.

'Your conditions will be considered, and word sent to you in Dun Camul.' Though he said Camulodunum when interpreting her words, she had used the real name for the place.

Maxentius made his salute; his bodyguard stepped behind him to lift the campstool as he turned heel and marched out of the roundhouse. The company followed. The Britons remained impassive, sitting on the floor.

CHAPTER TWENTY-SIX
THE FLAMING TOWERS OF ILLIUM

Torches lit the path leading down to the gate at the end of the strutted walkway. Maxentius' men, able to take it three abreast at most, headed out ahead whilst I clomped along at the back of the column, thoughts dashing about in my head like moths around a lighted taper ... Cartimand ... Her intriguing response to Maxentius' ludicrous offer. Surely, she wouldn't surrender to Rome? I had to get word to Claudia as fast as I could.

The sharp night air, the stars ranged like sentinels above us, and silence filled only with the sound of hobnails striking the planks as they we went. We'd almost reached the end of the walkway when, out in the darkness, somewhere to our right, we heard a scuffling noise. I listened for a moment, thought nothing of it, and back to my pondering I went. But the scuffling grew louder and now voices could be heard and muffled cries. The company came to a halt. The noise drifted towards us and two Brigante came into sight, dragging a small, whimpering man between them. I looked once and then again.

Ye gods ... Petronius!

Had he been terrified before, now, at the sight of members of a Roman unit lined up watching, and as a deserter who'd succeeded in escaping the clutches of Rome all this time he was very near collapse.

'Siva Ostorius!' Maxentius boomed down the column.

'Yes sir.' My mind was racing as I ran forward.

'What's happening here?'

Petronius and the Brigante had stopped in front of our little group, but only because we were blocking their path. The rest of the unit were well ahead, thank all the gods.

'This man's not a Briton, he looks like one of ours. What in the name of Zeus are they doing with him?'

I stepped forward. Maxentius, his bodyguards, a couple of the Macedonian auxilia and our young Iceni guide were behind me now. The youngster apart, no one seemed keen on getting anywhere near the menacing fellows.

'You,' I barked. And with that Petronius' head came up. His slightly podgy, good-natured face was shiny with sweat, or more probably tears.

'Look at me when I'm speaking. I, Siva Ostorius Scapula.'

He fixed his stare upwards and relief flooded into his eyes.

'Let him go.' I spat out the words in my best British, and on hearing their language spoken by a 'Roman' like me, so surprised were the two giants, that's just what they did. But they had to grasp out at their captive to stop him toppling over.

'Who are you?' I bent down and put my head close to Petronius' so that no one would see that his lips weren't moving.

No reply.

'Petronius, something I couldn't quite catch,' I shouted out, 'sir.'

Luckily for Petronius, and for me, that with the main body of the company stopped beyond the walkway, Maxentius was too anxious to give his full attention to the performance being acted out before him.

I continued my interrogation. 'And from which cohort?'

No reply.

'The XIV,' my voice rang out. 'And what are you doing with these men?'

My little friend looked close to toppling over again.

As if to hear him better, I put my ear to his mouth. 'Snatched from a foraging party, sir.'

'Why, in Hades, is he dressed like that?'

'Perhaps we should ask him later sir. Poor chap looks half dead.'

'Take him then,'

So I took him, simple as that. The two giants stood back and watched as I escorted him out of their custody, the single question left for them to ponder being, *If our captive was a Roman why then, pray Bel, is he dressed sensibly, like any normal man, in a pair of good woollen breeches, while the rest of them clank along in their strapped leather skirts, toes sticking out from the front of their boots?*

'I've got him, sir,' I said, trying to dampen down my panic. We were walking back through the high marshy reeds by now towards our camp, a smudge of lights in the distance, stars scattered over an indigo background.

I had a good grip on my little friend, bending towards him as we walked. 'Ye gods, Petronius, snap out of it!' for he was reeling along beside me. A few more steps and he began to right himself. He glanced up.

'Keep walking,' I told him. 'This is what we're going to do then, are you listening?'

'... huh.'

'We'll go a little further on. Look, see that point? Are you looking?'

'… huh.'

'When we reach that point, I'll let go of you. Do you hear? Don't move, bury yourself in the reeds. Then once you reckon we're far enough off, make a run for it. Get back to the ditch. Hide under the walkway. I'll go on as far as is safe, then I'll start shouting, let them think that you struggled out of my grip. There, to the left, that's where I'll point, no one's going to risk heading out after you. Now, did you hear me?'

'… huh.'

'Understand?'

'… huh.'

'Look.' I was shaking him now. 'You're alright. You've just had a scare.'

He nodded.

'Good. Right then, I'm letting you go. Fall. Fall down … And run.'

He did as he'd been told, and on I walked, a good twenty paces behind Maxentius, before I started to shout. 'By Saturn, sir, he's run off. The blighter's just run off.'

The torches stopped and six of the company looked back, Maxentius and the Iceni lad amongst them. What I'd just said was as puzzling to him as it was to our commander. *Now what would a soldier of Rome want to do, running away from his own folks like that, especially when they've only just wrested him from our clutches?*

He scratched his head. And Maxentius would have done the same had it not been for his helmet.

I stood for long moments trying to steady my thoughts and emotions, struggling to make sense of what had just happened;

my little friend crashing back into my life. What was he doing here? And why had he been alone? But Maxentius and his guards were well ahead by now and I had to drag myself onwards. A few steps, and I started to question my sanity. First Petronius ... but was what I heard now part of my utter confusion? For in my dazed state I imagined that I was being engulfed in great wafts of smoke accompanied by the sound of crackling carried on the wind. I stopped and turned to see behind us the contour of the dun like some enormous beacon fire aglow in the dark of the night.

Desperate to find my little friend before he burned to death, I started to run back through the reeds and could see that the smoke was by far worse than the fire, which, incredibly enough was contained to the buildings. This gave me some hope that he'd still be alive, but by the time I reached where the walkway should be, it had tumbled, blazing into the chasm and lay there, smashed and burning. But peering across the stretch of escarpment I could see that the gaping ditch had kept the flames at bay.

A sense of power flooded through me, a kind of mad desperation. Off I set, along the outside circle of the ditch, peering into the well of blackness. The contrast of the flaming dun made the dark seem darker still. If I had the slightest chance of finding Petronius, it wouldn't be by staying up there on level ground. So, with the walkway gone, I forced myself down the ramp and up the other side, towards the glowing heat of the place, my feet slipping and slithering against the plane of its dusty surface.

Here chaos reigned. The walls of the houses burned ferociously, spewing out great bursts of sparks, whilst their rain-sodden roofs smouldered; the combination of water and fire giving rise to clouds of acrid smoke, which wafted around me like a searing sandstorm. My eyes felt as if they'd been pierced by hot needles, forcing me to stop in my tracks.

Great crowds of Brigante rushed along the puddled paths between the houses. I pushed against the tide and, clad in full armour though I was, could just as well have been invisible for all the attention they gave me as they sped past. Out of the yellow smoke, a herd of pigs careered towards the rampart wall, honking and bleating, knocking me flat. And there I lay, my face pressed against the now hardening mud till they passed.

As if this wasn't enough, a sheep sprang frantically at me. I kicked out and, as I did, my foot pushed against what felt like a leg. Then came a voice.

'Siva, Stranger!' it seemed to be shouting.

So streaming were my eyes by now, I could see nothing through the smoke but I knew that voice more than I could ever know one. Cal pushed me forward and together we slid down into the sanctuary of the ditch. Sheltered from the smoke, my vision cleared enough to let me see him looking at me, much the way that I must have been looking at him.

He clasped his arms around me. We knelt there together for some time. A heartbeat boomed in my ears. I understood his fractured mix of words and tell them now in proper form.

'I waited till you were bound to be halfway to that camp of yours before I touched the flame. What brought you back?'

Mind in turmoil, I opened my mouth but nothing came out.

'Siva,' he shook me, 'listen, will you? What is it you've come back for?'

'You did this?' I heard my voice say at last.

'Of course.'

'I should have known you were here when I saw Petronius.'

He shook me harder. 'You saw him, did you?'

'Back there.' I pointed behind us. 'I rescued him if you could put it that way.'

Before I could finish my sentence, I felt the rough of his hands as he grasped my face and kissed my forehead. And, as he did, above the booming and crashing of buildings collapsing into the inferno, came the blast from a war horn. Maxentius had ordered his troops from the camp, and now they were out on alert. There being no time for words, I pulled the sunship over my head and looped it over his. He grasped my shoulder in farewell, scrambled back up onto level ground and disappeared into the night.

I laughed very loudly, then followed suit.

The first person I came across as I battled my way through the smoke was the Gaul, stumbling as badly as I, his face blackened, his braid singed to a crisp.

'Who did this?' he asked, a question of the rhetorical variety. 'Was it us?'

'I don't know.' I endeavoured to look as perplexed as he.

'I came back to find you. You just disappeared.' An act of courage and kindness; I'd find a way to repay him, but there was no time to tell him this now. I had to think fast. 'That little chap. I went after him.'

'Do we stay here, or what?'

Was there any use in telling him at this late stage of proceedings that despite my armour I was exactly like him? A person of no rank at all, apart from my scant knowledge of things that were British.

'We should go back. We're separated from the company. We can do nothing. Let's leave it to the auxilia.'

Happy to comply, he slid after me down that infernal ditch

and followed as I clawed my way up the opposite side. The smoke had lessened by the time we got halfway back through the field of reeds and we could see a phalanx of guards ranged round the perimeter of the camp, javelins in one hand, swords in the other.

'The tribune?' Having gulped down great lungfuls of burning smoke I could barely whisper to the one closest to us, but he understood and signalled towards a tent.

'What is all this?' Maxentius boomed when he saw us. As expert on all things British, I had to think fast, his fury was simmering, cold.

How to turn the whole ghastly but fortuitous episode round to set it to our advantage? By 'ours' of course I mean the Britons.

'It was meant for us, sir. I had a feeling that something was wrong, but there was no way to warn you. When we left, I thought we were out of danger.' And as I strung out my story it struck me that I was fast becoming a master of disinformation. 'I can't be certain but am as sure as I can; she wished to target us as we crossed the bridge. But the Britons aren't Roman. They plan in a haphazard way. Had it been us, sir, we would have known exactly when to set it alight. But they were too late, and by the time they did you had reached the other side of the bridge. And something else they didn't take into account was the wind. It blew the embers towards them. We saw what came next. The little Roman must have been one of their captives. He was trying to warn us. Now I think upon it, sir, he didn't run away, one of their arrows must have got him.'

Where was such a fantastical story coming from? Homer could have hardly done better. Perhaps I had missed my mission in life.

Now was the time to plant the seed deeper. 'Far from being an ally, she has declared war upon us.'

And as if to quell any doubt that he was in control of the situation, that he'd simply asked for my meagre opinion, he said, 'This could turn out nicely, freedman Siva.'

I knew what was bound to come next but looked at him as if at a loss. 'She has no choice but to beg our forgiveness. But we shall not give it. I will destroy her.'

Oh, he was clever enough, but I would have bet ten thousand silver denarii that he would meet his match.

The auxilia guard stood by the tent flap; Maxentius jerked his head towards the Gaul. 'Take him and find out what you can about this bloody attack before she comes into my presence.'

I doubted she would be doing that in any great hurry.

We turned and made our way back towards the still smouldering dun.

'How can we do that?' In contrast to my joyous state of mind, the Gaul looked thoroughly wretched. His life with the XX depended on his grasp of the situation. Here was my chance to help him now.

'We can't. We'll wander around and maybe we can pick something up. But if not, we'll just stick to my story.'

He seemed happy with this arrangement and for the third time that night I slithered down the now fire-cracked slope of the ditch. The auxilia at the other side held out their hands to haul us up.

'Any idea what it was?'

They shrugged, it wasn't their place to have ideas, only to follow orders.

Their rear rank captain came towards us through a hail of floating cinders.

'They've scarpered. Not a frigging one of them to be seen. I reckon it was some other set of barbarians ... now they're fighting amongst themselves.'

This was too close for comfort. 'No,' I said, 'I did think so myself but the commander has proof it was her.'

'But why burn your own place down?'

'An unintentional consequence, the wind blew the flames in the wrong direction.'

His head now filled with my concocted theory, he turned to his men and roared the retreat.

As we waited for them to assemble, all I could do was think about Cal and had to tell myself to stop smiling.

I returned to Maxentius' tent, accompanied by the unfortunate captain, where we were faced with his rage; the words lax, sloppy and ten of his men crucified to teach them a lesson – I felt I had to step in.

'Sir, if I may speak,' I managed, during a pause in his shouting. 'I hadn't thought it important to report that though the Britons have few skills in warfare, they do surpass us in one, the art of secrecy and deception. No one could have suspected what they had planned.'

Appeal to his pride, now. 'The mistake they made, at least in my opinion, was to believe that with the standard of the Victrix fluttering on the edge of their dun, and you not yet inside its protection, they had succeeded in their plan. It all came down to timing. They are a garrulous people who make long speeches, and knowing this,' which surely he hadn't, 'you spoke briefly and left before the order to fire could be given. You beat them at their own game sir.'

Had he been scrupulous enough to go over this tale he would have known it made no sense at all. But he wasn't and it served its purpose; Maxentius could go back to Dunum and turn his failings into triumph. The Gaul glanced at me thankfully; he and the captain, to say nothing of the ten poor unfortunates who would have drawn the short straws, were safe, if only this time.

No need to say that before even the smallest chink of light came into the sky, tents were dismantled, horses saddled and we were heading back south.

*

I was in the slave quarters, going over Cal's words. 'I waited till you were …'

He'd attacked the Brigante as a warning against joining Rome. But what if it was cleverer than that? What if they'd wanted the Brigante to think that Maxentius had given the order to torch them? What better way to make sure that Cartimand would swear to remain their enemy rather than become a vassal? What better way to make sure that she wouldn't join them?

No longer would Cal and his Catuvellauni allow themselves to be outsmarted. They had started thinking like Rome.

A sense of euphoria filled me; I must have laughed out loud.

'Are you alright, dear?' Polydorus looked at me alarmed. Poor, gentle Siva wasn't made for riding out with all those horrid, rough auxilia. And if they forced him to do it again, it would only be a matter of time before he cracked.

'Lie down for a while and I'll bring you a little infusion.'

I looked grateful and would pretend it had soothed me. How could he have guessed that I was on a mission, and raring to get started.

The first thing was getting word to Claudia.

By the time darkness fell I should have been exhausted. Sense told me to sleep; give myself strength for tomorrow. But that was the last thing I wanted. I went out to the watchtower instead. The lookouts, pleased to have an extra pair of eyes, welcomed me aboard.

It was a clear night; stars twinkled above us. I thought of Cal. Now I knew he was alive, still part of this world, I had an even greater sense of being one of his tribe, that he thought of me as a brother in arms. Until this past time my life had been nothing; I had tagged on to Marcus but now I had become the main character in my own story. Rome knew me as one thing, Britain as quite something else. Surely the gods had plucked me from the path upon which I'd been travelling to set me on this new one, had given me a second chance, if you could put it like that.

Till now the conflict with the Britons had been an uneven fight but even with its levelling out I felt a dreaded certainty that, as they had all over the world, the legions would be the victors.

Wars are won by brute force, or such had always been the case. But now there was another weapon for the Catuvellauni were beginning to think in a new way; only guile and outsmarting the enemy had a chance to prove me wrong.

No one knows when they will die, or where, and so I wondered if for me it would be back in the City, my ashes placed in one of the hollows carved into the wall of the Scapula tomb, or here in Britain, buried in some unknown place, deep in a forest.

I prayed it would be the latter.

CHAPTER TWENTY-SEVEN
ERIS, THE GODDESS
OF STRIFE AND DISASTER

At the prescribed time, I made my way down to the stables and thanked Fortuna; my auxilia friend was preparing his horse for its trip to the river.

He seemed pleased to see me.

'Do you mind if I tag along?' I asked. 'I need to get away for a while.' He understood the feeling.

'Heard you were up there with Maxentius.'

'Yes, I was.'

'They're stupid, those Britons. They can't even get a fire attack right. Ended up burning their own place to cinders.'

After he'd chuckled and I'd followed along, he said, 'I'm Servius, by the way. And this one,' he nodded at his horse, 'is Gracchus Sempronius.'

Where did these men get their sense of humour? To name a horse after the banished man who'd had an affair with Augustus's daughter, even if the name was the wrong way round, was a brave act indeed. But I supposed with the notion of facing death every day, humour was the only way to help them get through it.

'And I'm Siva.' I didn't add Ostorius, and, sensing I might

be doing a lot of this with him from now on, I chuckled again. 'Isn't naming horses against orders? And more importantly, exceedingly dangerous with that one.'

'Not if we keep it to ourselves.'

After this short conversation, and away from the babble, we walked silently as he led Gracchus Sempronius through the gate, and down towards the tweedy water meadows and the river beyond, Servius regaling me with camp stories of the hilarious kind. Swallows darted low in the sky, catching insects flitting about us.

'Just going to stretch my legs,' I said as off I set along the riverbank, and, thankful for the willows which gave me cover, disappeared out of his sight.

I found a place where the water was shallow, took off my hobnails and began wading through it. A few steps onward, it became deeper, a current of tremendous force popped up as if from nowhere; my old self would have struggled to go any further for the water was numbingly cold, but that didn't bother me now. The field on the opposite bank sloped upwards, and at the top of the rise stood Cogidubnus' house. It was much like his other, but very much smaller, the standard of the XX fluttering above it in all its glory.

By now I was desperate to be with Claudia again. I thought of how she had looked when she'd come with the sunship, her tiny bell earrings, her cheeks smudged with cinnabar, Maxentius chuckling, 'I have a feeling she was happy to see you.'

I quickened my steps towards the house. Two men stood at its entrance, one broad and well-armed, the other thin and dressed like a servant. He smiled and stepped forward. 'I have come to visit the lady Claudia,' I managed in my poor British.

'Please come this way, sir,' he replied in Latin, 'I'll tell her you're here.' He led me into a porchway, whilst the broad man set off with some urgency across the open field. I followed him along a low, dark corridor and into a long wood-clad room. Claudia appeared from a door at its end. My heart filled with joy but, 'Siva Ostorius,' was all she said. This was too cold a greeting, even for her.

Standing behind her, the guard gave me a look of commiseration and said, 'My lady, would you like me to leave you for a moment?'

'No,' she snapped, 'stay.' But changed her mind. 'Go then, I will call if I need you.'

And when he was gone, I smiled at her gently. 'Claudia,' but she didn't reply. Her cold and sullen demeanour had returned, whatever rapport had existed between us was well and truly gone.

'Don't even think of coming anywhere near me,' she said next.

This shocked me to the core. 'Claudia,' I said again and here she shouted for the guard. 'Please take this man away.'

Back along the corridor, stepping aside at the porchway, and with the same sympathetic smile the guard let me pass him. 'Good day, sir,' he said in a tremulous voice.

Head spinning, I bade him farewell and set off back towards the river, this time walking downwards rather than up.

Claudia Cogidubnus was certainly the strangest woman that ever I'd come across in my life. The morning we'd spent in the badgers' sett had tempted me into thinking that we were making some headway towards being friends, and, after all, she had risked everything to visit Maxentius, had brought me my sunship, had put her message in it. I had imagined that I might have been falling in love with her, but now this illusion was shattered; we seemed to be back where we started. Her manner had disconcerted me so badly I cast my mind to find a reason. Why tell me *find a way to come to me* if she didn't want to see me?

I was so trapped in my thoughts it was too late to feel the silence close in around me, to see the dead horses, blood swirling through the water, to hear the gates across the river clanking open. Trumpets blaring. Men shouting.

I stood, uncomprehending, but I should have run before the dark curtain blocked out the light.

CITY OF A DIFFERENT GOD
A.D. 46 continued

CHAPTER TWENTY-EIGHT
THE HOUSE ON THE QUIRINAL

The flopping of slippers; shuffling footsteps. Quintus was shaking me awake. I failed to hear the first words of what he was saying.

I tried to listen more closely. Why was he talking about weather? There would hardly be time to pull on my breeches … my cloak … hadn't he said I had a couple of days before the auxilia set off?

I was flying through a dark void.

I was a bird with outstretched wings.

But I didn't wake amongst the stars; instead I lay beneath a blue sky, in a place surrounded by pots of lemon trees. I gazed up.

Flashing images: I tried to catch them before they were gone.

A life past or a life just begun.

A whispering voice. *'Siva. Siva.'*

'Siva. Siva …' His voice had changed.

I blinked up at him, but it was Ares who stood above me.

'I'm sorry to wake you …'

What was he doing in Quintus' hut?

'… but something has happened.'

I did my best to fix my vision.

'... Man ... Door ... Message ... Important ... Siva, Siva. Can you hear me?'

Then he said, 'Petronius.'

I knew that name ...

A light shone above me, swinging in the draught.

'*I wonder if you'd be kind enough to bring me a little water.*'

'*Oi, Oi, what has we here, a gentleman of the Hebrew persuasion.*'

And now I could see ... the lamp was the sun; this was the garden. I only wanted to shut my eyes again and dream it all forever.

Ares' voice now, 'You must look at it, Siva. It's important.'

He held a square of something so small I could barely see it.'

'Look,' he said, 'it's your sunship.'

How could that be?

He helped me sit, balanced my pillows around me and held what seemed to be a scrap of cloth close to my eyes. 'Look what it is.' He shook me. 'Siva, it's your sunship.'

And peering at it I saw he was right, for drawn upon it was a curve above which hung a circle.

Visions of smoke billowing around me. Taking it from my neck, looping it over Cal's.

'Remember you felt yourself strong enough to walk out for a while. It was too much for you, we should have stopped you for when you came back you fell ill. We left you to sleep ... it's been two days now. Perhaps it is good that I had to wake you, only because a man came. He told the guards his name was Petronius, that he was with you in the White Lands. The White Lands,' he said. 'That he's got your sunship, Siva', he said again, 'he's got your sunship.'

It didn't make sense. I asked if I was still dreaming.

'No,' he said. 'You're awake.'

I looked around me; the garden was as it always had been. The din of the City swelled beyond it; a flock of birds swooped above me; if I was an augur, I'd know what it meant. I tried to pull my thoughts together.

'I'd have left you to sleep, but he wants you to meet him. At the Sandilarius crossing. They told him that you were unwell, but he didn't care. He said you must get there, even if you have to be carried.'

I swung my legs over the side of the couch upon which I'd been lying, and sat for a moment, and when I finally found my voice I said, 'But he's in Britain.'

The memory came then, falling from Fabius' litter, a little man shouting, 'Siva. Stranger. Look it's me. Siva. Look it's me.'

Mistaking my bewildered expression for one of disbelief, next he said, 'I'll get Demitrious and he can tell you himself.'

Who was he?

He looked at me, baffled. Could I not remember? Demitrious Siva ... one of the guards.

'Ah yes,' I said as if I had.

And off he sped.

I sat in a daze, and after a while I gazed about me; the garden was as it always had been, the trees in their pots, the crocks filled with water, the marble satyrs ranged between them. I tried to pull my thoughts together but there was no time, for Ares appeared with the guard called Demitrious who greeted me as if he knew me.

'Tell Siva,' said Ares, 'the man who came with the message, what was his name?'

Demitrious nodded. 'He said it was Petronius.'

'What did he look like?' came next.

'If you want my honest opinion, someone who lives on the street.'

'That's an overall description,' replied his interrogator, 'you need to be more precise. What height was he?'

'A little bit smaller than usual.'

'And the colour of his hair?'

'Grey … sticking up all over the place,' and warming to his task. 'He spoke with a Suburan accent and had a hood-like thing round his shoulders.'

Which was all that was needed. An energy filled me; the gods had sent him to me. I tried to batten down my emotion. I looked at Ares and though I'd asked him a moment ago, perhaps things had changed. 'Tell me again, is this real or am I still dreaming.'

'No Siva … I promise it's real.'

'You're to meet him at the Sandilarius crossing.' Demitrious repeated what Ares had told me, but here he added, 'He'll be there at sundown.'

I thought I heard Ares say, 'I wish you'd told me this before, we don't have to rush.'

When they left me, I lay back on my pillows and tried to untangle the images whirring around in my mind. Fabius' voice floated out of the jumble, *one who's returned from the region of Hades*, but how could my little friend be here as well?

It was warm; a perfume of lilies hung in the air. No longer able to lie in my torment I walked to the wall and looked down over the palaces and villas of those who governed the City. Pine trees spiked between them, the smoke of fires already lit wafted slowly upwards, the trundling of handcarts and babble of voices swirled around me and I thought of the stillness of Britain.

Pictures superimposed in my mind, facing Cal at the camp at dawn, dangling in the darkness of the pit, his arms around me, the horns of Taurus flashing below. Of the morning we'd set out to Vespasian's camp, of the frost-covered ground, the ghost-like trees, the opal sun, more like a white moon than anything else, and I longed to be there. A great sadness filled me.

And how could Petronius be here in the City?

I heard again the crackling of flames and saw his slightly podgy good-natured face, shiny with tears.

'Look at me when I'm speaking. I Siva Ostorius Scapula.'

Fixing his stare upwards, relief flooding into his eyes.

I struggled to retrace my steps; there was more to remember. What was the last thing, the last thing in Britain?

Claudia, her cold expression. Making my way across grassland towards a river, stillness around me. Dead horses lying in its slow-moving water. A whirring around me, then darkness and nothing.

And Petronius? How could he be here in the City? How could he have known I'd be on the Sandilarius ... when I hadn't even known it myself, and it was now that some of my old wariness returned. It was noon and Amun's rays shone down upon me, but even he couldn't grant me patience to wait.

I summoned enough strength to call for Ares; he came running, a look of panic upon his face.

'Why did he say to meet him at sundown?'

His expression changed from panic to pity, what little grasp of reason I'd possessed until now was fading before his eyes. But he sent for Demitrious even so. And when he appeared his answer filled me with relief. 'No, it was me. I was the one who told him to meet you then. I thought it would give you time to gather enough strength to get there.'

Sundown was one thing but I knew he'd be waiting long before then.

'I'm going.' I pushed my feet into my shoes and started along the path.

Ares rushed after me and pointed at my crumpled, sweat-stained tunic. 'You can't go like that.'

But appearances were the last thing on my mind.

He tried again. 'It's the festival of Neptune,' as if this would stop me in my tracks. I struggled to remember what that was, with a lack of success I may add. '… and the streets will be crowded. We should wait till things calm down a little.'

But these words had the same effect, and to this day I thank him for his next ones. As I turned away from him, I heard him say, 'Wait, I'm coming with you. But we have to be careful as we leave, Gratius is back from Cumae.'

Gratius. The name seemed to mean something to me, I thought for a moment and unlike Demitrious I knew who he was and said some ugly words.

Emboldened by my reaction to this piece of news, Ares abandoned his restraint. 'He's been tormenting us all since he got here; we'd forgotten how bad it could be. But look,' he said, 'if we bump into him, we'll say we're going to the temple, to thank Adione for your safe return.'

CHAPTER TWENTY-NINE
THE MADNESS RETURNED

Not a word came from Ares until we reached the foot of the hill, where we stopped by the fountain. And though I had walked all the way from Cogidubnus' house to May, and all the way back again, who would have thought it, for now my strength was completely gone. He forced me to sit on its edge while he filled the scoop with water. He handed it to me and tried to persuade me to rest for a little but I stopped for only enough time to drink.

Every step of the way my mind was in turmoil. Petronius. How could he be here? Had he come back with me? Why had he been on the Sandilarius when I hadn't even known that I'd be there myself. How had he known where to find me? I scoured my brain. Had I ever mentioned my master's house? 'Ye gods,' I all but shouted out loud, but thanks to Neptune and his feast day, the streets were as crowded as Ares had said, and he was the only one who heard me.

The further we went, the stronger I started to feel; if I'd been firm enough on my feet I'd have run, so desperate was I to find him.

'It's not far now,' said Ares, and he was right for the arch of the theatre loomed before us only a little way off. The

Sandilarius came first, however, which, festival or not, was always a throng of bustling hordes. He went first and pulled me after him through the crowds; it took us a fair time to get to the edge of the crossing. And when we were there, I squeezed his shoulder, and after I'd thanked him for helping me, told him to go back to the Quirinal; he couldn't be away gone for too long.

'But how will you manage?'

'Don't worry, I will,' I said, 'and there's always Petronius.'

'If you're sure.' He looked up at me with the greatest concern and when I smiled and he felt it safe to leave me he set off back through the teeming masses, but he'd taken only a few steps when I called him back.

'You wouldn't happen to have any money?'

He searched in the fold of his tunic and produced a few coins. 'I'm sorry,' he said, 'it's all I've got.'

I thanked him again and with what I could see was the greatest reluctance he left me to stand in a state of foreboding scouring the sea of faces. But after a moment I caught sight of a blue hood and my heart filled with joy. When I shouted his name, he dodged through the crowds, and when he reached me he tried to smile.

'By Sacred Jove,' were his first words, 'you looks in a worse state then me!'

We stood for a while, arms wrapped around each other, and when I found my voice, I said, 'Petronius, my long-lost friend, what in the name of all the gods?'

His eyes filled with tears and I knew that some hellish thing must have happened. As usual, the taverns were overflowing so we sat beside a horse trough. I put my arm across his shoulder and felt his despair. And when he spoke, he told me something that even before my mind had been reduced to its present state, would have been out-with my capacity to comprehend.

'Cal … 'e's been took.'

'What?'

''Ere,' he said, ''es been took 'ere.'

What could he possibly mean?

'Locked up, ain't he.'

But even though this made no sense, I heard myself asking him, 'Where?'

'Like I said, 'ere.'

Was he saying he was here, in the City?

But he wasn't listening. 'Captured 'e were.'

Had my madness returned? Yes, that's what it was, my madness had returned.

'Were in a battle with them there legions of yours and 'e were took. Putting him up in the arena, or so I'm thinking. Games is on for the feast.'

And somehow I knew this was real.

There are places within us, dark places better not to know about. And most people travel along the path of life, never having to look down into their depths.

This was more than all my agonies put together. We sat for a long time in silence before he spoke again, 'We 'as to get him out. And you is the only one as can do it.'

I held his gaze for a very long moment and heard my voice say, 'I will. I promised I will.'

He gave a weak smile and only now did I see how ill and gaunt he looked, and it hit me; to add to his misery he was hungry, so when he said, 'And I 'as more to tell you,' I thought it best that he should eat first and sent him to the tavern beside us.

For that brief moment, I sat in a stunned state trying to take in the horror of what my little friend had just told me and then to make some sense of it. Cal had been captured. He was here in the City. They were putting him in the arena. But when …? And who or what would he be facing? If it was animals he'd have no chance, but if a gladiator, he could have a little. Ridiculously and futilely, I began to think of those he might have the skill to defeat. A secutor but not a net man. Maybe a murmillo, but would he be strong enough to fight? What kind of wounds did he have? Was he with others, or was he alone? If only he could speak to me through the darkness of my mind, tell me where he was.

'Tell me where you are,' I whispered and was glad that my nightmare thoughts were brought to a close by the little man who'd come back with all Ares' coins would afford; wine, three sausages and some pies. And as I watched him thrusting them into his mouth, I knew I'd been right; he hadn't eaten for a very long time.

'How in the name of the gods did you get here?' I asked once the pies and sausages were gone. He slurped the wine as he told me a most incredible tale.

'Got me a lift in a boat to Over.'

Over, I seemed to remember, meant Gaul.

'Then one down the coast. Then I hid in another one to some sodding place called Massilia. Then I were arrested, then I escaped and hid in another one to here.'

And how did he get from what I assumed had to be Ostia?

'Walked, didn't I?

'By Numa,' I gaped at him. 'You walked? All that way?'

'Were nothing,' was all he chose to say.

And how did he know where to find me? I meant here on the Sandilarius when he'd seen me with Fabius.

'Didn't know nothing. It were the gods. When you fell out of that there litter, I asked someone if 'e knew who you was, an 'e asked a man with a monkey. An 'e knew. Said you was Publius Ostorius' slave an his house were up by some gardens or other. Didn't know where they was so he told me near the Vetus.'

'Dear Heavens … Petronius.' I thought about what Demitrious had said, that he looked as if he lived on the street. Where was he staying?

'With me brother,' he said, 'still 'ere in the City. But 'e ain't up to much.'

'Come back with me and I'll get you some money. It's my master's house or you could stay there.'

'Don't you worry, me old son,' he smiled. 'Money'll do the trick for me. But listen, I got something else to tell you. Cogi … what's 'is name's daughter, she's 'ere as well.'

If I'd thought I could take in no more, here I was doing just that.

And though there was little point in asking what he meant, I did anyway. Just to make sure.

'You mean in the City?'

He nodded.

It's said that the gods burden you only with what you can bear.

'Why?'

'Dunno, but she's 'ere, and that's a fact.'

'Where in the City?'

He looked at me blankly.

'You don't have even the slightest idea?'

He shook his head, and I felt that his spirit was fading. 'Couldn't do nothing to save him.'

I clasped his shoulder. 'But look what you have done; more than any man could contemplate. You got on three boats, walked all the way from the port. You're right about the gods, they set us both on the street the day you saw me. And when that didn't work you tracked me down. These are phenomenal feats. And now it's my turn, my little friend. I'll move Olympus to find him and I'll move Elysia to get him out of wherever he is. But first come back with me. I'll get you the money.' I was thinking as I went along. 'And then I'll go and find her.'

'Who?'

'Cogidubnus' daughter.'

He gave me a horrified look, but before he could interrupt my flow of thought, I went on. 'What happened to me, do you know?'

'Was attacked.'

'By whom?'

'Slingers,' he said.

'But where did they come from?'

''Er.'

What did he mean by her?

''Er. Well not 'er, 'er men.'

'Who's her?'

'Her, Cogi … what's 'is name's daughter. And they say she were the one who handed 'im over, then 'e were sent 'ere by that shitting bastard Vespasian.'

It was fury that kept me going. The fury that would make me remember where she'd told me she lived in the City.

We walked together back to the Quirinal, along the Sandilarius, up by the temple of Sallis, the fountain. It was late afternoon by now and though somewhat cooler, still too hot for those accustomed to the mists and snows of where we'd both come from. Climbing took energy we did not possess and so we stayed silent until we reached the Scapula house.

Petronius was the first to speak. 'Some place this is.'

I could only agree, and so caught up in my tribulations was I, I would have passed Demitrious without thinking. But he stood when he saw me. 'How did it go? Did you find him?'

'Yes, yes thank you, I did.'

'And?'

'All is well.' But I could see that he knew I was lying.

I thanked him again and without saying more crossed the atrium, his eyes surely boring into my back.

One of the old boys saw me. My mind must have started working again for I remembered his name was Charmides. 'Ah Siva, I heard you were well enough to go out, you look a little better.' I didn't have time to wonder what I must have looked like before.

I thanked him and without saying more, dashed along the corridor and into my old, familiar room where I emptied out my bag of coins. I picked out five denarii, enough to last him for a fair while; better to have given him those of small value, anything larger might be considered suspicious. But five coins of some worth were easier to hide.

Back through the atrium, luckily there was no Demitrious, another guard sat in his place by the door and headed back out onto the street where I handed over the coins. This was more money that ever he'd had all at once in his life. And thinking of how he might be challenged about being in possession of what amounted to a month's wages, I told him, 'If anyone crosses you, send them to me.'

'You's a good 'un, Siva, and we thanks the time Cal found you.'

This touched me very greatly, and I told him so. 'But you're the one to be thanked. You led me into my new life, and for that I'll forever be grateful.'

He gave a modest smile.

'Go to the Sandilarius every day from now,' I told him. 'Get there early and stay until late. Only because I don't know when I'll be able to meet you but I will. I promise. And if something should happen to prevent me, I'll send a boy called Ares to find you.'

I would have thrown my arms around him, but for the fact we were on the Quirinal. Instead I grasped his shoulder and heard my voice say, 'Don't worry, my friend, I'll find him.'

He turned to go, then turned back again, and feeling under the neck of his tunic pulled something over his head. 'Almost forgot, didn't I?'

And as I looked at the sunship, all I could say was, 'But I left it with Cal ... at the fire.'

And I knew we both remembered that night, how I'd saved him from Cartimand's guards and no matter how bad it had been then, that we wished we were back there.

'Gave it to me,' he said, 'for safes keeping.'

CHAPTER THIRTY
CLOSE TO THE TEMPLE OF PORTUNUS

Back in the house, past Demitrious now back in his place, giving him a little wave, I sat on my bed. 'Think Siva. Think.' But I was too anguished to do much of that: Cal was the one and overriding person in my life, Claudia quite another. I had dared to think of her as the woman of my heart, but it was ripped open now. She'd been playing a part all this time; she had set a trap for me and I had been caught.

I saw the dead horses in the river, Gracchus Sempronius among them. But I had to clear my mind of all this for it hit me, no longer was she an odd and curious ally of the Britons, she was their enemy, which meant that as she was well and truly a part of Rome, she would know where he was.

But where was she, that was the first thing I had to work out.

'Think, Siva. Think.' And when I did, I remembered she'd told me that her father had a house in the City but where had she said it was? Once I'd have remembered without effort, but now I had to go over the times we had spoken. Or perhaps when we'd spoken the longest.

Not on the night when she curled my fingers around the sunship.

Not on the night I'd come to her with Cal.

Not when she'd taken me to the badgers' sett. *There's no time to talk about all that now.*

The next day then, after she woke me. It could only be something to do with her father … then I had it. *If he's lucky, they might leave him our house by the Tiber. It's close to the temple of Portunis and isn't grand enough for snatching.*

The gods were with me still.

I crashed back through the house, tumbling tables, across the atrium, thanking the gods that once again Demitrious had abandoned his post by the door, down the steps, taking them three at a time, past a *group of* tambourine players, surely the ones I had cursed so badly, down to the fountain, the Clivus Salutis, turn left at the theatre, along by the river till I reached the Aemilius bridge.

The house was close to the temple of Portunus, but which one was it?

I approached the guard at the first door I came to. 'Excuse me but would this happen to be the house of a Claudius Cogidubnus?'

He signalled to his right with his thumb, and I was faced with a high ivy-clad wall, at the end of which was a barred iron gate. The only way in was by pulling the bell that hung outside it.

This was the moment I realised how I must look, standing there in my crumpled tunic, stained even more now with sausagey fingermarks, hair on end, my feet stuck into unlaced shoes.

Back I went then, round the temple, along by the river, turn right at the theatre, the Clivus Salutis, the fountain, the hill. Up the steps, into the atrium, the house boys standing in silence, staring, the tables, now back as they had been before. Charmides stood at the end of the corridor, his eyes betraying his thoughts, *Poor Siva. Poor, poor Siva.*

He followed me to my room and asked if he should tell Ares that I was back.

I almost said yes, but he would want to know what had happened, and though I was desperate to tell him, there was no time. 'It's late, I'd hate to disturb him, and I'm in a terrible rush.' Amazed at what I could drag from my brain, I told him that something had happened, that I had to visit the father of an officer still back there in Britain. I pulled at my revolting tunic. 'He's patrician; I can't go like this. I need a toga. I wonder if I might borrow Marcus.'

'Are you sure?'

I was.

'But it hasn't been chalked since he left.'

My hair. Comb it. My stained tunic, off. A fresh one on.

Charmides stood holding the length of creamy cloth. And now he was helping me, draping and tucking. My head was too muddled to realise that this was the first time I'd looked like a Roman.

'Thank you,' I said.

He looked at me, sadly.

Walking this time, since a toga and running are two things apart, and added to this the fact that I'd never worn one before. Back past the house boys, through the atrium, down the steps. The tambourine players, the fountain, the Clivus Salutis, the theatre, along by the river, the guard at the first house, the ivy-clad wall.

The bell beside the iron-barred gate, I pulled it. When nothing happened, I would have pulled it again, but I had to be patient, I had to seem as if I were normal.

A whole lifetime later, a figure appeared. A very old slave bent almost double. He peered through the gate with rheumy eyes.

'Sir?' he said.

'Greetings,' I answered, all civility and good manners. 'I have a message for the Lady Claudia. I wonder, is she at home?'

'Yes … but …'

'Would you be so kind as to tell her one Siva Ostorius Scapula …' mere mention of that name and the old slave's mouth opened wide '… recently returned from Island Britain, would like to have a quick word. I wouldn't disturb her at this hour but the message won't wait, I'm afraid.'

He made a little bow and scuttled back along the path.

A moment later he was back, accompanied by a large man. The large man was a Briton, no doubt about it, though how he was dressed, in a tunic with swirling yellow patterns, was the least British thing I could think of.

A key was produced, the gate opened, then locked behind me.

Through a shadow-filled courtyard, the Briton leading the way, the old slave scurrying behind us. Out of darkness, through a lamp-lit atrium and into a room beyond it. At the far end a small figure stood very still.

I strode towards her, booming out for all the City to hear, 'How very good it is to see you, Claudia Cogidubnus, and after all this time.'

She saw the madness in my face and turned to make her escape, but she was too late for I had her by the wrist.

The Briton was beside us by now. 'Everything all right, my lady?'

I answered for her. 'Never better. Never better,' and though I used Latin, the very fact that I'd understood what he'd said … well.

'A little stroll, wouldn't that be nice?' I tightened my grip.

The big Briton thrust his face against mine, and whilst Claudia, knowing what was bound to come next, reassured him that all was well, that I was a friend of her father's, that she had to go with me, that she wouldn't be long, I unfastened the key from his belt.

She walked silently beside me, through the courtyard to the end of the path where I turned the key in the lock and we were out onto the dark of the street.

A wayward wife, an unfaithful lover, that's what anyone foolish enough to be about at that time of night would think when they saw the impassive patrician in his toga calmly pulling the bare-footed woman behind him.

I turned into the market of Cuppendis and we were engulfed by the perfume of roses. The flower sellers were gone, its stalls were empty at this time of night. I stopped by the first one and pushed her inside it, and when I looked at her with disgust, she scowled and shouted, 'It's not what you think!'

'How do you know what I think?'

'I do, I know.'

'Come on then, tell me.'

'You think I betrayed you.'

'I don't think Claudia, I know.'

'Then you know wrong,' she kicked out at me.

A mixture of despair and fury rose up inside me.

'Go on,' she stood defiant; her face blotched with anger,

her hair stuck to her forehead, 'kill me, if it makes you feel any better. But if you do, you'll never know what happened.'

I let her go on talking. 'It wasn't me, you idiot. It was Cartimand. She was the one who sent her men to kill you and she was the one who captured Cal and gave him to Vespasian.' She held my gaze. 'You have to believe me.'

I crouched on the ground all covered with petals, Marcus' toga unravelling as it slipped from my shoulder.

She knelt beside me; her breath was warm against my face. 'Why do you think I've come to Rome? It's the last place I'd ever want to be.'

Language had escaped me.

'To find you, that's why. You know what happened to you, don't you?'

The horses in the river, the blood, the trumpet sounding the alarm, the gate banging open, darkness closing in around me.

'Don't ask me why, but she thought you were the one who planned the fire. She set a trap. Her men attacked you at the river. They were going to kill you that day when you came … it's why I acted as I did. I wanted to make you leave as soon as I could. The troopers found you … they came down just in time. It was Cartimand,' she repeated. 'She gave him to Vespasian as a bribe to keep her lands.'

I looked up and saw her fierce, unsmiling expression was gone, and in its place the tear-stained face she'd tried to hide from me the night she thought Cal was dead.

Her next words were not what I'd have imagined. 'Please help me, Siva. Please help me. I said I had come to Rome, but that's not exactly true; I was sent here. My father banished me … he was going to send me to Gaul but I pleaded with him to let me come here … because I wanted to find you.'

This shocked me to the core.

'Someone told him that I was working against him. He called me to him and asked me to explain. I was so stunned by what he said, and there wasn't time to think clearly, so I denied it. He didn't believe me ... why would someone accuse me of such a thing for no reason? But I could tell that he didn't entirely believe them either, and so he sent me to our house near the camp until he decided what to do. To begin with, our own guards were there. They were given orders to keep me inside. They thought it was for my safety. I was distraught.

'I asked them to let me visit Tribune Maxentius, but, of course it was you I wanted to see. I used the sunship as a reason. When Cal had recovered enough to go back to the White Lands, he wanted to get it back to you. That's why I had it. After we met with Maxentius and I gave you my message, I prayed to the gods that you would come soon. I was desperate; I had to tell you what had happened, that I had been banished. But then I heard that he'd taken you north, to speak with Cardimand. Then I heard about the fire. That she was sure that you were behind it. I thought I would never see you again. I thought you would never come back. But you did, thank the gods.' And here I could see she was crying.

Every sense in my body seemed to stop. I put my arms around her and felt her tremble.

'I was desperate; I had to warn you that she, and all our enemies, wanted you dead. They'd been told you were spying against them as well.' In her distress, she repeated what she'd just told me. 'Then you went to Cartimand with Maxentius. Then there was the fire.' She paused to find the right words. 'She was sure that you ... and I ...were behind it. She sent her men to the house. My father's guards were bad enough, but hers were more like gaolers. When you came to see me, I had to make them believe that we had nothing to do with each other. They thought I was guilty … if it seemed we were friends they'd have known that you were as well. But I didn't know they'd been given their orders already. My poor servant tried to help me but it was too late.' I saw his stricken face again.

'Cartimand's guard went off to tell them that you had arrived. When you left, they were ready with their slings. I don't know why they started firing before you reached the river, but they did and the horses were killed. When my father heard what had happened, he knew that he couldn't let Plautius believe the charge of setting her place on fire that was bound to be made against me. He had to prove he was loyal to Rome, and so he started a rumour that it hadn't been Cartimand who ordered his men to attack you, but me. And that's why he had to send me away.

'Then there came news of what had happened. I was distraught because I'd put my message in the sunship … and I knew that when your unit returned you would come. And when you did, I couldn't let them see the slightest hint of friendliness between us. I had to get you away as fast as I could. I knew nothing of what would come next. Please believe me, you've got to believe me.'

I smoothed her hair and looked into her eyes.

'I do. I believe you, and as far as Cartimand's concerned, she hated me from the moment she saw me.'

'But you were there with your tribune. Wouldn't they hate him more?'

'No, it was before then, when I went to May. She was there. Caradoc sent me to reason with her, but she wouldn't listen. And as far as the fire is concerned, Cal was the one who did it, he hoped that Rome would think it was her for if they did, they'd destroy her.'

She was quiet for too long a time. 'That's why she had to give them a gift as valuable as him … She had bought him from the Atrebante and offered him up to Vespasian.'

Exhausted by our emotions, we sat for a moment, and then I said, 'We met, just after he'd set light to the place … he was entirely back to his old self, even after what he'd been through.' We smiled because we knew what that meant.

I told her about the bridge walkway, the wind blowing the flames back into the compound.

'That night when you brought him to me, I felt I could see Britain dying.' There was a long pause. 'I was in love with him, you see.' Another pause. 'But he didn't know it.'

My heart went out to her then; she had loved Cal and she had foretold the future, and only now did I understand her wild reaction to her fear of the terror that was to come.

They're putting him in the arena.'

She grasped my hand and looked into my eyes. 'We have to save him.'

'I will die trying,' I said.

And as she looked up at me, her face crumbled. 'Oh Siva, I'm ashamed. I've treated you so badly. I beg you to forgive me. I want to explain.'

I unwound my arm and took her hands in mine, no need to encourage her to speak, her words poured out in a babble, it was hard to keep up with what she was saying.

'The first time I saw you wasn't when you think. It was at Samhain. I knew nothing about you before then, but when they told me that you were with them because you'd been caught by a raiding party, had changed sides and had agreed to work for us, I began to distrust you. Britons know little about Rome and her tactics, but I do. How could a man from the legions join us so easily? But I was prepared to give you a chance, but then you didn't meet me on the cliffs. And then you came back with Cal. I thought it was a trick of some sort. I thought of so many wild things. That he would be used as bait to take them to Caradoc. But I had no choice, I had to send him away; he couldn't stay in my father's lands.'

So she hadn't trusted me.

And now her hostile reaction towards me made sense. I had always laid faith in my intuition, but it had let me down.

'The boys took him back to the White Lands and when they returned, they told me that Caradoc thought of you as his saviour and I knew I'd been so wrong.' I unwound my arm and took her hands in mine.

'I had just arrived here, when I heard what had happened to Cal. I knew who you were and I knew how to find you, but I couldn't put you at risk. It was an agony, I was distraught … but now you've found me.'

'They're going to put him there … to fight.' Her voice was very small.

'We won't let them do that,' was all I could think to say.

Silence closed in around us and then came the question, 'You don't know anyone who owns gladiators, by any chance?'

I was about to say 'No' when it hit me.

We sat there together until first light came into the sky. She was dozing, her head against my shoulder, but when I moved, she woke.

'What are you going to do?' she asked.

'Get him out from wherever he is.'

'How?'

'I have a friend. If he can't help us, no one can.'

I kissed her head, her hair smelled of jasmine. 'And you?'

'I have to go home.'

We walked back to her gate. I looked down at her. 'Let's meet at the same place tomorrow night … if you can get away.'

'I can do anything I want,' said she.

As we parted, I asked, 'You said you saw me at Samhain?'

She wrapped her arms around me and laughed. 'Haven't you worked it out yet?'

I hadn't.

'Do you remember someone hitting you with walnuts? She didn't wait for an answer. 'It was me.'

It wasn't till after we parted that I realised I hadn't told her about Petronius.

CHAPTER THIRTY-ONE
FABIUS LICINIUS RUFUS

It was too early to summon Demitrious with his key and I really didn't want to anyway, so I scaled the garden wall and got in that way. I stretched myself out on the couch, still there in the garden and thought for a while, and when I knew what I'd do, I walked back into the house. The first person I met was Charmides, carrying a tray. He stopped in his tracks.

'Siva,' he said, 'where on earth ...'

'Don't worry,' I told him, 'I'm all right now,' which was true for hope had sprung into my heart.

He looked at me with unbelieving eyes.

'Really I am. But I have to get this thing off. Would you give me a hand?'

And after he had, I put on a fresh tunic and he helped me shave. I'd have hired a carriage but it was morning now, the City gates would be shut to traffic, and so I walked all the way to the Fontinalis across Mars Field and along the Via Tusculanum.

It wasn't yet mid-morning when I got to Fabius' place. Funnily enough, he was at home. I couldn't help noticing that the new slave boy who let me in had a golden leaf stuck in his hair. Fabius was stretched out in his bed; it was strewn with plates of fruit and crumbs from a pulverised cake. He was suffering, I could tell.

He peered at me from under a circlet of the same golden leaves. 'Darling Siva, what a wonderful surprise.'

I got straight to the point. 'Fabius, old friend, I need your help.'

He pulled down the covers and patted a space, and when I had settled myself beside him, he chose to remark upon my appearance. 'Venus save me, you look like a corpse warmed up. The world is not a place where you should be gadding about. Stay here with me forever,' he said, 'and I shall look after you. Have some cake, you look positively starving.'

He shouted, 'Hyacinthus,' to which the same slave boy appeared. 'Bring Siva some breakfast.' He turned to me. 'What would you like, my favourite person?'

'I'll have some after I've told you why I'm here.'

'You can eat and talk can't you, or have you left that facility somewhere back in the wilds of Britain?'

I tried to hurry him along. 'With every moment that passes, I'm closer to disaster.'

'Some fruit, some cheese, some eggs ... one of these patty cakes.'

I thanked the gods that Hyacinthus had picked up something of my panic, and helped by saying, 'Oh dear.' And as Fabius told me to fluff up his pillows, 'I need to be comfortable whilst I'm listening,' he scuttled off and reappeared with a tray piled high enough for a tavern.

'The floor is yours.' Fabius took the circlet from his head and put it on mine.

'Am I right in thinking you own gladiators?' An unnecessary question, for I knew he did, though only the favourites, who always won and had their names plastered over walls, even those in the forum.

'Well, well,' he gave me one of his looks, 'are you thinking of changing profession? What would suit you … let me see, you could be a pharaoh tussling with a pack of lions … or would that be cheetahs if we were thinking of Egypt. But that wouldn't work as you're not really that anymore. Maybe a retiarius, I fancy you could be quite good with a net.'

Which was the last thing I wanted to listen to, but I had to let him go on like this for a while for what I was going to ask him to do was the most dangerous thing that he would ever face in his life.

When he let me speak, I said, 'No one knows what I'm going to tell you, but I was captured when I was in Britain.'

It took a moment for this to make traction in his mind. He sat up and blinked. 'When? By whom?'

'A tribe.' And to suit my cause, I began to think in a theatrical way. 'I was with a group of auxilia. We had pitched our tents at the edge of a forest. It was only just light when we were set upon.'

He shrank back, clutching his neck.

'There were sixty of us, fifty-nine were slaughtered.'

He let out a bleating sound.

'I'm the one who wasn't.'

'In the name of all that is sacred, how did you manage to escape?'

'I didn't. Someone saved me.'

'Did they appear from the forest at just the right time?'

Best to say yes. 'I owe him my life, and more besides. But now he's been captured by Vespasian; he's putting him in the arena.'

Nothing came out of Fabius' mouth; this was the first time I'd seen him struck silent.

'I need to save him. I'm begging you; please can you help me?'

He thought for a moment. 'If you're using the words *I'm begging you* there's no need to add please. It's one or the other. But in case you're wondering, yes, I will.'

My life had returned.

'So tell us about this chappie, won't you?'

'His name is Calgac, and he belongs to the Catuvellauni.'

Only now did I realise how little I knew about him. But I needn't have worried about this, for Fabius only asked, 'What in the name of Mercurius do these words mean?'

'Calgac, Swordsman … Catuvellauni, War Chiefs.'

'My, oh my,' he said again, 'it all sounds so exciting.'

Placing a finger to his lips, he said nothing for a while then, 'But you should ask Ares. He and his friend have joined this silly new cult everyone's raving about. It's led by some idiot fisherman called the Pebble.' He grinned at Hyacinthus; for he knew what was about to come next.

'Not Pebble,' Hyacinthus said wearily; it was obvious he'd heard his master say this word a hundred times if not more. 'The Rock,' and turning to me, he added, 'but his real name is Peter.'

'Whatever it is, it will all end in tears. Come on then, do tell … we want to know about this rock person.'

I had a feeling that Hyacinthus might have abandoned the conversation at this point, but he'd heard my story and what he said next was for my sake.

'He might be able to help you, but I can't really say. I'm just a newcomer, Ares has been with his temple for longer than me.' Did he say Ares? Surely the fates were with me still. 'He comes to the rescue of poor folks, especially those who're in trouble with Rome.'

'Then he's the very one we want,' Fabius exclaimed. 'How do we find him?'

I explained to Fabius what Hyacinthus clearly knew that he was one of our own group of slaves up there on the Quirinal.

'You must talk to him, say that I told you to do that,' said my new friend in need.

'How long do we have?' I thought to ask next. There was nothing that Fabius didn't know about the games; what if it was only till tomorrow?

'Now, let me see, until Saturni. Which gives us three days. Let me work out a few odds and ends with Hyacinthus. He's bursting to help us. And whilst you're waiting, take a bath ...' he looked me up and down, 'you really need one.'

How many times had I dreamt of this place. The steamy water, the finches in their cages. And when I'd been in my own one, hanging from the side of the hut, could I have imagined that one day I would ever be here again, but in my tortured state would not be able to enjoy it.

'Behold! A clean man come to join us,' Fabius announced, when I emerged, raffia slippers upon my feet. 'Come and join us my sweet, we have worked out a plan. I will let my clever darling speak.

'It's my master's task to free your friend from where he might be, that's something only he can do. But once he's safe we must find a place to hide him. This is where Ares fits in. You'll have to ask him; I can't tell you more.'

Fabius drew his eyebrows together. 'Have a little lie down first, you need to gather your strength.'

CHAPTER THIRTY-TWO
PETRONIUS

I would have run all the way back to Ares but first came my little friend.

I had allowed myself only the shortest of whiles to lie back upon Fabius' cushions, but that was enough to get me to the crossing in a somewhat revitalised state. And now, with the games only three days away, it was even more   crowded.

He stood in the same spot as yesterday. As I approached him, I thought of how changed he was compared to the first time I'd seen him; then filled with energy and purpose, a distinguished member of his tribe. Now, drained and bedraggled, blending in with all the poor folks passing him by as he stood watching for me. How could they have guessed about his high status, the fact that he'd sat with men you might refer to as kings? Or that he'd taken part in ceremonies presided over by those Rome called Druids? That he'd carried golden boxes filled with captives' hair? How could they have known about his part in Caligula's shipwreck?

But I did.

His face filled with hope when he saw me and I thanked the gods that I was able to seal his trust in me; things weren't as hopeless as they'd been before.

'My friend,' I said, hugging him to me. 'I may have the tiniest piece of good news.'

I told him about Fabius and Hyacinthus. How they had taken on the mission of rescuing Cal as if it were a game filled with risk and excitement.

'There's not much more to say at the moment. Rest, eat and get your spirit back. Where, exactly, does your brother live, in case I need to find you quickly? You said it was west of the Viminal.'

'Top floor of the fried dough shop,' he said, 'next to the vinegar stall.'

'It might be a couple of days until I'm able to meet you again.'

He nodded.

'And oh,' I said before I forgot, 'I called on Claudia Cogidubnus. I don't have time to explain it all.' But I told him as fast as I could. The important thing was that she hadn't betrayed me, that it had been Cartimand.

His mouth gaped open.

'In fact she was betrayed herself. One of her father's men told him that she was working against him. And so, in order not to lose face with Rome, he started a rumour that she was the one who had ordered my death. And then he banished her. I'm sorry, my old friend, I'll tell you more when we have time, but at the moment there's someone I have to talk to.'

I handed him a few more coins. His eyes opened wide. 'Find yourself an inn … there's one somewhere round here. It's called the Peacock'

He looked down at his raggedy clothes. 'But …'

'Tell them that Siva Ostorius has recommended them to you. And if there's a problem to take it up with me.'

And with that, I set off back to the Quirinal.

CHAPTER THIRTY-THREE
A PLACE TO HIDE

The gods were with me for I caught a fleeting glimpse of Ares in the garden watering the fig trees. I made my way across the atrium and called softly to him. He put down his can and came to sit beside me.

'Ares,' I said, 'I have something to tell you,' after which I spewed out my story. He knew that the little man he'd taken me to meet had come from somewhere called the White Lands. But he didn't know they were in Britain.

'He came all the way to bring me some terrible news.'

I told him about my capture, and how my life had been saved by a man that Rome had just taken captive.

'He's here in the City. They're putting him in the arena.'

He looked at me, horrified.

'The reason I'm telling you this is because I think you may be able to help me ... help him, is what I meant to say.'

'I'll do anything I can, but I don't understand ...'

'I have a friend. His name is Fabius Licinius Rufus. I think you know him.'

He did.

'And you know Hyacinthus even better.'

He did.

'I hope you don't mind that he told me you may know of somewhere we could hide him after Fabius rescues him, because that's what he's going to do.'

Ares looked at me blankly; did he have any idea what I was talking about, or perhaps he preferred not to get involved with something as dangerous as this.

I thanked the gods that after a moment he said, 'There's a man who goes by the name of the Rock.'

'Hyacinthus told me a little about him. Do you think he might be able to help us?'

I can't describe my relief when he said, 'Yes.'

'How could he do that? What I mean is, would he be prepared to do such a thing?'

And after a moment, 'He would be more than prepared,' said Ares.

'Would you be comfortable in telling me who he is?'

'He's the leader of the new religion. He comes from a place called Galilee bringing news of a man he calls the Saviour. He preaches love. Rome is afraid of him. They think he wants to become the new Caesar, but they're wrong. Being Caesar is the last thing he wants. What they should be afraid of instead is the fact that he's not afraid of them … or anyone else for that matter.'

My heart sank at this. Hyacinthus had only been trying to help, and Ares was too. But what could a man who preached love do to save Cal?

I grasped his arm and thanked him for spending time to tell me all this. I would leave him to get on with his watering, but as I stood to go, he said, 'Wait …'

Time was passing. I couldn't spend another moment talking about new religions and men who came from places like Galilee.

Then he said, 'You don't understand.'

I had wasted so much time until now, what was another moment?

'There may be a place he can hide ... you have to listen.'

So I did.

'Some powerful Romans, even Senators, follow this man. I'm not permitted to give you their names, but I can tell you one ... his name is Cornelius Pudens. They have houses. People in fear of their lives can hide in them, before they're helped to escape from the City.'

I struggled to find my voice, but Ares knew why. 'If you like I'll ask him, but I know the answer will be yes.'

Just at that moment, Demitrious appeared; a message had been delivered by a boy with a golden leaf stuck in his hair. He held a small roll of parchment towards me. It read *My dear boy, come to my place tomorrow at daybreak we're going to a slave prison.*

CHAPTER THIRTY-FOUR
THE WHISPERER

Though it was only the edge of evening, so desperate was I to tell Claudia what had happened, I made my way to the flower market. With the hope I now had, my dark despair was held at bay and I realised that I was incredibly hungry. I stopped by a food stall on my way and, thinking of those I'd turned down at Fabius' place, bought some meat patties and two small flagons of wine. Uncaring as to the stall-girl's horrified look, I rammed the patties into my mouth, gulped down the contents of one of the flagons – this action took no more than ten counts – and found my strength returning.

Walking along by the river I let my mind soar; there was a way to save Cal. And I was saved too. Fabius may have been vain and indulgent, but there was a huge heart under his bluster. I thought of the times I had sat on the benches of the Marcellus watching him entertain the audience who'd laugh so loudly at his outrageous performances he'd have to pause for the guffawing to die down enough to be able to start on his next joke. I was blessed to have such a friend.

And though it wasn't yet dusk, she was already there. The lingering heat of the day pulsed around us but strangely enough she was swathed in a cloak that seemed much too large for her.

When I reached her, she threw her arms around me.

I was sorry if she'd been waiting for long.

'No. No. I came early. I wanted to see you so much.'

'Do you notice anything different about me?'

She shook her head.

'Look at my face.'

She looked.

'I'm smiling.'

This was a little too much for her.

'Could there be a reason?' I asked.

She thought for a moment, but I had to help her.

'Maybe something to do with Cal?'

And now she was smiling too.

'Come, let's celebrate,' and as the market was still in full swing, with flower stalls everywhere and gentle chaos all around, I led her away, too exalted to take much notice of the fact that as we went, she hugged her cloak close to her body. We reached the river and sat beside the temple of Portunus.

'Before I start, let's pour a libation to the gods ... I don't mind if it goes by way of our throats.'

The wine was good, as is often the case when bought from these little family booths, and just what we needed. As I passed the flagon to her, I felt I had to ask, 'Aren't you hot in that cloak?'

But instead of answering yes or no, she opened it enough to let me see a long flat object wrapped in linen, and even before I had taken it from her, I knew what it was.

I unwrapped the linen, and there it was. I felt my heart stop, my happiness drain. I saw his eyes again, his face, the snake coiling its blue painted way across it.

'One of his men brought it to me. And now it's yours.'

A long moment passed. 'He called it the Whisperer,' I said.

Its hilt curled at each end and etched into its long blade were patterns; a curving line ran down it.

'That's the river,' said Claudia, 'protected by Sul.'

I knew this but let her go on.

'The goddess of water,' she looked at me with startled eyes, for she had just thought of it, '…and the sun.'

He and I were linked in a way I couldn't have imagined.

Would she remember what I had told her in the badgers sett, that when he ambushed us he was about to kill me like the others but he saw my sunship and that's what stopped him.

I took it from the neck of my tunic and we gazed upon it, and upon the Whisperer too. It was mine now … what had I done to deserve such a wonder. I was struck with a shuddering sadness.

Claudia saw this and shook me. 'I can't wait any longer. You have to tell me what's made you so happy.'

It took me a moment to push my emotions away.

'It was when you asked if I knew anyone who owned gladiators. It may seem strange, but I do. His name is Fabius Licinius Rufus … you might have heard of him.

She shook her head.

'He's an actor and the most loved man in Rome. He makes people laugh so much in the theatre they almost fall off their seats. He's fabulously rich and owns many things without caring much what they are. When you asked me that question it struck me. And so I went to see him. He's going to help us. He says he knows where Cal must be. That he'll get him out.'

She let out a little scream and hugged me, then she kissed me on my cheek. 'Thank the gods … oh thank the gods. But if he can't?'

And echoing what she'd said the night before, I told her 'He can do anything he wants.'

I was happy to see her laugh.

'He's taking me to a slave prison tomorrow. When we've found him, he'll think of a way to get him to safety. He says it's too dangerous to tell me how he'll do it.'

She thought for a very long time.

'But here's something else, his slave boy has joined some new cult, and so has Ares, he's one of the boys in our household. It's led by a man called the Rock, who's protected by a senator. Ares is sure they can hide him ... after he's been rescued. I'd trust Fabius with my life, not just because he's a friend, but because he rose up from poverty and knows what misery is like. And Ares and Hyacinthus because they're good boys.'

A moment passed; I could see she was thinking.

'This cult, is it more like a religion?'

'I'm sorry but I know nothing about it. Only that they worship a god of love.'

At this she looked extremely excited. 'Do you remember when we were in the badgers' sett and I asked if your sunship had anything to do with a new faith, only because it might have had been linked with fishermen ... And fish?'

I struggled to think and when I had I said, 'Yes.'

'That's their symbol. I've heard all about it. People are flocking to join them. Of course they say it's simply a fad, that it will fade out but I don't think so.'

'Do you know about this man called the Rock?'

'Only that he's the most unlikely leader you could find. He's simple and doesn't speak Latin too well.'

'It seems he comes from Galilee.'

'Where's that? I've never heard of it.'

'Judea ... somewhere close to the coast.'

'So strange,' she said.

'Ares is taking me to speak with this senator fellow, after I've been to the prison. He won't give me his name until he gets permission to do so. I've a feeling it's all quite secret. But there's one last thing to tell you. Did you ever come across a small Roman chap who'd joined Caradoc?'

'Yes,' she said, 'but only once.'

'Well, he's here now too. He came all the way from the White Lands to tell me that Cal had been captured. He's staying with his brother in the Subura. I'll bring him with me the next time we meet.'

She gave a gentle sigh, and I knew it was at the thought of the little man making his long journey back to the City, a place he surely hated as much as she did. I put my arms around her and we sat for a while, linked together in our sadness, gazing down upon the scene set out before us; the marble buildings, and those of stone, the shiny new bridge stretching across to the slums of the poor. How long would it take for the place they called Camulodunum to look just like this?

We were ready to go. As I lifted the Whisperer, she looked at me. 'Perhaps you should take my cloak to hide it.' And she was right. I had forgotten that weapons weren't allowed in the City; you could carry only the smallest of knives.

And on the steps of the temple, we stood with open hands as we uttered the prayer.

Divine Portunus Mater
May you look favourably upon us.
We pray to you that … and here I said …
you might free the friend
of our hearts

And lead him to safety.

We hoped she'd remember that we'd poured her libation already.

And though it wasn't a correct thing to do, out there in the open for all to see, I drew her to me and kissed her.

*

Ares was waiting for me in my room; he looked anxious. 'How are you?'

'Better, much better,' I told him. 'And I thank you for all you have done for me. I would have been dead without you.'

He shrugged and gave a shy smile. 'Oh, it's nothing.'

'It's everything, Ares. It's everything.'

Humbled by my words, he changed the subject. 'I've arranged for you to meet our benefactor at his house tomorrow after dark. It's not far from here. I hope you don't mind that we've taken the couch away from the garden. Now that you're better, we thought you'd like to be back in your room.'

And they were right, for here, away from curious eyes, I placed the Whisperer on my bed. If someone had told me that one day it would be with me here of all places, I'd have thought they'd partaken of some kind of mind-bending potion.

I looked upon its perfection and cast my mind back; I pictured it in Cal's hands the day we had fallen into the boar pit, and before then at the camp at dawn.

And as I gazed upon it, it struck me how little Rome knew about the Britons. Their wild, drink-crazed conduct is well reported but I had heard their music, played after nightfall, had seen the beauty of even the simple things they used, or carried with them; their ploughs and hoes and brooms and baskets, all crafted with care. And their fine things etched with secret patterns known only to themselves, their edges and hidden portions engraved with the same intricacy as those areas meant to be seen, interwoven marks of such delicacy, loops and spirals, the edge of a bowl, the rim of a beaker, the mouthpiece of a trumpet. Of all civilised men, I knew how privileged I was for I'd glimpsed beyond the ostentatious show of gold on arm and neck, had seen the decorated under-edge of a torc boss, the patterns on earrings, arm and ankle cuffs, the minute scratchings on the little bells which sewn into the hems of garments would be hidden from sight though not from hearing.

And colour. At first their strange mix of shades had seemed garish. But as I got used to it, I'd begun to wonder why, back in the southern lands, I couldn't have imagined green and purple and red lying so peacefully together in the same cloth.

I had also learned all manner of things relating to their idea of the world; how their trees and rivers and sky possessed spirits of their own, of gods who lived in secret places, in stones, or in wells, or under the ground, and their great celebrations, like Samhain, much like Saturnalia, though less taken up by debauchery.

I wondered if I'd ever use it and my mind, calmed by thoughts of freeing Cal, slept with it beside me.

CHAPTER THIRTY-FIVE
WHERE IS DARDANTIUS?

We set out from the southern gate on one of the hottest days I'd yet experienced in the City and travelled out along the Appia. The pine trees spread their branches above us, giving at least a little cover from the sun. Some way south the carriage was ordered to stop. Hyacinthus helped his master to clamber down; we left him to guard the carriage and off we set.

It was noon by now, and stifling. The sky was bleached the colour of milk. Lizards clung to stones; the air was filled with the sound of cicadas. A stony path led us forward. The hills were a shimmering blue in the distance; olive groves sheltered goats and goatherds asleep. As Fabius lumbered stoically beside me, beads of sweat trickled down his face from under the brim of his sunhat.

White walls emerged from the shimmering haze a little way ahead. A figure on a mule appeared; it seemed he was coming in our direction. An arrow, then another, zoomed through the heat-laden silence, to land a scant foot in front of us.

'Oh sacred gods!' cried Fabius, 'we're facing up to a madman.'

As our would-be assassin heeled his mule forward, Fabius made a heartfelt plea. 'Steady on, old chap,' said he.

The mule rider, Mauritanian, head bound in twisted, colourful scarves, now within hearing distance, shouted at us in a thick accent, 'You may trespass no further. Go back to where you came from.'

'Have you the slightest idea,' Fabius screeched back at him, 'whom you are addressing?'

The Mauritanian forced his mule to a halt, not the response he'd been expecting.

'I'm making this hike, and most uncomfortable it is, in order to visit Dardantius. Dear Dardantius, I happen to own him, as a matter of fact. This being the case, it follows that I own you too. So bugger down from that mule, my good fellow, and help me aboard.'

Which is exactly what the mule rider did. With Fabius' posterior bulging on either side of the unfortunate animal's back, we set off once more towards the mirage.

The white building solidified, and at a distance of about forty or so steps from a hole cut into its wall, we were hit by a smell of shit and sweat and boiled pig swill. Fabius pinched his nose between his forefinger and thumb.

A fat-bellied man, clad in leather breeches and nothing else, came wandering through the gate.

'Where is Dardantius?' Fabius released his nose for long enough to enquire. 'I want to speak to him. Now.'

'Oh, my lord,' replied fat belly, recognising a rich man when he saw one. 'He's in the City, readying things.'

'And who is in charge?'

'I am, sir.'

'Oh never mind, you'll have to do then.'

'Yes, my lord.'

'You have a Briton here, I understand, who goes by the

name of Calg … something or other.'

'A prisoner sir?'

'Pray what else would you find in this place?'

The fat-bellied man shuffled his feet. 'I can't give you an answer to that, I'm afraid, sir. The men held here have no names. Numbers my lord, but not names.'

My insides churned; I was desperate to throttle the fat-bellied chap and rush through the gate. But Fabius was in control, and he was a master of ploy and deception.

'Forget about names then, you numbskull. A Briton. Do you have a Briton?'

'I think we may, my lord.'

'Let's force our way then, Siva my sweet, into the midst of this ghastly stench.' He flapped his hand at the fat-bellied man. 'Lead on, dear chap,' he instructed. 'Lead on.'

Inside the gate, ten or so rows of cages, twenty per row, with inside each one five men, maybe more.

The wretches inside those facing the gate looked like spectres from battles fought at the beginning of time; starved and filthy, some dressed in rags, some naked.

'Lion fodder,' fat belly explained. 'But perhaps, my lord, you'll find your Briton further to the back. Those picked for fighting are kept there.'

Fabius took off his hat to fan his face. 'Oh you go, Marcellus, I can't take one more step.'

In the guise of Marcellus, whoever he was, I made my way down the left-hand row. A guard, well covered in body armour made of chain, kept two or three paces behind me. Men peered from between the bars of the cages, desperately pleading. Words came at me in different languages.

At the end of the main rows, two sections of railed fence

curled in semicircles towards the western wall, forty or fifty cages in all, one man to each. I started along the left-hand arc, taking it as fast as I could. I reached the end and started on the opposite one. The seventh cage, and I found him, crouched by the rail to which he was fastened, eyes closed, face raised to the sun. I took a tentative step towards him, then another. He opened his eyes and glowered up at me and my blood ran cold. I was back in the forest grasping his wrist, dropping the sunship into his palm.

'Cal … Cal,' I whispered, 'it's me.'

With this, he was on his feet, thinner than before, hair tangled, dirty. No whirling whorls of blue on his skin, no snake curling over his cheek, no golden cuff. No torc. All gone now, all things of yesterday. But still he was Cal, still strong, still him. His face: large nose, slanted lips, not beautiful in a soft, gentle way, a face I knew more, could know more, than any other.

For a moment he stood like a man in a daze, then he stepped towards me, his ankles shackled and bleeding. Blood meant nothing, and everything, to him and I felt a sorrow so deep.

The guard was too close behind me. If I'd had the chance, I'd have broken his neck. But I hadn't reckoned on Fabius, that devious manipulator of events. A scream came at us from somewhere close to the gate, and looking through the maze of cages, I saw him stretched out on the ground, sunhat awry, screaming like a stuck pig. My guard turned heel and raced back to where the drama was unfolding. And now, save for his fellow captives in the cages to left and right, we were alone.

He smiled and I saw his front tooth was broken. I pressed against my side of the cage, stretching my arms out.

He did the same, then he said – and I put this into my own words – 'Look up at the sky, Siva Dark Stranger.'

I followed his finger and what did I see but the moon. A moon adrift in the daytime sky.

'It's a moonship,' I said. 'Here to protect you through the black side of this time.'

'Or to carry me to my death.' And before I could say more, 'I know you're the one who's so terrible afraid of dying, but death is different for me.'

'I'm here to talk about life,' I said, 'so listen. At first light they'll take you from here to a fighting ground. Listen to me, Cal, are you listening?'

'I'm listening, of course I am.'

'Before you get there, you will be rescued. I have a friend who will,' I wanted to say bribe but knew no British word for this, 'give gold to a man called Dardantius, who will take you to a place that is safe.'

He clasped my fingers through the bars. 'I will wait.'

'I too,' I said.

'Until the stars fall from the sky.'

'Until they fall,' were the words I replied as the guard came clomping back towards us.

'There's one other thing.' I had to speak quickly and prayed he'd understand. 'Petronius is here. He came to find us.'

Engulfed by emotion, it took a moment for my words to sink in.

'I'm going to him now, to tell him we've found you.'

'Look after your master,' said fat belly, as Hyacinthus helped Fabius back into the carriage. 'He took an awful cramp in his leg.'

CHAPTER THIRTY-SIX
THE MOONSHIP

I wasn't in a good state when Ares led me down from the Quirinal and along to the Vicus Patricius. I could feel my feet dragging.

The white ghost-moon of that morning had risen, and now was full and round; the type I had called an Osiris moon, but forevermore would be a moonship to me.

'You're tired.' He looked at me with concern. 'When all this is over you must get some sleep.'

But it wasn't sleep I needed, only to know that Cal would be saved.

'Promise you will.'

I could barely reply. The thought of his cage, his face battered and bruised. *Pull yourself together, Siva,* I spoke firmly to myself, *you're no use to him in this state. You've only one chance to get him out. If you go on like this, you'll fail and he'll be out there facing up to who knows what.*

I thought of how he had looked the last time I'd seen him in Britain with fire raging all around us, his expression of triumphant jubilation. How I had strung the sunship round his neck. Those joyous days would return if I conducted myself in a decorous manner. It wasn't any old person with whom I would be pleading for help, but a man of great status. I had to present myself as a serious and sober person.

The house which was halfway along the street belonged to a different era, and like all old houses it stood a little way below level ground. In contrast to my master's pristine and polished villa it had a slightly neglected feeling about it, which helped to put me at ease. A few steps took us down to a portico supported by pillars on either side. I followed Ares along a path, which led to a plain wooden door of a type that might be the entrance to a tradesman's store, in front of which sat a boy. He and Ares greeted each other; it was clear they were friends. He asked if his master had returned from the forum, and if so, could he bring him the man in dire need, whom Hyacinthus had told him about.

'I think he's ready to see you but let me just check.'

It took barely a moment before he returned and led us along a dark corridor filled with the smell of incense, of a type used against mosquitoes.

We entered a room flooded with light from torches in a garden that stretched out behind him. The doors were thrown open and now I understood the need for the incense; the smoke of which filled the space here too.

A small, thin man, surrounded by piles of tablets and scrolls, not unlike those on Quintus' desk, stood up to greet us. He looked at me with great sympathy when he saw my condition, and though I had tried to disguise it, it was clear that he'd noted the pain in my eyes.

'My name is Cornelius Pudens.' He gave a gentle smile. 'I hear you have a problem.'

He signalled Ares to pull up two chairs and place them before him. Next, he asked if he would kindly go to the kitchen and ask for some refreshments to be sent. 'No need for cooking, anything they have to hand.'

This I found most extraordinary; when did a master speak to a slave, even should they belong to someone else, in such a courteous fashion? 'But something substantial would be nice. Sausages, perhaps,' which made me think of Petronius. He looked at us for our approval, I replied that he was too kind. 'And perhaps don't bother heating them, cold will be fine.'

With Ares gone for the moment, he settled himself and looked at me. 'Please tell me, how may I help you?'

Kindness is never a good thing when one is distressed. I closed my eyes and tried to stall my nerves. I had wondered how much I could tell him without causing problems for Fabius, but now I knew I need not worry.

'I want to rescue someone who's being put up for the games.'

We all knew what that meant, no need to explain.

'Tell me about him.'

'He's a Briton who was captured and taken here. He's important to me; he put himself in great danger to save my life.'

'He sounds like a good man … so you were in Britain?'

Just then the sausages arrived and handed round; Pudens took one to put us at ease, though it was clear that he'd eaten already.

'I have a friend who will rescue him,' I started, 'but we need a place where he can be hidden. If only for a short while.'

'I will be honoured to help you,' he said. 'We have young Ares here; I'm sure he won't mind acting as go-between. Only tell him where your friend lives and he can deliver information back and forward. The first thing I need to know is which games we are talking about. There are three coming up over the feast days. We have to arrange when your man will be rescued and when we are able to take him from Rome. There will be other points to think about, he turned to Ares, 'but that can be done by our messenger here. You only need to take care of your side of things; we'll do the rest.'

I lay on my bed, glad to be back in the calm of my room and it was only now that I thought of my dream; Cal in a carriage with Fabius, travelling along the Via Patricius, the very same road that Ares and I had just walked along. I had often feigned to possess second sight but now I knew I did.

CHAPTER THIRTY-SEVEN
GRATIUS

Ares had told me that the plan to save Cal had been arranged and had gone to deliver the news to Hyacinthus and tell him where he was to be taken once he'd been rescued. He seemed incredibly happy to do this, I felt that he regarded the task trusted to him by Cornelius Pudens with great humility, as a badge of honour. 'But I am sorry, you know I can't tell you where this is. At least for the moment.'

I smiled. 'Of course you can't,' I reassured him, 'it is for all our safety.' And here a wondrous thought flashed into my mind. 'I know I must separate myself from all this, but I wonder if someone else might be permitted to join him.'

Ares gave me a worried look.

'I'm only thinking about Petronius. He speaks Latin and the language of the Britons, and he could help you. He would be ideal.'

'Would you like me to ask Cornelius Pudens? He might not agree, but at least we can try.'

Filled with hope, I went to the Sandilarius, and there was the man himself, in his usual spot, anxiously looking in the direction from which he knew I would come. His face filled with relief when he saw me. I gave him my usual bear hug and said, 'I think we've done it.'

We sat ourselves down by the horse trough, and I began to spill out the news, but so quickly he could barely follow me.

'Slow down, me old mate.'

But it was a hard task indeed.

'We found him ... he's in a slave camp ... they let me speak to him ...'

... 'He can still speak?'

I couldn't be so cruel as to tell him the truth. 'He seemed in a fairly good shape after what he's been through, and his spirit was strong. I told him that we would rescue him ... And I told him that you had come to the City to find him. This meant more to him than anything else I could have said.'

And just like Ares, a humbled look washed over his face.

It was hard to speak slowly for I had so much to tell him. I speeded up my speech. 'The man I told you about, my friend, has arranged for him to be rescued on the way to the arena. This can only be done outside the walls, and then he'll be taken to somewhere I'm not permitted to know about, but only for the sake of safety. I don't know if it's for mine or his.'

*

Ares had come back with a message; all was in place I should be at Fabius' house the next morning as early as I was able. And though he wasn't as good at the task as Charmedes , with his years of experience, he helped me wrap and fold Marcus' toga around me in a vaguely acceptable manner.

Light had not yet appeared in the sky but Demitrious was already at his post by the door, but as I approached him I heard footsteps, and turned to see Gratius behind me, desperate to know who had dared leave the house without his permission.

It took far longer than a moment before he realised who, exactly, I was. He drew his eyebrows together and looked me up and down, and, though he was facing an entirely new Siva, he wasn't going to let that change his loathing of me.

'And where do you think you're off to at this time in the morning?'

Of course with my mind on different matters, his question took me unawares, and where the old me would have stumbled to find an answer, I stepped as close to him as I could and said, 'Out.'

And though this flummoxed him, he came up with another. 'And why are you wearing Marcus Ostorius' clothes? Where are your own?'

I stared at him with a hatred beyond compare. 'It's absolutely no business of yours.'

He faltered, 'I need to remind you that I am in charge whilst the master's away.'

I adopted a snarling tone. 'Then take it up with him when he gets back.'

As I strode past Demitrious, who gave me a very broad grin, I wondered why I hadn't stood up to our tormentor a long time before.

CHAPTER THIRTY-EIGHT
THE CIRCUS

'Tell you what we're going to do. No, let me correct myself, my sweet, what I'm going to do. You must keep well out of all this … you're hardly inconspicuous. And neither am I. My fame, forgive me please change that to infamy, may stretch from Patavium all the way south to Licea. Nothing they choose to do to me has the slightest prospect of tarnishing my reputation, in fact it would add to it most enormously. Fabius Licinius Rufus who freed the gladiator from the clutches of the powers that be. My oh my, after my little adventure you won't get a seat in the Marcellus. They'll be standing three deep in the aisles.'

I didn't know if this was bravado, after all he was an actor.

'When I get my hands upon your Briton, we will take him to somewhere he cannot be found. And you must stay away from there, or you will lead them to him.'

Should I confess about my plea to Ares, if Petronius might be allowed to join him … He misinterpreted my silence.

'I cannot tell you where he is … No I will not. For all that I love you, since your ignominious metamorphoses I am not sure I entirely trust you to act in the way you might have once before. But tell you what I will do, darling boy, when he is safe and enough time has passed, I will give you a clue as to where you may find him, and it will be for you to puzzle it out.

'The plan, then, is this. He could not be seized in the slave prison. And neither can he once they've ensconced him in the arena. And therefore, just in case your Ares hasn't been clear, he'll be snatched from the slave carts somewhere in between. And so we must check that they've not double-crossed us ... we'll go in before the games start. Make sure that our plan is fulfilled, in other words that he's not there.'

But what if he was? I pushed the thought away.

And by way of answer, Fabius produced an old and bashed bag. I knew it was filled with silver coins because he had told me.

*

Hyacinthus carried it as we jostled our way along the crowded throughfare that led to the circus where we took shelter behind the booths selling wine and flowers to be thrown at the stars of the day.

'My dear.' Fabius looked at me anxiously. 'I ask myself, is this really worth it?'

Hyacinthus came to the rescue producing a phial of something or other. Fabius tossed it back and after a moment or so returned to his old self. Armfuls of yellow blooms were bought and quoting his rude and hilarious poetry, he handed them, one by one, to members of the oncoming crowd. Thus we were able to wend our way through the multitude.

Forced to trundle along at a snail's pace, I felt my heart would burst. We reached the great gate; the crowd in front of us pushed its way through it; we followed on. The circus stretched out before us, no horses no chariots no charioteers, for today was the games.

I had only ever been there with Marcus. The races were bloody but what was about to happen here now was in a different league.

'Hello there, my good men,' Fabius swept forward, majestically, scattering his greetings like largess and, reaching the brutes he'd been addressing, now came the questions. 'That rascal, Dardantius. Have you seen him?'

No, they hadn't.

'Oh, not to worry. I'm sure you can help. Tell you what I'm looking for; a Briton. Fighting today. Ring a bell, by any chance?'

But no, it didn't. They went to look anyway but came back; no one remotely like a Briton was in any of the cages.

'I'd know if they were lying,' Fabius assured me. But to calm me, he asked them again. 'This barbarian fellow, are you sure he's not here? Really sure?'

They gaped at him, puzzled looks on their faces.

He turned to me. 'Look my sweet, if he were here, we'd know. Believe me. I pay them too much in bribes not to know.' He looked at me with thankful reassurance. 'And if I'm right, and he's not here, well what a good thing it is. Rejoice, I say, rejoice. You can but put one and one together. Please, my dear, don't fret.'

Just then one of Dardantius' fellow rogues was spotted, standing on the sand by the fighting pit, too obviously cursing that he'd been spotted. 'Well, well,' he said as he approached. 'If it isn't Fabius Licinius Rufus.'

Next followed a conversation that had much to do with the lining of pockets. Standing there, listening, I felt I would burst.

But there was method to my old friend's sudden interest in paltry sums of cash. 'I say Turpillus. You don't happen to have laid eyes upon a Briton, selected for one of the fights?'

Turpillus answered right away. 'Yes,' he said, 'as a matter of fact I have.'

My heart stopped beating.

A look of suspicion washed over his face. Next he asked, 'Why?'

'Wagers, Turpillus, wagers.'

'Well,' said Turpillus, trying to keep the glee from his voice, 'missed your chance then, haven't you?'

'Come on, dear chap, do tell.'

'Not here ... it was somewhere else,' was all he said.

'Oh, you know, you're such a cheater,' Fabius smiled. 'How could we ever believe you. We'll just have the tiniest check.'

The horde surged forward, but Fabius led us in the opposite direction and took to a stairway leading down. Down, down I followed Hyacinthus, an impossible feat in Marcus' toga. Fabius stumbled behind me, so close I could feel his breath on my neck.

We were underground now. A stinking, hellish place of low ceilings and noise, but Fabius seemed entirely at home.

'Water. A stool,' shouted he.

A young boy arrived, stool in one hand, pitcher with a cup suspended from it in the other. The stool was placed behind us, the pitcher handed to me.

Fabius sat himself down, and after he'd taken a sip or two from the proffered cup, he signalled to Hyacinthus who handed over the bag of coins. The boy took it without even raising an eyebrow.

'Dardantius!' instructed Fabius.

The boy scampered off. Moments later he reappeared, still holding the bag.

I was wracked with utter despair.

Fabius got up from his stool; I sensed something bad in the air.

'He's come down with the ague,' said the boy. 'Varrus told me to tell you.'

'Bring him to me … this minute.'

I hardly dared look at Fabius, his expression might tell me the worst.

Varrus appeared, a skinny nervous looking creature and after enormous bribes had been offered, we were led through great subterranean chambers.

'Look inside them all, my darling,' said Fabius, 'and shout if you spot him.'

'There are only seventeen cells, but he must have told you if your man's here it's where you'll find him,' proclaimed Varrus. 'Take your time, you've two hours at least.'

I turned from Fabius and forced myself forward. Small and low-roofed, the cells held fifty or so in each, the majority filled with men like the poor unfortunates out in the Appian camp; but five held, not gladiators as I'd imagined, but those who seemed capable of putting up some kind of fight … being killed straight away was far too tedious for the crowd. These combatants were armed with wooden shields, some had swords, others had pikes.

I peered through the bars of all seventeen cells, and then I went back and peered again.

He wasn't there.

And though my heart went out to the poor and wretched prisoners, my soul soared upwards. Up and up as far as the stars. Shaking now, unable to speak, I vomited onto the sand, saturated already with blood and piss.

Aware of a presence behind me, I turned and there was Fabius.

'He's not here.'

'Well, if you're like this under present circumstances, I wonder how you would be if he were.'

CHAPTER THIRTY-NINE
SUL

Filled with euphoria of a type that cannot be described, I sped back to the Sandilarius, quiet now for everyone was at the games, and there was Petronius waiting just as he had for all these days. One thing had changed, however, his face was scrubbed and his hair combed.

I was still thirty or so steps away, and desperate to put an end to his torment, I raised my arms in a gesture of victory.

I reached him but before I could tell him that it was sure now Cal had been saved, he pulled at my toga. 'Gods preserve us, you looks like one of them lot.'

'But I'm not, I'm still me. And what's more,' I shook him in jubilation, 'All's well. They've saved him.'

My little friend leaned against me, his nightmare was over; the pain and struggle since his capture had been masked until now and I felt his strength fading. He seemed in a daze as I helped him to the horse trough where we sat in our usual place.

'He wasn't in the cages, which means they got him away.'

'You sure about that?'

Yes I was sure. 'I was the one who went down there to look. I chose not to tell him about all the poor, wretched men I had seen there, he couldn't cope with anymore misery.

'Now, is the time for celebration,' I said, 'Ares will be here soon.' He looked at me blankly. 'Remember … the boy who made all this happen. And then we'll go and meet Claudia and you can be the one to tell her.'

I left him sitting wrapped in his joy and went to the food stall to buy a measure of wine to drink as we waited, but as I looked at the range of offerings set before me on the counter an idea popped into my head. I added to it two flat oil breads, olives, onions, eggs with garum, chickpeas and snails wrapped in cabbage leaves. They'd be cold by the time we got there, but who could possibly care. And when I returned, I sat down beside him and laid my pack on the ground. 'We'll eat when we get to where we're going.'

He looked at me, slightly worried. 'Where's that?' But there was no time to answer for a voice came from above.

'I prayed that I would find you here.' We looked up and there was Ares. 'I think you will know it, but I wanted you to be sure. They have him,' he said, as he sat down beside us. 'They took him before the slave cart reached the Appian gate.'

Confirmation, if any were needed that my life was returned to me, and to Petronius too. 'I thanked all the gods I could think of when I knew he wasn't there. I don't know what we would have done without you, and this is Petronius and he doesn't either.' Petronius stood and they greeted each other. 'He has a wondrous story to tell but let us wait till we get to where we're going.'

As we approached the Temple Claudia saw me. And then she saw Petronius. As she came running towards us, he seemed to become peculiarly bashful – the first time I'd seen him like this – and though we had decided that he should be the first one to tell her, I had to step in. 'He's safe,' I said and when I took her in my arms she cried happy tears and when she had recovered enough I added, 'And this is Petronius, though I think you know each other already. And this is Ares, our saviour.'

We made our way down to the water's edge. By now the red globe of the sun was sinking below the Janiculum. We sat amongst the food and drank two of the three flagons of wine between us and poured the third one into the river.

'This is to Sul,' I said, 'goddess of the river that runs along the whisperer's blade' and Ares and I sat and listened as Petronius and Claudia spoke together, hesitantly at first due to his sudden bout of self-consciousness, then with such speed we found it difficult to keep up with their frenzied conversation; her father, her banishment, his journey, how he'd seen me on the Sandilarius when I'd fallen out of the litter, just about onto an oil vendor's head. How he'd managed to track me down.

It was Ares' turn now; he wanted to know about my strange metamorphoses. 'When you came back you looked like a different person. You had changed so much we could hardly recognise you.'

Not wishing to drag him into the danger of knowing about my stay with the Britons, that I had been given the honour of joining them, 'Army life,' was all I could think to tell him. 'Army life.'

Which spurred Claudia to think. Here was something of monumental importance, as far as she was concerned. 'What were you like before?' she wanted to know.

And the only one who could tell her was Ares. 'Beautiful,' he said, 'with long plaited hair. As if he belonged to a different world. The place where his sunship came from … and he was quite thin.'

''E were thin first time I saw him, 'an no doubt about it.'

She laughed at this unimaginable fact but then a new thought hit her; she turned to Ares, 'Are you allowed to talk about this new religion?' I knew she'd been desperate to ask him, and he was desperate to tell her about the man they called the Rock, how he saved those who were in trouble with Rome. How people flocked to hear him speak, how so many were joining his cause.

She looked at me, 'Do you think Cal will?' But I felt she knew the answer.

And now Ares said that he had asked Cornelius Pudens, and if Petronius wanted, he could join him … a joyous shock to my little friend.

'Any place 'e is,' was his reply, I want to be with 'im.'

CHAPTER FORTY
UNTIL THE STARS FALL
FROM THE SKY

We were a strange little company; a pale-skinned lady of high rank, a slave boy, a veteran of Caligula's legions and a priest of the temple of Amun Ra. Autumn was making its mark and there was a chill in the air.

Through the City Gate and along the Appia, past its tombs, nestled between its rows of pine trees that cast pools of shade, as we kept to the edge of its cobbled way, Petronius holding Claudia's arm, not so much to steady her as to encourage her onwards.

We followed our fellow travellers towards a group of spreading bushes in the centre of which stood a small circular building. And inside we had never seen anything like it; we thought this would be much like a temple but it had none of the serious aspects of a Roman ceremony or Egyptian worship, for that matter; joyful voices rose in a crescendo, people laughed and children ran around.

Ares and Hyacinthus appeared beside us. A man stepped through the doorway. We wondered if he might be the Rock but Hyacinthus said no, that he was one of his companions. 'Blessings be upon you,' they said.

And now, at the far side of the congregation, we saw Cornelius Pudens. He smiled at us and made a sign, as if drawing a cross in the air.

'It's to remember a man who was crucified,' said Ares, which seemed peculiar to me. But it was also a sign that Petronius should leave us and follow him, for he was going to be with Cal. Claudia put her hand to his face, and as she had told him a hundred times before, 'Remember to tell him that we will come as soon as we are allowed.' And I was hit by a very great sadness for though her words had been bright and hopeful, I knew that I might never see that brother of my soul again. But at least Petronius would tell him all that had happened since the day that I'd stood in front of his cage, and he had stood inside it.

She hugged our little friend, and I did too. But before he stepped forward to leave us, I put the sunship into his hand.

'It's for you and for Cal,' I told him. 'When you look at it, wherever you are, to remember what we've been through together and to know that we will love each other, until the stars fall from the sky.'

A glimmer of something close to hope tiptoed into my soul. Until the stars fell from the sky.